Marissa gave a little shiver, a frisson of excitement, and rose to her feet. She approached the small card table where Valentine was waiting and allowed him to draw out a chair for her, calmly arranging her skirts about her as she sat.

"Is this part of your promise to show me about pleasure?" she said, clasping her hands before her and watching his face.

But instead of answering her he said, "Here are the rules. There must be no touching, not until the game is over."

"No touching?" she cried, unable to keep the disappointment out of her voice. For Marissa, the act of touching his skin was a pleasure in itself.

He smiled and threw the dice. They landed on four and two. "Now your turn," he said softly, gathering them up again and handing them to her.

Marissa held the dice tight in her hand, feeling the excitement growing inside her. She couldn't decide whether she wanted to win or lose, but when she threw and the numbers were revealed— a three and a two—her disappointment made her realize what her true wishes were.

"I lost," she said, raising her eyes questioningly to his.

His triumphant smile made her shiver again. "And I won."

Romances by **Sara Bennett**

A Most Sinful Proposal

SARA BENNETT

AVON

An Imprint of HarperCollinsPublishers

This is a work of fiction. Names, characters, places, and incidents are products of the author's imagination or are used fictitiously and are not to be construed as real. Any resemblance to actual events, locales, organizations, or persons, living or dead, is entirely coincidental.

AVON BOOKS
An Imprint of HarperCollins*Publishers*
10 East 53rd Street
New York, New York 10022-5299

Copyright © 2010 by Sara Bennett
ISBN 978-0-06-133917-2
www.avonromance.com

First Avon Books paperback printing: April 2010

Avon Trademark Reg. U.S. Pat. Off. and in Other Countries, Marca Registrada, Hecho en U.S.A.
HarperCollins® is a registered trademark of HarperCollins Publishers.

Printed in the U.S.A.

10 9 8 7 6 5 4 3 2 1

This one is for Andrew. No matter how many years go by, he's still my little brother.

A Most
Sinful Proposal

Prologue

Miss Debenham's Finishing School
Graduating Ball
1837

Marissa Rotherhild waited until the laughter and chatter faded. Olivia Monteith had stunned them all with her plan to marry Wicked Nic Lacey, and although she was excited for her friend, Marissa had her own news to share.

The five members of the Husband Hunters Club settled. All of them were from respectable and wealthy families—well, almost all—and all were expected to marry to please those families. The Husband Hunters Club had been formed because the five members found their fate disagreeable; they wanted more from life and marriage and they were determined to get it.

"I have decided on the husband I want for myself," Marissa announced, when all eyes were upon her. "The Honorable George Kent."

There was an awkward pause, not exactly the sort of response Marissa hoped for. Olivia reached to clasp her hand and her voice was earnest. "I know

George Kent is very handsome, and I am aware of several girls who have a tender for him, but Marissa, you are the cleverest person of my acquaintance and the Honorable George does not have the reputation of a learned man. Won't you grow bored with him?"

"Olivia is right," Tina Smythe spoke forthrightly. "George Kent is a social animal, hardly an intellectual. And he's a flirt, isn't he? Do you really want to marry a flirt, Marissa?"

"Of course not. You don't understand. So what if he is a little forward? There's no harm in it. He is fun, good company, and he makes me laugh." Marissa's lovely face grew earnest. "His being different from me is the point, don't you see? I grew up in an atmosphere where laughter was rare and discussions at the dining table revolved around mosses in Scotland and lichens in Wales and the latest insect-eating plants to be discovered in the . . . the Amazon!"

She took a deep breath. "My parents are not here at the graduating ball tonight. Do you know why?"

The girls glanced at each other and shook their heads.

"They are on an expedition to the Continent, to investigate a rare fern which has been seen growing in the crevices of the Pyrenees."

Marissa blinked back sudden tears and shook her head. "I understand their passion, really, I do. I could be the same, if I let myself. But I want to be different, don't you see? I want a husband who will make me laugh rather than impress me with his knowledge of botany. I want a husband who will bring the sunlight into my life. And I believe with all my heart that George Kent is the man to do that."

Lady Averil nodded in agreement, but Eugenie wasn't so certain. "You are a bluestocking, Marissa, we all know that, and although I agree that sometimes opposites can attract, they do not always end happily ever after."

"Yes, yes," Marissa said, impatiently tossing back an ebony curl. Her dark eyes glowed. "If this was a whim I would agree with your concerns, but I have met George several times." She blushed under their sudden scrutiny. "Lately he has been attending my parents' botanical evenings and he always singles me out. He appears to enjoy my company as much as I enjoy his. Indeed, sometimes he makes me quite giddy," she added, with a secret smile.

"George Kent attending botanical evenings?" Olivia repeated, raising her eyebrows in wonder.

"His brother, Lord Kent, is an authority on roses," Marissa explained, "although I have never met him. He keeps to himself and spends every moment studying his chosen field. George more or less brought himself up after his parents died and he was left in his brother's care. So you see, in many ways, we have a great deal in common."

Olivia smiled. "And I see you have considered your choice very thoroughly, dear Marissa. I'm sorry for doubting you. I suppose the next question is how do you intend to hunt and capture George Kent?"

"Well," Marissa met their curious eyes, "I have been invited to his house in Surrey next month for a weekend party, so I should think there will be plenty of time for hunting while I am there. The only problem is that my grandmamma will be chaperoning me, and she tends to be a little . . . overwhelming.

I don't want her to frighten George off before I can marry him."

The girls exchanged glances. They'd all met Marissa's grandmother. Lady Bethany came from an era when life was far more liberal and unfortunately she wasn't reticent about describing her Bohemian escapades, most of which today's more moral society considered very improper. Marissa, who loved her grandmother dearly, knew how confronting she could be to those who had never met her.

"Perhaps I can lock her in her room," she murmured to herself, and then blushed when she realized she'd spoken aloud.

"George will just have to get used to Lady Bethany if he becomes part of your family," Eugenie said firmly.

"I'm sure George won't mind," Marissa replied quickly. "It is his brother who may decide to take offense. Lord Kent, from what George says, is old and very stuffy."

Olivia raised her glass. "I want to make a toast. To the Honorable George Kent, and may Marissa find her heart's desire and marry him!"

"To Marissa and George!"

Solemnly the toast was drank, and another member of the Husband Hunters Club was set upon the path to her future.

Or so she thought . . . .

Chapter 1

Abbey Thorne Manor,
Surrey, England

The first Lord Valentine Kent knew he had guests was when his butler, Morris, told him so. Not that Valentine even knew Morris was hovering behind him until the butler loudly cleared his throat, a signal that he had been waiting for some time to be noticed. Valentine frowned, the magnifying glass in one hand, the specimen of *rosa foetida* on the table in front of him. The single yellow flower had arrived this morning from one of his contacts, carefully packed, but the sea journey had caused some damage—salt water stained a corner of the box and the inside was damp. He'd recognized the flower immediately and with the familiar pang of disappointment.

There was a second parcel, as yet unopened, from a name he didn't recognize. Valentine did not find this unusual. He received letters and parcels from all over the country containing specimens or descriptions of specimens for him to name. He was one of the leading experts on roses. But his true passion was one particular rose, a rose which was first brought to England seven hundred years ago. It was his quest, his Holy Grail, his lifelong ambition, and he had an uneasy feeling that it was becoming an obsession.

Morris cleared his throat even more loudly. Obviously the man wasn't about to go away. With a sigh of frustration, Valentine turned to face him. "What is it, Morris? I warn you, it had better be a matter of life or death."

"I apologize, my lord," Morris droned, his bloodhound face drawn down into apologetic lines. "I am always loath to interrupt you when you are busy, my lord. But there is a young lady here to see Mr. George—"

"Then, Morris, I suggest you fetch Mr. George."

"Believe me, my lord, I have tried," Morris replied with feeling. "Unfortunately Mr. George can't be found, and yesterday he was most specific that when this particular young lady arrived she must be treated with courtesy."

Valentine sighed again. Damn George! Why wasn't he here? The last thing Valentine wanted to do was make polite with a stranger. No doubt she was one of George's silly little flirts, all hair and no brain. George had inflicted someone similar on him once before and he'd made his younger brother swear he would never again invite anyone to Abbey Thorne Manor without first informing Valentine and allowing him enough time to escape to his rooms, or, if necessary, to leave the house altogether.

"Who is this young lady who must be treated with courtesy?" he said gruffly, rising to his feet and shrugging his dark blue jacket back on over his white linen shirt, allowing it to settle comfortably across broad shoulders.

Morris gave him a glassy look.

Valentine was used to his butler's silent disapproval when it came to his preference for comfort over fashion. The jacket was an old favorite and a little shabby, the top buttons of his shirt were undone, and he'd neglected to put on a neck cloth this morning. Well, he told himself irritably, it was just too bad. George's flirt could take him as he was or not at all.

"Her name, Morris."

"Eh, Miss Marissa Rotherhild, my lord," Morris said, dragging his eyes away from his master's ragbag appearance. "She's in the yellow parlor—"

"Rotherhild, Rotherhild . . . Why do I feel as if I know that name?"

Frowning, Valentine set off at a brisk stride, down the stairs and along the gallery, in the direction of the inappropriately named yellow parlor.

His thoughts turned back to George. The boy needed a firm hand and a tight leash and Valentine, his elder brother and in many respects a stand-in for their father, had always done his best. But now that George was of age and had come into his own money he did very much as he liked. If the boy would take an interest in something other than horses and gambling and women, Valentine would breathe a sigh of relief, but so far George showed no signs of doing so.

Not that there was any malice in him. Good-tempered, smiling and handsome, George was in no way a bad person. He was, if anything, too good-natured and easygoing. Valentine, who'd grown up during the war with Napoleon, couldn't remember ever being as young as George sometimes seemed to be. Of course George thought *he* was far too stuffy and serious. Valentine always disputed it but now he wondered if there was some truth to George's accusation. With a frown he tried to recall the last time he'd laughed for the simple joy of living, and found he could not.

Morris darted ahead of him, slightly out of breath, to open the parlor door. Valentine hardly broke stride as he entered the rather chilly room where George's young lady was waiting. His eyes narrowed as he realized, with annoyance, that there were actually two women. One elderly and rather regal, with graying dark hair and a pair of black eyes with a surprisingly unladylike expression in them as she surveyed him. And the other . . .

The other was the most beautiful woman he had ever seen.

For a moment he stood and stared, at a complete loss for words. His shocked and startled gaze noted her thick, curling dark hair, fastened up in some deceptively plain style beneath a jaunty little bonnet, her skin—smooth and pale as cream—with a tempting smidgeon showing where her dress buttoned below her throat. She lifted her head to stare back at him, her large brown eyes framed by sweeping lashes, and her lips opened slightly, like unfurling rose petals.

"Miss Rotherhild, my lord," Morris murmured at his side, as the silence stretched on.

Valentine realized he was being rude, and worse than that, his thoughts had turned poetical. The last time they did that . . . Well, he'd sworn never to allow it to happen again.

"Miss Rotherhild," he said, sounding gruff. There was a pulse beating in his head, and a warmth spread over his body, making him aware of every inch of flesh and blood and muscle. Of being male and very much alive.

"Lord Kent." Miss Marissa Rotherhild was watching him with a serious gaze and she came forward, holding her gloved hand toward him.

Valentine stared at the hand until he felt a slight bump against his back—Morris of course—and hastily took her fingers in his and raised them automatically to his lips. Her glove, and the flesh beneath, smelled of violets and woman.

"George . . . eh, that is, your brother invited me to your house party this weekend, my lord."

Through the fog in his brain Valentine made sense of her words. "House party?" He belatedly dropped her hand and spun around to fix his butler with a piercing look. "Morris, what is this about a house party?"

Morris paled. "My lord, I swear I know nothing of any house party! I would not dare allow such a thing to occur without your permission."

Marissa Rotherhild glanced at her elderly companion with some anxiety.

"Where is George?" Valentine went on in a grim voice. "Find him, Morris."

Morris managed a shaky bow before trotting hastily away on his mission.

When Valentine turned back to face the room, he found two pairs of dark eyes watching him with an intensity that was unnerving. "I'm sure we can sort out this misunderstanding as soon as George can be found, Miss Rotherhild and . . . eh . . . ?"

There was an uncomfortable silence. Marissa said, "I beg your pardon, my lord. I haven't introduced my grandmother, Lady Bethany."

Valentine found himself under scrutiny from the lady with the lined face that had once been as beautiful as her granddaughter's. "How do you do, Lord Kent? You have a fine old house. People with houses like yours should open them up. If you're not having a weekend party then you should be."

"I prefer my solitude, Lady Bethany."

Marissa surveyed him seriously from beneath her little hat. "I hope you won't be too cross with George, Lord Kent. It must be a misunderstanding. I'm sure he would never do anything to upset you on purpose."

"George is a thoughtless young pup," he retorted sharply.

She blinked. "Oh no, you're wrong about your brother. He's . . . he's quite wonderful."

She blushed deeply as she realized what she'd said, and her elderly companion hid her mouth with a gloved hand, as if she might be laughing.

Valentine had never been jealous of George, he had no reason to be, but now there was a strange tightening in his chest. Marissa Rotherhild was too good for his thoughtless brother. Suddenly, Valentine found himself considering ways to steal her all for himself.

* * *

Lord Kent was not at all like George, Marissa thought in bewilderment. George was always fashionably dressed, neatly turned out to the last button, and here was Lord Kent looking as if he'd been sleeping in his clothing. He hadn't shaved, either. Marissa could plainly see the prickly stubble on his jaw, the same honey color as his hair, which was also rather long and untidy. Her fingers itched to comb it back from his brow and, surprised by the strength of that urge, she folded them into tight fists, just in case she actually acted upon it.

"George has clearly made a good impression on you, Miss Rotherhild," he was saying, with a note in his voice that made her think he might be making fun of her.

"I'm sure George makes a good impression on everybody he meets, Lord Kent," she replied rather coolly.

"My daughter and son-in-law are under the impression George is an enthusiastic botanist," her grandmother spoke behind her. "He is invited to all their meetings and has been attending regularly."

Lord Kent's eyes widened. They were very blue, Marissa thought. Piercingly so. In fact, she could not recall ever seeing eyes quite that spectacular shade of blue. Someone had once described the Aegean Sea to her, and she thought that perhaps Lord Kent's eyes were that exact color.

"George interested in plants?" he cried. "Good Lord, whatever next?"

"Do you mean the boy isn't an enthusiast?" Lady Bethany said with a touch of satisfaction. "I thought as much." She sank down into a brocade covered chair, evidently tired of waiting to be asked by Lord Kent who seemed to have forgotten his manners.

"George never said he was an enthusiast, Grandmamma," Marissa said, casting her elderly relation a quelling glance.

"Well he certainly gave a good impression of one," her relation retorted, completely un-quelled. "Professor Rotherhild was even considering taking him on a trip to see the lichen in Yell." She shuddered. "That's in Shetland, Lord Kent, and a more windswept and godforsaken place you would be hard-pressed to find."

Lord Kent, who had been listening to their exchange in silence, suddenly spoke. "Rotherhild! I knew I had heard the name before. Of course. Professor Rotherhild is one of Britain's foremost experts on lichens and mosses."

"My father," Marissa said quietly. "My mother prefers insect-consuming plants. She has several in the conservatory and feeds them with—"

"Please, Marissa, I beg you, don't remind me." Again her grandmother shuddered. "My daughter does not take after me, Kent. I cannot think where she got her love of such unpleasantness."

Lord Kent's lips twitched and he looked down into Marissa's face with those eyes. "And what is your specialty, Miss Rotherhild?" he asked her in a deep voice.

"I have no specialty, Lord Kent."

"Well, that is a pity."

"I find that being in the presence of my parents

has dulled my own enthusiasm for botany. George says . . ." But she remembered in time that what George had said wasn't very complimentary to his brother, and changed the sentence to, "George says not everyone feels the same way about plants."

"Does he indeed?" Lord Kent fixed her with his piercing gaze, as if he knew she wasn't telling the entire truth.

He was correct. The truth was the first time she'd met George he'd said that growing up with Professor Rotherhild, in her case, and his brother, in his, had instilled in them a fierce determination to keep as far away as possible from anything even vaguely resembling a plant.

"Your brother?" she'd asked George, surprised and pleased that they had something in common.

"He's an obsessive rose collector, Miss Rotherhild."

"At least roses are attractive to the eye, and the nose."

"Oh, but the thorns!"

They'd laughed, and Marissa had felt as if she'd finally found someone who understood her predicament. And, indeed, as they conversed she learned that he had grown up in similar circumstances, suffering through dinners where heated discussions took place over obscure plants and hardly being noticed at all while her parents read aloud from the latest paper on their favorite subjects. Her grandmother sympathized but she didn't really understand. For her, other people's foibles were amusing, grist to the mill of her caustic tongue, but Marissa was unable to laugh at her parents' peculiarities. She felt ignored and isolated, even though she knew they did not mean to be cruel. Now George had made her feel she wasn't entirely alone.

Indeed, it was as if she'd found a soul mate.

That was why it had been so important for her to come to Abbey Thorne Manor for the weekend party. George was the man she wanted to marry, she was absolutely certain of it, and when he'd extended the invitation she'd been determined to use the weekend to convince him that she was the perfect woman for him.

And now he wasn't here to greet her and from the way Lord Kent was acting it was possible there may not be a weekend house party taking place after all. George had mistaken the date or, worse, forgotten her.

She was reminded, painfully, of the day her parents forgot to arrange her tenth birthday party, so engrossed were they in their latest find, and she had to explain to several disappointed friends that there would be no food and no cake and no games. The echo of her humiliation was still fresh as she'd faced the pity and scorn in their eyes.

Lord Kent sighed. Marissa glanced up, startled, wondering if he'd read her feelings in her face. He was staring at her with something like sympathy, but to her relief he did not ask her what the matter was.

"Do sit down, Miss Rotherhild. If anyone can find George then it is Morris—he knows all my brother's hiding places. We will soon unravel this mystery."

Marissa perched on the edge of a chair beside her grandmother and clutched her reticule in her gloved fingers. Lady Bethany reached out and gave her hand a squeeze.

"Never mind, my dear. At least we have had a jaunt into the country, and just think, if we'd been at home in London we may have been forced to travel deep into Scotland to help collect your father's lichens and mosses. I doubt I could survive another visit to Yell."

That was true, Marissa thought, but it still didn't help to make her feel any less disappointed about George.

And how was she going to tell the Husband Hunters Club that she'd failed to capture her chosen husband before she'd even begun?

"Ah, Morris. Any news?"

Marissa looked up, hope shining in her eyes. But Morris's mouth was down turned and he shook his head with a gloomy air. "I'm very much afraid Mr. George is nowhere to be found, my lord."

"You've looked everywhere?"

"I have."

"Should you . . . should you begin a search for him beyond the estate?" Marissa asked, stumbling over her words, as it suddenly occurred to her that George may be in trouble. Yes, that must be it! She should have known it. George was missing. He would never abandon her like this unless there was something wrong.

Morris and Lord Kent exchanged a glance.

"I very much doubt a search will be necessary," Lord Kent said, his tone thoughtful, "but we shall see what the day brings. Now, Morris, can you arrange for some rooms to be prepared for Miss Rotherhild and Lady Bethany? And inform Mrs. Beaumaris we will have extras for luncheon. There is no reason for them to travel all the way back to London just because my feckless brother isn't here to greet them. They have come for a weekend party and we shall have a weekend party."

Morris looked as if he'd been skewered but swiftly rose to the occasion. "I . . . certainly, my lord."

Lord Kent nodded, and then gave a brief bow to the women. "If you will excuse me, ladies, I have some business to complete. We will meet again at luncheon."

The door closed behind him and the two women were alone.

"Should we stay, Grandmamma?" Marissa asked tentatively. "Perhaps we should make our excuses and leave. If we take our time returning to London my parents will have left by the time we arrive."

But Lady Bethany was adamant. "No, Marissa, we are not leaving. I want to stay. I declare I haven't been so amused by a situation for years. Our host is a one of a kind."

"Well, Lord Kent *did* seem very . . ."

"Underdressed, dishabille? Indeed he did. Not your usual English gentleman to be sure, but very manly, my dear. He quite melted my insides, and I haven't felt like that since . . . well, such fond memories are not for your innocent ears."

Another of her grandmother's wicked recollections, Marissa thought wryly. Was Lord Kent manly? Certainly there was something about him that was very earthy. The unbuttoned shirt and the triangle of masculine throat she couldn't help but notice, as well as his unshaven jaw and ill-fitting jacket. She had a strong desire to brush him down and straighten him up.

"So, it is agreed. We will be staying?" Lady Bethany said with an arched eyebrow and a twinkle in her eye that hinted she knew exactly what Marissa was thinking.

"Yes," Marissa replied primly, "I do believe we will."

Chapter 2

Abbey Thorne Manor was a treat. George had spoken of it to Marissa but she hadn't realized until the carriage brought them into the quiet serenity of the Surrey countryside and she saw the mellow red bricks and half-timbered upper stories of the old moated manor house just how beautiful and ancient his home was. As she recalled he'd been far more interested in his London town house.

"The countryside is all very well," he'd said, with a hint of wickedness in his smile, "but it dulls in comparison to the excitement of life in London."

At the time Marissa had been quick to agree, but now as she stood in her room, overlooking the moat and the countryside beyond, she wondered how it would be to live her life in such a place as Abbey Thorne Manor. Her family resided in London, when they weren't out and about on field trips. Their house was large and untidy but there was no tradition, no heirlooms or family portraits. Her father didn't believe in hanging on to the past, and her mother usually went along with her father's wishes. What would it be like to be George and his brother, descendants of a family who'd lived in the same house, on the same piece of land, for centuries? Wistfully, she decided it must give them a wonderful sense of belonging, of knowing who they were. Until this moment Marissa hadn't quite understood it was a feeling she was missing in her own life.

"Who would have thought a rattle like George Kent would come from such delightful beginnings?"

Lady Bethany's voice startled her. Her grandmother had removed her hat and gloves and set out on a journey to inspect Marissa's rooms. Her elegant, upright figure showed nothing of the weariness most older ladies would be feeling after such a journey, and her dark eyes darted about her. She murmured her appreciation when she spied the ormolu clock on the mantel, and lifted the pince-nez which hung on a fine gold chain about her neck so that she could examine it more closely.

"So, where do you think he has got to?"

Marissa met the sharp eyes that missed nothing and deliberately made her tone light. "I have no idea, Grandmamma. Perhaps he was called away on some business and did not have time to let us know."

"Mmm, perhaps he was. Although if that was the case, my dear, one would think he would have left word with his brother, or the servants."

"Not—not if it was extremely sudden and—and urgent."

It was a poor effort, and Lady Bethany rightly ignored it as she perambulated toward the window, gazing thoughtfully through the small glass panes. "The brother is nothing like George, is he? Has George spoken much about him?"

Marissa didn't trust her grandmother's airy tones,

eyeing her suspiciously and wondering where this was leading. Lady Bethany kept her eyes trained on the view.

"George said his brother was much older than him, and that he more or less brought him up after their father died at Waterloo. Lord Kent is a keen botanist. George calls him obsessive."

"One doesn't see Lord Kent about in London society. Is he married, do you know?"

"I think he is a widower."

"Ah." She smiled.

"Grandmamma, he is far too young for you," Marissa retorted.

Lady Bethany smiled. "Wicked girl, I wasn't thinking of myself."

"Then who—" But suddenly it seemed more sensible not to prolong the conversation; whatever machinations were going on in her grandmother's head were better left unspoken. Lady Bethany had a reputation for meddling and although Marissa supposed she meant well the outcomes to her plans were not always the ones she'd imagined. Look at her own parents. Lady Bethany had decided upon a rich and handsome gentleman for her daughter, but instead found herself with a son-in-law whose hands were perpetually stained green from handling the mosses in his ever-increasing collection.

Lady Bethany was leaning forward to peer down toward the gatehouse, and the stone bridge that spanned the moat. "I thought Lord Kent said there wasn't a house party planned for this weekend?"

"Yes, he did say that."

"Well, a gentleman on a rather fine bay has just ridden over the drawbridge."

"George—" Marissa began, hardly daring to believe.

"No, my dear, it wasn't George. He was more mature than George. I wonder who it could be? There isn't another brother we haven't met? Or an older relative?"

Marissa swallowed her disappointment. "No, there are only two brothers and I don't know of any elderly relatives. Perhaps we will learn his identity at luncheon, Grandmamma."

"Perhaps we will. I must say I am looking forward to luncheon a great deal more than I ever expected to when we set out for Surrey." Lady Bethany gave her an innocent smile and wandered off. Marissa watched her go, eyes narrowed suspiciously. Her grandmother was up to something, and Marissa knew her well enough to be extremely uneasy.

If only George was here!

With a sigh she turned again to the window as if she expected to see him galloping wildly toward her. Where could he have gone? And why? She'd so looked forward to being here with him, to him showing her his home, to their conversations, and the way he made her laugh. He was so different from her parents and their circle of friends.

Marissa had been positive George was as attracted to her as she was to him. She was so certain she would not have to try very hard when it came to hunting him and making him hers. Now she was thrown into confusion and doubt.

To be honest she didn't know if she was capable of hunting a man, especially if he didn't want to be hunted. She knew more about the mating habits of plants, such as they were, than she did about people. Lady Bethany may have told risqué stories but they meant little to Marissa—it was because she'd never felt the passionate emotions her grandmamma remembered with such fondness. Until she met George she had begun to think herself incapable of anything warmer than a formal, cool fondness, and a dispassionate intellectual curiosity. It was a frightening vision of her future, never to care enough or feel enough for her husband beyond liking, and perhaps not even that, if some of the marriages she'd seen were anything to go by.

With George everything had changed, and suddenly she'd been able to hope for a truly happy and passionate future.

But now George had vanished, and taken that hope with him.

"Kent, I can't tell you how glad I am that you are at home. I thought you might be on one of your rose visits to the Continent."

Valentine returned the brisk handshake. "Jasper. What brings you here?"

Lord Jasper was dressed as neatly as a pin, and when he lifted his hat his scalp glowed through the remaining strands of copper hair as if it had been polished. Bright and watchful hazel eyes and a thin-lipped mouth completed the picture of a man not given to impetuous behavior. His next words explained everything to Valentine.

"Did you know that Von Hautt was in England?"

Valentine's brows snapped down.

Jasper gave his cautious smile. "I thought not, my friend. Well he is. And I have heard that he is hot on the trail of *your* rose."

Valentine appeared startled. "The Crusader's Rose? I have been looking for the Crusader's Rose for twenty years, and my father was searching a lifetime before me, but we have found no trace. The trail has long gone cold. I thought I was the only one who still believes it exists . . ."

"Von Hautt is aware that if he found the Crusader's Rose his name would be made. He would be famous. And it appears he's now come into some information that may well give him what he wants."

"What information?" Valentine scoffed.

"A list of names."

Valentine fixed him with a piercing look. "Names?"

"The names of the men who traveled to the Crusades with your ancestor, Richard de Fevre."

Long before Abbey Thorne Manor was the home of the Kent family, there had been a motte and bailey here, belonging to the de Fevres, an ancient family related to Valentine through his maternal side. By the twelfth century the wooden tower had been replaced by stone, and it was from here that Richard de Fevre had set off on his journey to the Crusades. Richard was a pious man who believed his fight to free Jerusalem from the Saracens was a just one, and before he went he took a vow of chastity, swearing it would not be broken until he returned home— Valentine had often wondered what de Fevre's wife thought of that. Richard had traveled with some like-minded companions, neighbors of his, and by luck or miracle they had all survived and all returned.

Usually when crusaders returned from the Holy Land they brought back gold and jewels, rugs and tapestries, or even grisly souvenirs of the Saracen dead, but Richard brought back something else.

A rose.

It was said that this rose was far more beautiful than any other ever seen in England. It shone with all the colors of the sunset. De Fevre grew it in his garden and there it remained, regenerating through the ages, until last century when it was destroyed by one of Valentine's ancestors. But legend had it that de Fevre didn't bring just one rose back from the Crusades, he brought two, and he made a gift of the second plant to one of his companions as a reward for saving his life. It was possible—probable, Valentine liked to think, because of the rose's ability to self-seed—that this second rose still existed in the garden of that unknown companion's descendants.

Valentine had made it his life's mission to find the Crusader's Rose and restore it to his family.

And now Baron Von Hautt was on the same quest, but for far less altruistic reasons.

"Where could he have found such a list?" he said with quiet anger.

Jasper shook his head. "I don't know, Kent. I thought you might. You have received nothing recently?"

"No. Only . . ." Valentine paused, remembering. "Wait a moment. I received two parcels this morning but I have only opened one." Quickly he moved toward his desk, finding the object—a square brown paper package with his address written in a shaky hand on the front. The name on the back was unfamiliar to him.

Without hesitation he tore the package open. A bundle of moth-eaten looking papers spilled out and, fastened to the top, a single sheet covered in the same shaky writing as the address.

"Ah, now that is interesting." Valentine scanned the sheet. "This is from a Seth Bonnie, who says he was my father's orderly during his time with the regiment." Valentine looked up at Jasper, as though suddenly struck. "I believe I do remember the name now I see it in its proper context."

"Why is he writing to you after all this time? Your father died at Waterloo, didn't he, Kent?"

"Yes, he did." He continued to read. "Bonnie says he was in possession of some of my father's papers and always meant to send them on, but he was badly wounded at Waterloo and by the time he'd recovered the papers were long forgotten. He only found them again very recently. He has been sorting through his belongings in preparation for 'the final bugle call,' as he calls it." He read on. "Bonnie says that a man, a stranger, came to see him. A Prussian." His voice grew sharp.

"Good God, Von Hautt!" Jasper cried.

"Yes. He asked Bonnie if he could see my father's papers—that was when Bonnie remembered he had them. The Prussian examined them, but Bonnie made certain he did not leave the room. He says he didn't trust the fellow. But Von Hautt made notes. Bonnie has been thinking it over and now he's concerned he did the wrong thing in allowing a stranger to look at my father's papers. So he's sending them on to me."

Jasper joined him by the desk. "Is there a list, Kent?"

Valentine began to flip through the bundle, pausing once or twice, and then drew out a crumbling piece of parchment. His handsome, austere face broke into a smile. "I do believe there is, Jasper."

At that moment the luncheon gong sounded.

Startled, Valentine looked up, and found himself strangely torn between the newly discovered list and the memory of Marissa's dark eyes.

"Kent?" Jasper was frowning. "The list, man!"

"I have guests," Valentine said, and set the paper down carefully on his desk.

"Guests? What guests? Who cares about guests when we are in pursuit of the rose?"

Valentine shrugged uncomfortably, knowing Jasper would not understand his sudden loss of the single-mindedness that had always accompanied his quest. "They are George's guests, actually."

"Then let George deal with them! You might be holding the key to the Crusader's Rose in your hands and you're worrying about some uninvited guests?"

But Valentine felt anticipation stirring within his heart, anticipation that had nothing to do with roses or plants of any kind. It was so long since he'd felt like this he didn't know how to explain it to himself, let alone Jasper, so he didn't try.

"I owe them a duty as their host. We will eat luncheon, Jasper, and then we will be free to take up the quest."

Jasper shook his head in frustration, but nevertheless he reluctantly followed Valentine to the door. Once outside Valentine turned the key in the lock and tucked it into his pocket. "Von Hautt doesn't know the English countryside like we do," he soothed his friend. "It will take him longer to find out where de Fevre's companions lived all those centuries ago."

"But he has a head start."

"Nevertheless, we will triumph, Jasper. Suddenly I am sure of it." And he gave an uncharacteristically reckless laugh. He would be thirty-four next birthday but right now he felt like a youth, the blood pumping through his veins, his body powerful and strong, his mind clear.

Was that because he finally had a strong clue to the whereabouts of the second Crusader's Rose? Or was it because he was about to take luncheon with the beautiful Marissa Rotherhild?

Chapter 3

Marissa nibbled delicately on a piece of chilled salmon and looked across the luncheon table at Lady Bethany. Her grandmamma rolled her eyes. Neither of them spoke. A hush had fallen over the four persons gathered and no one seemed willing to break it. Lord Kent, still looking as if he was dressed to dig ditches, had introduced them to his friend, Lord Jasper.

If it was possible to have an exact opposite, then Lord Jasper was his. Nearly twenty years older than Lord Kent, neatly clothed, every stitch in place, and with a precise way of speaking, Jasper inquired politely as to their journey. But it was obvious his heart wasn't in it.

Then Lord Kent inquired as to whether they were happy with their rooms. Twice. And neither time did he seem to listen to their answers.

It was all very strange.

"You haven't heard any distressing news, my lord?" Marissa asked tentatively.

Lord Kent and his friend turned to her with such sharp, intent expressions that she was startled into dropping her fork.

"What do you mean?" Lord Kent demanded.

"I mean . . . I thought you might have heard from George," she said, unsettled and attempting to compose herself. "If that is the case I wish you would tell us to go, my lord. We would not dream of intruding upon you if—"

"Oh." Lord Kent turned to Lord Jasper and exchanged a look that Marissa found extremely suspicious. There *was* something!

"Kent, do put my granddaughter's mind at rest," Lady Bethany said, setting down her own knife and fork. "She has a somewhat vivid imagination."

"Grandmamma, you know that is not true. If anything I have a very limited imagination."

But Lord Kent had already taken the words to heart and set out to ease her fears. "No, Miss Rotherhild, I haven't heard from George. I can't imagine where he's got to."

Marissa glanced from him to Jasper, and found she didn't believe it. They were lying to her. The question was, why?

"Does your brother often go off without telling anyone?" Lady Bethany asked mildly, but her gaze was watchful.

"He is a grown man and considers himself past what he calls 'fussing.' He was named for my greatuncle, who was an amateur explorer, and George likes to think himself of a similar fearless character, although as far as I can make out, most of his exploring is done in Covent Garden."

Jasper gave a snort, hastily turning it into a cough.

Marissa was not such an innocent that she didn't

know what Covent Garden was famous for, besides opera and ballet—the strumpets who stood about looking for gentlemen to buy them for an hour or a night. She felt defensive on George's behalf; she wanted to tell Lord Kent that George would never do such a thing. But even as the urge rose in her, doubt joined it. George was a flirt, the sort of man who always noticed a pretty face and a neat ankle, and it was quite possible—in fact more than likely—that George did spend time in Covent Garden. She would sound naïve if she declared him innocent of the charge, but there was one point she could argue on his behalf.

"Indeed?" she said at last, with a distinct chill in her voice, fixing Lord Kent with her dark gaze. "I think you are wrong. George would make a very good explorer."

He gave her a limpid look from his blue eyes. "Do you, Miss Rotherhild?"

"Yes, I do."

"I find this an interesting study, Kent," Jasper said in his precise way. "Does this mean any man, or woman," with a nod to Marissa and her grandmother, "named for another will take on some aspect of their namesake's personality? For instance, my first name is Charles and I was named by my mother for a crusty uncle with a great deal of money. Does that mean I will become as irascible as my uncle Charles?"

Kent gave a deep chuckle. "Definitely, Jasper."

"You need to fight against it," Lady Bethany said, amused. "Be contrary. Ask yourself what your namesake would do and then do the opposite. I was named for a rather prim great-grandmother who never did anything without earnestly seeking the advice of her chaplain. I like to think I am her complete opposite, but it has taken a great deal of hard work."

"Grandmamma," Marissa said with a sigh, but wasn't surprised when she was ignored.

"Then I think I am safe where my uncle Charles is concerned," Jasper replied, his eyes sparkling. "Unless I suddenly develop a liking for small, smelly dogs and black stout."

They smiled at each other with growing interest, and Marissa knew her grandmamma was about to make another conquest. How did she do it? Marissa had often wondered how her grandmother managed to ensnare gentlemen—what was her secret?—but until George and the Husband Hunters Club came along she hadn't considered asking for advice. Perhaps now she would . . . if George ever came home.

Looking up she noticed that Lord Kent was observing the older couple with the same bemusement as herself. In an effort to distract him, and herself, she said, "Tell me, my lord, who were you named for?"

His expression changed abruptly, his eyes narrowing and his mouth tightening. He was actually frowning at her, Marissa thought in surprise, not sure whether to frown back or give a nervous giggle. Obviously she had touched a raw spot.

It was Jasper who came to Marissa's rescue. "Forgive my rude friend, Miss Rotherhild. His forename is a matter of great embarrassment to him."

"Jasper," Kent growled a warning.

Marissa thought it served him right if he was embarrassed. He shouldn't have said those things about George. "Come, my lord, I'm sure your secret can't be so awful . . . can it?"

Jasper gave a helpless lift of the shoulders. "Tell them, Kent. I don't know why you make such a fuss. It only draws attention to it."

Lord Kent took a gulp of his wine and set the glass down heavily on the table. "At the time I was born my mother was going through a romantic phase," he said, sounding extremely reluctant.

"Oh dear, you're not called Cupid, are you?" Marissa pulled a mock sympathetic face, enjoying herself immensely. "Or Pan, perhaps? Although he was half goat, wasn't he, and I'm sure you're not—"

"No, Miss Rotherhild, I'm not."

Marissa bit her lip and waited.

He took a breath. "I am named for a saint. My birthday falls on the fourteenth of February."

Lady Bethany clapped her hands together in glee. "St. Valentine's Day! Valentine Kent. It is, isn't it?"

Marissa could not think of a more inappropriate name for George's brother. *Valentine?* The saint of lovers, of kisses and flowers and happy endings. It was quite ludicrous. He should be called something prosaic like Jack or Henry or—

His deep voice interrupted her thoughts. "As a boy I longed for a simple manly name like Jack or Henry. You can imagine the bullying I endured at school." He spoke matter-of-factly, but Marissa was sure she heard an undercurrent in his voice that spoke of painful memories. Did George's brother have a sensitive side? And was his unhappy childhood the reason he'd channeled his intellect into the study of roses? Perhaps it had been wrong of her to force him into revealing his name like that, although she couldn't regret it after what he'd said about George.

Jasper launched into conversation, regaling Lady Bethany with the tale of a man named Admonition. But Marissa was only half listening. She was watching Valentine Kent.

He was smoothing his cuffs, although they were so creased she didn't know why he bothered. Didn't he have a valet? Her gaze lifted to the tilt of his head and the dark sweep of his lashes, so long they were almost feminine, if one discounted the masculine cheek they brushed against. His nose was similar to George's, but not nearly as straight. There was a bump in it, as if he'd broken it at some time. Fighting the bullies who teased him about his name? By the breadth of his shoulders she thought he was probably handy with his fists.

Marissa's gaze traveled down the length of his strong arms, coming to rest on his hands. They were large, like the rest of him, but with long fingers rather than the blunt and broad digits one might have expected. One might even call them artistic— surely that was the sign of a sensitive soul? The idea disturbed her. She felt unsettled, confused, and— more disturbingly—aroused.

What would it feel like to have those fingers on her?

As the shocking thought took hold, he looked up at her. Hastily she glanced away, but not before being startled once more by the amazing color of his eyes. Indeed, looking into them had made her feel quite giddy.

This was George's brother, she reminded herself. He was nothing more to her than that. George was the one she was interested in. George was the one she intended to marry.

"Who were you named for, Miss Rotherhild?" Valentine's voice was soft, for her alone, and the husky quality of it sent an involuntary shiver down her spine.

Marissa took her courage in both hands and forced herself to look up. He was closer than she'd expected, leaning toward her. There was a hint of a smile on his mouth, and suddenly she found it difficult to draw air into her lungs.

"I've told you my secret; it is only fair you tell me yours," he added, dropping his voice even further. That shiver rippled across her skin.

The effect he was having on her was beyond anything she'd ever experienced. George made her laugh, but when she was with him she never felt like this. Intellectually, she didn't know quite what to make of it.

"I have no secrets," she said sharply.

He is George's brother, she told herself firmly, *and unimportant except for the connection he has to George.* But that wasn't true any longer. Something had changed. Suddenly she was conscious of him as a man in his own right, and a most attractive one.

"No secrets at all?" he said, with that half smile that seemed to tease and admire her at the same time. "I find that difficult to believe, Miss Rotherhild. All women have secrets."

"Then I am a sad disappointment to my sex, my lord."

His astonishing eyes narrowed as his gaze slid over her. "You are far from a disappointment to me, Miss Rotherhild."

Was he flirting with her? Marissa thought. And why didn't she put a stop to it immediately? Why was her heart beginning to beat faster with excitement, like a bolting horse, running?

"You are only making me more curious, Miss Rotherhild," he purred. "I will find out."

Yes, she thought, *I believe you will.*

"Were you named after a rare botanical specimen?"

"Thank goodness, no."

"Ah, you don't have your father's interest in botany then?" He quirked an eyebrow at her.

"Definitely not. George and I are at one on the subject of botany, Lord Kent."

"I see." Did he appear a little disappointed? But before she could decide he was speaking again. "Then who are you named for, Miss Rotherhild? Please, keep me in suspense no longer."

"I am named for no one but myself," Marissa said, feeling her cheeks growing pink. "My parents don't believe in reusing family names. We are all different and unique and we should be given a name to celebrate that fact." She lifted her chin. "Marissa. My name is Marissa."

A spark lit his eyes. "Marissa. It suits you."

"I expect you think of people as roses," she said quickly, to stop him from embarrassing her further. "George told me that . . ." She bit her lip, suddenly conscious that once again what George had said was probably not something he'd expected her to repeat to his brother.

Valentine smiled his fascinating smile. "Go on, Marissa," he invited her. "I am always interested to hear what George says about me when I'm not there."

"I assure you it was nothing you could take offence to," she said, her color higher than ever. "George said he believed you thought of him as a climbing rose that needed constant pruning in case it escaped the trellis."

He considered her words. "I rather think George is right."

And as she found herself once more caught in the brilliance of his eyes, Marissa could not help but wonder what sort of rose he saw in her. Something irritating and thorny, or one of the more dull, domestic varieties? A pity she didn't quite dare to ask because suddenly she desperately wanted to know.

After luncheon the two men removed themselves to discuss "business." Remembering the nuances of their conversation, the strangeness of their manner, Marissa could not help but think there was something wrong despite their assurances that there wasn't. Her fears regarding George raised their head again, and the more she considered, the more convinced she was that she was right. Why else would George abandon her like this after inviting her for the weekend? Could Lord Kent—she must remember to think of him as Valentine—have been instrumental in whisking George away? But why would he do that? Was he playing the overly protective brother, as George seemed to suggest, shielding him from a woman he didn't consider good enough for him? But that didn't fit. Marissa had been positive that when Valentine came face-to-face with his guests in the parlor he was utterly taken aback by their unexpected arrival.

"Marissa?"

Lady Bethany was watching her with interest. "You are miles away, my dear. Whatever are you thinking of?"

Marissa shook her head, realizing that she was in danger of being as wildly imaginative as her grandmother had accused her of earlier. "Nothing of importance, Grandmamma." She smiled. "Valentine is a very unlikely name for Lord Kent, is it not?"

Lady Bethany smiled back wickedly. "I think it very suitable, Marissa, but then I have a great deal more experience of life than you. Now, I believe I will go and take a nap. What will you do?"

"I'm not tired so I will probably read or—or walk in the garden. Go and have your nap, Grandmamma, so you can look your best for later."

"And why would I want to look my best?" Lady Bethany asked cagily.

"You can't pretend to me you aren't enjoying Lord Jasper's company," Marissa said.

"Nonsense," Lady Bethany retorted, her voice sharper than usual.

Marissa was surprised at her grandmother's reaction. Her flirtatious manner seemed to have quite deserted her and there was a serious expression in her eyes. Marissa had never seen her worldly grandmother take any of her conquests seriously.

"Very well then, you loathe Lord Jasper."

"Now you're being ridiculous, Marissa. I am going to lie down."

After Lady Bethany had gone Marissa knew exactly what *she* was going to do. She was going in search of Valentine and Jasper, and one way or another she was going to discover exactly what they were keeping from her.

Chapter 4

There are six names on the list," Valentine said, holding the chewed and crumbling piece of parchment gingerly, as if he thought it might disintegrate at any moment.

"The five companions who went to the Crusades with Richard de Fevre, as well as de Fevre himself," Jasper added thoughtfully.

"Exactly." Valentine grimaced as a flake of parchment fluttered to the desk. "I think we should write them down, Jasper, before this thing turns to dust. There's a pen and ink over there . . . that's it."

"Number one?" Jasper asked, pen poised.

"Sir Wilfred Montfitchet."

"And two?"

"Henry Fortescue."

They went through the list, Jasper questioning the spelling and Valentine peering intently at the faded writing on the old document. He had no doubt this was what Von Hautt had been after when he called on Seth Bonnie and asked to see Valentine's father's papers. The first real clue in decades and Von Hautt had to find it first.

The rose is mine! he wanted to shout. *You have no right to it!*

But unfortunately, legally, that wasn't so, although morally he was positive no one had more right to make such a claim.

"So any one of these men could be the companion who saved de Fevre's life? The one to whom he gave the second rose?"

"It appears that way.

"How on earth did your father get hold of this?"

Valentine frowned in thought. "There *are* family papers. I've been through them myself, searching, but couldn't find anything. I see now why. My father must have found the parchment and it was in his possession and then after his death, Bonnie held on to it." He thought again. "He must have taken it with him for safekeeping."

"Good lord," Jasper said drolly. "You call Waterloo safekeeping?"

"You didn't know my father," Valentine replied, studying the new list Jasper had made. "Some of our family papers had already gone missing—sold off—and he didn't trust anyone when it came to the Crusader's Rose. My grandfather was none too fond of the whole matter, and as you know another of my ancestors destroyed the rose in the first place because there were too many strangers coming to the house, interrupting his peace and quiet. His vandalism and the rose's loss to the world inspired my father to take up the quest."

"And now his son is following in his footsteps," Jasper murmured. "He would be proud of you, I think."

Valentine remembered his father as a man in military uniform with a severe moustache, but he'd had a warm smile. His mother had died shortly after George's birth, but she'd seemed to be always sickly, reclining on sofas and wincing when her young son came rushing into the room to tell her of his latest adventure. He remembered making her shriek once when he opened his cupped hands to show her a large and slightly battered insect he'd found in the garden.

And later there was Valentine's wife. He'd had high hopes for a happy marriage, he'd been deeply in love, but it was not to be. Their marriage was short and miserable, and not something he planned to repeat. All in all, he decided, he hadn't had much luck. It was about time fate handed him a good card in the game of life.

"I wish—" he began.

There was a noise outside the room. Both men froze, listening. It had sounded very much like a sneeze.

Was one of the servants eavesdropping? thought Valentine. What the devil did it mean?

Rising from his chair and striding quickly across the room, he wrenched open the door.

Marissa Rotherhild had turned to run, but it was too late. He reached for her arm, halting her so suddenly that she stumbled and swung about, falling against him. The shock of her soft body against his, the scent and feel of her, rendered him momentarily unable to move or think. Breathing hard, he stared down into her pale face as her expression turned from surprise to wariness.

"What on earth do you think you're doing spying on me?" Valentine roared.

Her eyes grew wide. He could see every lash surrounding them and the lush melted chocolate brown of her irises.

"I wasn't spying on you." But her voice sounded uncertain. She licked her lips and the sight of her pink tongue sliding over the soft flesh went straight to his groin. For some reason this infuriated him even more than finding her outside the door.

"You were eavesdropping, Miss Rotherhild!" He pulled her harder against him, looming over her. "All this talk of George was just a blind, wasn't it? I knew you were too good to be true. You're spying for Von Hautt. Admit it, damn you!"

Her eyelashes fluttered and she sagged in his hands, almost as if she was about to faint. He didn't need Jasper's murmured admonishment to bring him to his senses. Shocked by his own uncharacteristic behavior, Valentine wrapped his arm about her waist, supporting her. Had it really been so long since he'd been in the company of an attractive woman that he'd lost the ability to function as a gentleman should?

"Miss Rotherhild. Marissa. Please . . . I beg you . . ."

Just for a moment she rested her head against his chest, while he cradled her in his arms, and he felt the strangest feeling. As if the world had ceased to exist beyond the two of them. And then she placed her palms against him and gave him a determined shove. He stumbled back a step, releasing her, and the spell was broken.

She was watching him warily, her hands clasped

together now, her fingers white at the knuckles. "I don't know what you're talking about. I came to this house at George's invitation, just as I told you. I have not been spying on you, Lord Kent. I have never spied on anyone in my life."

"I apologize," he muttered. He hadn't meant to grab her like that, but seeing her there, thinking she might be on the side of his enemy, had sparked an anger in him he hadn't known he was capable of. It was the disappointment, he decided, of discovering her perfection might be so badly flawed.

"Where is George?" she said, looking into the room as though expecting him to appear from between the books on the bookshelves.

He stared at her in complete bewilderment. "George? I've already told you that George isn't here."

The color had returned to her cheeks and her eyes sparkled with emotion. Whatever weakness she'd felt in his arms a moment ago had been banished. There was courage in the tilt of her chin and the set of her shoulders. Courage and beauty in equal measure.

"I don't believe you. You're lying to me. You were so secretive over luncheon, it was obvious there was something you were both keeping from me."

"Miss Rotherhild, I promise you I am not keeping anything from you. George comes and goes as he wishes. Despite the old adage, I am not his keeper."

"But there is something," she said stubbornly. "I know there is *something*."

Valentine shook his head. "It seems we have both been laboring under a misapprehension. Jasper and I do have a secret, but it has nothing to do with George."

Her look was skeptical, as if she was unprepared to think anything but the worst of him.

Valentine hesitated. He knew his quest for the Crusader's Rose was none of Marissa Rotherhild's business, but it wasn't as if it was a secret. The botanical community knew of his obsession—they probably had a good laugh at his expense. He remembered what Marissa had said at dinner, about her lack of interest in botany. *George and I are as one on that.* But surely the daughter of the famous Professor Rotherhild must have inherited something of her father's extraordinary zest? It was childish perhaps, but he wanted to find out.

"Come," he said, "and I will explain."

He held out his hand to her, but she would not take it. He accepted the snub—he deserved it after all—and stepped aside to let her by. After a brief hesitation curiosity got the better of her and she walked past him, her nose in the air, the hem of her skirts brushing the toes of his shoes. He followed her to the desk, where his father's papers lay spread about.

"Sit down, Miss Rotherhild," he said, coming up behind her.

She cast him a suspicious glance and he had the urge to brush his thumb over the protrusion of her bottom lip. Just before he kissed her. But of course he did neither.

"I promise not to manhandle you again," he said quietly. "Please sit down and I will confess all to you."

She ignored the tease in his voice and took her time arranging her skirts to her satisfaction, before folding her hands in her lap and striking a waiting pose. Her perfume drifted toward him and he was once more confounded by the reaction of his body. This was George's young lady and he should not be thinking of her in such a way, but he couldn't seem to help it.

"Kent?" Jasper was watching him with a trace of impatience, probably wondering what on earth was going on in his friend's head.

Valentine cleared his throat and regained control. He pointed to the parchment. "Before you, Miss Rotherhild, is a document that has been in my family for centuries. My father took it with him into the army, and when he died his batman took it into his keeping. It has only recently come to light—in fact, I received it in the post this very morning."

Marissa looked down at the grubby parchment with some distaste.

"Read it," he instructed her.

Dutifully she leaned forward to peer at the faded writing. Jasper promptly presented her with his own list and with a grateful smile she examined the names he'd copied in his neat hand. When she'd finished she looked up, gaze traveling to Jasper and staying there.

"Who are they?" she said, ignoring Valentine.

But Valentine wasn't having that. "Have you heard of the Crusader's Rose?"

Reluctantly she turned to where he still stood, tilting her head to look up at him. "No. Should I have?"

"Not necessarily. Suffice it to say that the Crusader's Rose is one of those mysteries that has become legend in botanical circles. Think of the Holy Grail, and then transfer it to the world of the rose collector. Everyone who wants to make a name for himself wants to find the Crusader's Rose."

"And you are one of those people?"

Valentine smiled without humor. "The rose belongs to us. It was brought back from the Crusades by my ancestor, Richard de Fevre, but unfortunately it was destroyed in 1735. However, we know de Fevre gave a second rose to one of his companions, one of the men who traveled to the Crusades with him. De Fevre stated that this man had saved his life in the Holy Land, and the legend says that the man then grew the rose in his own garden. Presumably it grows there still."

"Rather a large presumption, Lord Kent. The Crusades were in the twelfth century?"

"Yes, the Third Crusade, and probably the most famous one, was in the twelfth century. It was led by Richard the Lionheart."

"And you expect a rose to live for all those years?" Her voice was disbelieving.

"Of course not. But the Crusader's Rose was known for its self-seeding capabilities. There was always a vigorous young bush to take over when the older one began to wane. And if it survived here at Abbey Thorne Manor then why not elsewhere, too?"

"And these are the names of the other men who were de Fevre's companions?"

"Exactly. I believe this list to be part of a collection

of documents that were once held here in my library. Most of the collection was broken up and scattered, sold."

She was silent, taking it in, and he watched her curiously. If she and George were really as one then she would stand now and excuse herself and leave them to it. The quest would hold no interest for her whatsoever.

Her dark eyes lifted to his and they were full of brilliant intelligence; Valentine had to remind himself very sternly that he had promised not to touch her.

"But . . . what makes this particular rose special? Why is it so sought after?"

She was interested. She wanted to understand. There was nothing more exciting to Valentine than a woman with an inquiring mind, especially when she was inquiring about his favorite subject.

"Let me explain, Miss Rotherhild. Until very recently all the roses we grew in England were summer or spring flowering—that is, they only flowered once a year. The Crusader's Rose flowered several times throughout the spring, summer and autumn, a truly remarkable feat in Medieval times. And its color was very different from the white and pink colorings we were used to. The Crusader's Rose was golden orange—in fact, de Fevre claimed the hue reminded him of the sun setting over Jerusalem."

There was a glow in her eyes. "Oh," she murmured, her lips curving up at the corners, clearly enthralled with the picture he'd painted. Then, as if suddenly realizing she was showing interest in something she'd claimed bored her, her face went blank. When she spoke again her voice was carefully devoid of enthusiasm.

"But this is supposition on your part, is it not? You never actually saw the rose yourself? Not if it was destroyed in 1735?"

"No. But there are plenty of statements to back up the story. People came from far and wide to admire the rose. That was the reason my ancestor destroyed it. He claimed he was tired of strangers trespassing in his garden, and after a party of gentlemen from France appeared outside his library window and began exclaiming over the beauty of the rose, he decided enough was enough. He ordered the rose be dug out and burned, and any seedlings similarly destroyed. No one dared disobey him—he wasn't a very pleasant man—and when it was done everyone believed that was the end of the Crusader's Rose."

"Except it wasn't." Jasper was leaning forward as if he was hearing the story for the first time.

"When my father was a boy a manuscript turned up at an antiquarian bookseller's in London. It was incomplete and my father was certain it had once belonged to the de Fevre collection in our library. Historians concluded the manuscript was part of a larger document which told the story of de Fevre and his companions, but the important thing is, it mentioned the fact that there were two roses. Unfortunately, although it spoke about de Fevre handing one of his companions the other rose as a thank-you for saving his life, the name of that companion was completely illegible.

"That find inspired my father to begin his search for the rose, a search I have since carried on. When my father died I made a promise that I would do everything in my power to find it."

The spark of interest was back in Marissa's face.

"Kent is on a mission to restore the Crusader's Rose to its rightful place at Abbey Thorne Manor," Jasper said.

Marissa blinked. "You sound like my father when he's on the hunt for some rare specimen," she said with a grimace. "I'm afraid botanical missions are of no interest to me."

And yet even as she spoke she was leaning forward to inspect the list of names, a crease between her brows.

"What do you intend to do now that you have found the names? Visit each house and search their gardens?"

"That is my plan, yes," he said stiffly.

"Then I'm sorry to lack enthusiasm for your plan, Lord Kent, but what if the house is gone, fallen down, pulled down? What if the family moved far away and took the rose with them? What if—"

He interrupted her impatiently. "My family still lives in the same place, if not quite in the same house, and if my ancestor hadn't destroyed the rose in a fit of pique, it would still be here. You forget, these were not men who moved in the highest circles in the land. They did not play with kings and queens; they were not powerful except in their own little patch of country. There was no reason to take their land or homes from them for being on the wrong side in a political struggle. After the Crusades they stayed put and quietly farmed their land and raised their children. There is every possibility that the rose is still to be found, flowering away unnoticed, in some quiet corner of the county."

Jasper gave a grunt of agreement and Marissa turned back to the list, as if she might find more arguments in the arrangement of the letters.

Despite feeling a degree of irritation with her, Valentine found himself examining the delicate nape of her neck, noting the way wisps of her dark hair curled against her pale skin. There was the glint of ebony combs amongst the thick tresses, and his fingers twitched as he imagined removing those combs and allowing the heavy mass to fall into his hands. Burying his face in her hair, in her scent.

He almost groaned aloud.

"So if the rose still exists you will find it," she was saying, unaware of his struggle. "I wish you luck, Lord Kent. I'm sure the Crusader's Rose will make a very nice addition to your garden."

"You think it a waste of time," he said coolly. "Far better if I were spending my time at race tracks and in card hells, like George. Now there's an occupation for a gentleman."

Her cheeks flushed and her eyes sparkled. God, she was beautiful. Far too beautiful for his brother . . .

Marissa fought her anger and won. She gave a little shrug. "I have been on more expeditions than you can imagine. I've stood in the burning sun and the driving rain. I know how it works. And I have no desire to take part in your expedition, Lord Kent!"

"Well, that is unfortunate," Valentine drawled, "because as my houseguest I intend taking you on a little expedition tomorrow, Miss Rotherhild. I promise there will be no burning sun or driving rain, just a civilized jaunt to a pretty nearby village and a brief ramble through a garden. My expeditions are nothing like Professor Rotherhild's. You may even enjoy this one so much you will want to go on another."

"What if I don't want to go?" She wasn't smiling.

"You can wait here for George if you wish. I'm sure he will appreciate your concern and patience in sitting quietly at the window, watching for his return. Would you like me to burn a candle in the window to show him the way home? When he's tired of doing whatever he's doing and remembers he has guests, that is."

The emotions played over her face and he read them accurately. She didn't want to be seen as patiently awaiting George's return, she was too proud for that, and despite loyally sticking up for him she must also be angry with him for forgetting her. It was altogether too easy for Valentine to persuade her to his will.

"Oh, very well," she said crossly. "I will come with you on your expedition. But I warn you, if it so much as drizzles I demand to be taken home. I loathe being rained upon."

Jasper looked at Valentine, his eyes dark with laughter. "What say you to that, Kent?"

"Very well, Miss Rotherhild, I accept your conditions. And I think you are being very wise in not waiting for George's return."

"George would be here if he could." She shot him a combative look. "Something must have prevented him."

Valentine heaved a sigh. "I swear to you I don't know where my brother is, nor have I locked him up in the dungeons. I wish you would understand that George can look after himself very well. He always has."

She said nothing.

"I'm sure Miss Rotherhild will be a useful addition to our party," Jasper began mildly. "Although there is the possibility of Von Hautt . . ."

"Von Hautt? You mentioned that name before. You accused me of being his spy. Who is Von Hautt?" Marissa demanded, clearly requiring an answer.

"A fellow searcher for the Crusader's Rose," Valentine replied briefly. "He is a hot head. I do not believe him to be dangerous but he can be a nuisance."

"I am not afraid of danger." She spoke with scorn, lifting her chin, and once more Valentine found himself completely captivated. This was the woman he wanted at his side as he searched for the rose; it was a pity she claimed not to care for his quest.

But that didn't mean, given a little time and effort, that he could not change her mind.

"You see, Kent, Miss Rotherhild isn't afraid of danger," Jasper said, with a droll look.

"I doubt we will suffer more than a few rose thorns in our fingers," Valentine replied, forcing his gaze away from Marissa, and beginning to shuffle the papers back into a pile.

He should feel guilty. But it wasn't as if he was going to steal Marissa from his brother—well, not unless she wanted to be stolen—and besides, George was showing a singular lack of interest in her. She was his houseguest and it was up to him to keep her entertained, that was all.

But he knew he was telling himself lies. When

Marissa smiled at him with her warm, dimpled smile he felt himself go hot all over. She was making him do things, think things, he couldn't remember doing or thinking in years.

Truly, he was entering dangerous waters.

Chapter 5

During dinner, the expedition was discussed again, and when Jasper informed Lady Bethany of their intention of setting off the following morning for the village of Montfitchet, she said that if they were going searching for a rose then she had better come, too, to keep an eye on them all.

Jasper expressed his pleasure at her joining them and raised his glass in a toast. "To the quest!"

"To bringing the Crusader's Rose home to Abbey Thorne Manor!" Valentine added.

"Where it belongs," Marissa finished, before she thought to stop herself.

He smiled knowingly at her over his glass and she felt her heart give an odd, uneven thud.

He'd removed his neck cloth again, and the neck of his shirt was open. When he leaned back in his chair she could not help but notice his shoulders and the way his hair curled about the strong column of his neck.

He was very masculine.

He was the sort of man women noticed and watched and dreamed of marrying.

Marissa felt embarrassingly warm and flushed

being in his company, but she refused to accept there was anything out of the ordinary with that. Even the fact she wanted to touch him, and she wanted him to touch her, was surely not so very wicked. Marissa knew about fast women, she and her friends had discussed the subject at length, and decided that as long as one only used one's feminine attributes on the man one loved and wanted to marry, then it was acceptable to be "fast." The question was, did her wanting to run her hands over Valentine's shoulders and back and wind them around his neck fall within those guidelines?

He wasn't the man she wanted to marry. He wasn't the man she was in love with.

Like most girls of her station Marissa was a virgin. Although she had had her share of stolen kisses, some more pleasurable than others, she'd never experienced the dark pleasures of the flesh. What happened in the marriage bed was vague, and until she met George she'd not considered it overmuch, but she was sure he would make her laugh and they would muddle through somehow.

Now she found herself thinking of Valentine instead of George and she didn't feel like laughing one little bit.

She was shocked by her own thoughts, but she was also intrigued and unsettled.

They'd only just met!

She hadn't wanted to be part of his search for the Crusader's Rose, but when Valentine spoke of it the passion sparked like fire in his blue eyes. In response, something flared inside her, too. He made this adventure exciting—Valentine Kent was exciting.

How could she explain that to the Husband Hunters Club?

"Oh, by the way, I plan to marry George, but in the meanwhile I thought I might become infatuated with his brother . . ."

Her friends would think her flighty, but Marissa knew she'd never been that sort of girl. She was serious and cautious, more inclined to intellectual pursuits than balls and parties. For some reason Valentine Kent was having an odd and uncharacteristic effect on her.

Not that it would last. He was everything she had sworn to reject. A botanist with a quest, a man who found expeditions to find plants the highlight of his life, a man who poured over musty old books and dried specimens and whose conversation consisted of names in Latin. If she married such a man it would be as if she never left home.

George was her choice; George would give her a life completely different from the one she had. So what if he enjoyed a game of cards or a horse race? At least he would never force her to stand in a downpour armed with nothing more than a notebook and pencil while he crouched over plants exclaiming, "Magnificent. Look at this, Marissa. Have you ever seen anything more beautiful?"

Marissa gave a little shudder at the thought. The next time she turned her eyes to Valentine on the other side of the table, she found she could look at him with almost complete indifference.

After dinner, Jasper and Lady Bethany went out for a stroll in the garden before retiring. As she rose from her chair, Marissa's grandmother raised her thin eyebrows and gave her granddaughter a questioning look.

Marissa didn't need her to say what was on her mind. She was wondering why Marissa had involved herself in this expedition when she usually went out of her way to avoid such tedious adventures. She would want an explanation.

Restless and unsettled, Marissa rose and went to the window, gazing out over the moat and the park beyond. There was a copse of trees, dark against the fading twilight. They looked a little sinister, especially when a cloud of rooks flew up from the boughs and began a noisy protest.

"Jasper and your grandmother seem to be getting along very well," Valentine said from the room behind her.

"Yes."

"Is your grandfather alive?"

"No." She cleared her throat. "He died a long time ago, before I was born. My grandmother has been a widow longer than she was ever a wife."

"And she never remarried?"

"No, the single life suits her. She comes from a generation when marriage had little to do with love."

"Does it ever?" he asked in a quiet voice.

"I suppose not. It's just that . . ." Marissa found her tongue growing tangled, "well, my friends would rather not marry at all if they cannot find a man they . . . they admire enough to . . . to love."

"And what about you, Miss Rotherhild?"

He wanted her to bare her heart to him? Marissa

wondered how on earth she had strayed into this topic. But perhaps it was a chance for her to reaffirm the Husband Hunters Club and their aims. She took a breath and turned to face him, her back to the window, her fingers gripping the sill behind her.

"I admire your friends for their idealism," he spoke first, his gaze on hers steady and unreadable, "but unfortunately the world we inhabit does not value love in the making of a marriage."

"That may be true of some people, Lord Kent, but not all."

He raised a cynical eyebrow. "In the world we move in marriages are made through practical considerations—wealth, land, family connections. Love matches are accidental, or else unhappy failures."

"George says—" She bit her lip.

Valentine raised his other eyebrow. "What words of great wisdom has my dear brother spoken on the matter, Miss Rotherhild? Come, do enlighten me."

"Only that if you are going to spend most of your life with someone then surely it is better if you are fond of that someone."

"But then again might it not be better if one did not give one's heart too deeply to one's partner? Death is indiscriminate and if one's partner were to die, the pain would be almost more than one could bear."

He sounded bleak and suddenly Marissa remembered that Valentine had been married himself. Here she was blathering on about love and marriage and it was obvious he had loved his wife and still suffered deeply from her loss. How could she be so stupid? Nevertheless, as she opened her mouth to apologize, it occurred to her that his argument was flawed, and really she could not let it pass.

"So you believe one should encase one's heart in ice and avoid feeling too deeply in case one is hurt?"

"It makes sense."

"Or bury your emotions by taking on a task so intellectually stimulating that you never miss love at all. Something like a . . . quest to find the Crusader's Rose?"

His eyes narrowed, his mouth thinned.

Marissa's fingers gripped the sill harder, waiting for his anger to wash over her.

Footsteps came hurrying toward the room and Jasper appeared, flushed, his hair standing on end, and then her grandmother arrived behind him, wide- eyed and gasping for breath.

"Kent, you'll never believe it," Jasper burst out. "The utter gall of the man. The sheer arrogance—"

"Jasper . . ."

"It defies belief, Kent. If I could have caught him I swear I would have—"

Valentine poured a glass of brandy from the decanter, handing it to his friend. "Drink this, Jasper, and then tell me, slowly, what on earth you're talking about."

Lady Bethany had tottered to a chair and collapsed into it. "How very . . . exciting," she managed. "I don't think I've attempted to run like that since the Earl of Southmoor cornered me in an arbor at Vauxhall Gardens."

Thankfully, Jasper found his voice and interrupted her wicked reminiscences.

"He was standing outside in the park, Kent. Staring in through the window at you and Miss Rotherhild. I tell you it was him. I'd recognize him anywhere."

"Who, Jasper? Who?" Valentine cried in frustration.

"Von Hautt."

Valentine froze, and then strode across to the window, reaching it just as Marissa turned to also gaze out into the darkness. The soft summer breeze stirred against her cheek, bringing with it the scent of mown grass and the hum of crickets. His shoulder brushed hers and she felt his indrawn breath, and when he turned his head to meet her eyes she could see his own were full of passion and excitement.

"Are you sure you want to join me on tomorrow's quest, Marissa?" he said softly, for her alone. "I will think no less of you if you wish to bow out."

"But you told me Baron Von Hautt was not dangerous," she accused.

"I lied."

Her eyes narrowed at his unrepentant smile. "So Baron Von Hautt *is* dangerous?"

"Yes, I believe he is. I believe he will do anything in his power to beat me to the finish line."

He expected her to turn tail and run. Marissa had no intention of being seen as a coward, and besides, she wasn't afraid of Von Hautt. His possible presence made tomorrow's expedition far more exciting than any botanical adventure she'd been on with her parents. "I will not be bowing out, Valentine."

Some emotion flared in his gaze at the sound of his name on her lips, but before she could decide what it was he was turning away, moving back into the room.

"Which way did he go, Jasper?"

"Into the trees. He probably had a horse tethered there." Jasper was pouring himself another glass of brandy, and Lady Bethany gestured for him to pour one for her, too.

"Well, at least now we are prepared for him," Valentine said grimly.

"As prepared as we can be," Jasper added. "The damnable thing of it is I was just this moment telling Lady B about the theft you suspected Von Hautt of committing, and then there he stood."

"Theft?" Marissa looked from one to the other.

"Von Hautt has been a thorn in my side for many years," Valentine admitted, grim-faced. "Do you remember the manuscript I told you about, the one discovered in the antiquarian bookshop? It was sold to a private collector and kept in his house under lock and key, but last year it was inexplicably stolen. It just so happened that Von Hautt had been a houseguest a week before. He'd shown great interest in the manuscript while he was there, and seemed to think he could restore the illegible name with some chemicals he'd brought with him. Understandably, the owner refused to allow him to tamper with the document."

"So he took it anyway," Marissa murmured.

"Oh, he denied the theft, and it couldn't be proved, but only a fool would believe him innocent. There have been times when I thought I had a clue to the rose and set off to follow it, only to find Von Hautt had arrived before me. It would not surprise me to hear he'd paid someone to spy at Abbey Thorne Manor. That would explain how he always manages to be one step ahead of me."

Lady Bethany finished her brandy and heaved herself out of her chair. "I believe I will retire. Marissa?"

With one final glance at Valentine, Marissa came to her side, tucking her grandmother's arm into her own. They murmured their goodnights and left the room.

"Good Gad, I don't know if I can stomach too much more excitement," Lady Bethany murmured, as they climbed the stairs. "One moment we were enjoying a quiet moment in the garden and the next Jasper took off like a hound after a hare. I swear for a man his age he is very fit."

Marissa eyed her grandmother sideways. "I hope you are not planning to seduce Lord Jasper, Grandmamma. It could make things very awkward."

"Why? Because you have your sights set on George Kent?" Lady Bethany retorted. Her mouth twitched into a wicked smile. "Or is it Valentine Kent? I'll grant you he is very manly, but take care, Marissa. He is a man of the world and you are barely more than a schoolroom miss."

"I thought men of the world liked schoolroom misses," she said airily.

"In romance novels, perhaps."

"I am not at all interested in Valentine Kent, Grandmamma, so you needn't worry. He is George's brother, that is my sole consideration."

Lady Bethany paused outside her door and took her granddaughter's hands in hers. "That reminds me, my dear. Jasper was speaking of Valentine's wife. It seems she made him miserable—one of those cold, puritanical women—and he has sworn never to marry again."

Marissa felt inexplicably low, but told herself it was empathy for Valentine's misery, as she kissed her grandmother goodnight and retired to her bedchamber. The candlelight flickered over the beams on the ceiling and the draperies around the bed, as she settled back against the pillows.

Why did everything suddenly seem so complicated? Why couldn't George have been waiting to greet her when she arrived? If he'd been here she wouldn't have noticed Valentine and she wouldn't be having these thoughts about him. Intensely physical thoughts.

There was a definite spark between them. Perhaps their expedition tomorrow would give her a chance to practice her feminine wiles on him. In preparation for her hunting of George, she hurriedly reminded herself. A rehearsal. Because, of course, George was the one she planned to marry.

Marissa closed her eyes, smiling, allowing her imagination free reign. She pictured herself touching George, kissing him, rolling naked with him across a vast bed.

She began to giggle.

That was the trouble with George, it was impossible to imagine herself being serious in his company.

She closed her eyes again and suddenly it was Valentine with her on the vast bed. She was no longer giggling, in fact she felt breathless and excited.

Shaking off the fantasy, she blew out the candle and shimmied under the covers.

George was the man for her, she was sure of it, and as soon as he returned to Abbey Thorne Manor she would persuade him of it, too.

Chapter 6

Montfitchet, according to Valentine's copy of *Guidebook to Surrey*, was named for the Montfitchet family who had owned it from Norman times. Thus far it was the only village he could find with any connection to the men who went to the Crusades with Richard de Fevre, but even then the information was infuriatingly sparse.

"Perhaps the vicar of Montfitchet will know something of the history of the family," Valentine said, as they made their way through a leafy tunnel of elm trees, their branches meeting above the road as if they were holding hands.

"What you need is a scholar." Marissa rode at his side on the well mannered mare he had provided for her. Her grandmother and Jasper were in the carriage some way behind, preferring a more leisurely mode of transport. "Someone who has studied the land-owning families of Surrey in the twelfth century and knows what became of them."

"You're right," Valentine said. His own horse danced restlessly, taking exception to a patch of dappled sunlight. He tightened the reins. "I have a friend in London who may be able to help. I'll write to him."

Valentine had spent a restless night. Von Hautt's appearance was unsettling and he couldn't help but wonder what the villain was up to. The thought of him anywhere near Marissa made his hands bunch into fists as, he told himself, his protective instincts came to the fore. More likely and less chivalrously, he admitted wryly, he was like a dog, forbidden to touch the succulent morsel but at the same time unwilling to share it with anyone else.

Today she was wearing an emerald green riding outfit, with a jaunty little hat perched on her dark curls. He could barely take his eyes off her. The tightly fitted garment accentuated her narrow waist and the flare of her hips, not to mention the rounded curve of her bosom.

Whenever she mentioned George he had the perverse urge to pull her into his arms and kiss her until she forgot all about his wretched brother. He wanted her. Yes, that was the trouble. He wanted Marissa Rotherhild all to himself despite knowing it was impossible. A woman like Marissa did not have an affaire; she married. And even if she was willing, Valentine wasn't. Apart from the question of George, and their incompatibility when it came to botanical pursuits, he had been married once and he wasn't planning to do it again.

Ten years ago he had believed himself deeply in love but it had turned out badly. Vanessa might be dead, but her poison lived on. No, even if he could, he would not willingly place his head in that yoke again.

Again his gaze slid to Marissa. As if aware of his scrutiny she turned her head and smiled. Just for a moment he read an invitation in her dark eyes, but he knew he must be mistaken. Marissa was an innocent—her talk of love last night had proved that beyond doubt—and she deserved a man without the sort of shadows that blighted Valentine.

Damn it, she deserved someone like George.

Montfitchet village sprawled over the main London road and boasted a coaching inn, a blacksmith, and a shop. It was clear that this was now the hub of the village, and not the church, which was about half a mile away. It stood on a hilltop, a squat building with a blunt steeple that looked as if it had sprouted from the landscape rather than been built. When they reached the lych-gate that led into the churchyard, Jasper and Lady Bethany chose to remain in the carriage.

"Better not overwhelm the poor fellow," Jasper said, not quite meeting Valentine's eyes. "You and Miss Rotherhild go and see what you can discover about Sir Wilfred. I'll stay here and keep Lady B company."

Irritably, Valentine bit his tongue on the words that sprang to it. Had Jasper forgotten why they were here in Montfitchet or was he really more interested in Lady Bethany? He would have thought the pair of them too old for an affaire. Or was one never too old? He reached to help Marissa down, releasing her the moment her toes touched the ground. Even so, the feel of her trim waist and the scent of her skin remained with him as he ducked beneath the lych-gate and headed up the path between gravestones sprouting like crooked teeth from the green grass.

The church door opened beneath his hand and he stepped into the dim, cool interior. He felt Marissa's fingers curl about his arm and resisted the urge to shake her off. Predictably her touch caused his pulse to begin to pound. Feverishly.

I really must conquer this ridiculous infatuation, he told himself. *Surely a man of my maturity and intelligence can find a way to snuff out the flame?* Here he was, annoyed with Jasper for not giving the quest his full attention, while he was behaving in an equally ridiculous fashion.

"Oh look!" Her voice startled him back to the moment. She brushed by him, tugging his arm so that he had no option but to follow her. Set into the floor were two life-sized brass memorials, the images of a knight and his lady. Their features were worn smooth, but Valentine wasn't the least surprised when they made out the name "Montfitchet" at their feet.

"Do you think it's Sir Wilfred?" she whispered.

"I don't know. Possibly."

"The rose might be close by. Could it be so easy?"

He gave a reluctant smile. "Why are you whispering?"

"I don't know. Churches always make me feel like whispering." She smiled back, her head tipped to one side, as though trying to read him. There were smudges under her eyes, as if she had slept as badly as he. The urge to smooth them away, gently, with his fingertip was so strong he began to wonder if he could trust himself.

A sound from the vestry was a welcome distraction, and this time Valentine led the way, trying to ignore the fact that her hand was still tucked safely into the crook of his arm.

The vicar was busy stacking some heavy, leather-bound books into shelves. He straightened at Valentine's greeting, and turned with a friendly smile. He was a tall, thin man with untidy hair and a lined, comfortably-lived-in face.

"I say, more visitors. I'm afraid you've missed the service . . ."

Valentine was impatient for answers but Marissa was more polite. "We were just admiring your church," she said with her smile.

The vicar turned to her, Valentine thought wryly, as a blind man to the warmth of the sun.

"It is Norman, you know," he said with enthusiasm. "Well, most of it. The spire was struck by lightning and had to be rebuilt last century. At the time it was hoped it was only a temporary replacement, and that a taller spire would be constructed when the funds were available, but so far no benefactor has stepped forward."

"Oh dear."

Valentine interrupted their head shaking. "There are two brass memorials let into the pavement to the right of the front door. A knight and his lady. Can you tell us who they might be?"

He answered promptly. "The knight is Sir Wilfred Montfitchet and the lady is May, his wife. I believe Sir Wilfred was a crusader. He brought home enough booty to fill the Montfitchet family coffers for a hundred years or so, but eventually it ran out and then they died out. Although not before they had paid for a handsome screen for the church, and a couple of really beautiful candlesticks. I'm afraid the candlesticks are locked away—"

"We are looking for the original Montfitchet manor house. Do you know if it is still standing?"

The vicar's eyes widened. "Why, what a . . . a coincidence! It isn't often I am asked the same question twice within half an hour. But perhaps you are acquainted with the gentleman who has just left?"

Valentine felt the hackles rise on the back of his neck. "There was someone else asking about the Montfitchets?"

"Yes." At his tone, the vicar's friendly manner began to wilt about the edges and his face creased with concern. "Surely you ran into him in the churchyard? He's only just left. Foreign gentleman with gray hair and a red . . ."

"Von Hautt," Valentine growled. "Baron Von Hautt."

"He didn't mention his name," the vicar ventured, wilting even further. "I did tell him where the old manor used to be—well, it was a castle, actually. It's a ruin now. If you go to the far end of the village, beyond the inn, you'll see one of the remaining towers standing in the field to the left."

Valentine turned to go, taking Marissa with him.

The vicar called after them. "As I told the other gentleman, Mr. Jensen takes an interest in the history of the village. He will be able to answer your questions much better than I. He lives in the white cottage just down the hill. You can't miss it. There's a rather fine vegetable garden at the front and an old apple tree . . ."

"But how did the baron know . . . ?" Marissa said, as they hurried down the aisle.

"I told you, he is always one step ahead of me." Valentine paused, his head tilted, back and shoulders rigid. "What *is* that?"

Then Marissa heard it, too. Angry voices from outside the church. One of them sounded like Jasper. When they reached the porch Valentine set off at a sprint across the graveyard toward the lych-gate, but Marissa froze, staring in horrified amazement at the scene before her.

Lady Bethany was still seated in the carriage but Jasper was on the ground beside it, nose to nose with another man, and they were shouting. Or at least Jasper was. The stranger had steely gray hair but paradoxically his face was that of a man in his thirties. He also wore a red kerchief knotted about his throat and a caped coat covered him from shoulder to toe.

"The arrogance of the English is beyond belief!" he shouted back, his voice slightly accented. "You think you own the world and everyone in it. All is part of your empire."

At that moment Jasper glanced up, saw Valentine coming, and grabbed at Von Hautt's shoulder. "Here he is, Kent!" he roared. "I've got him. No escape for you this time, Von Hautt. See how you like the inside of one of our English prisons."

Von Hautt struggled with him, but Jasper wouldn't

let go, and then there was a loud explosion.

Jasper stumbled back against the carriage wheel and Lady Bethany screamed. Marissa pressed her hands to her mouth in disbelief. Von Hautt had a pistol in his hand, a curl of smoke still lingering about the barrel. The next moment he was running up the lane that led from the church and over the hill, with Valentine in pursuit. A moment later Marissa heard the sound of a galloping horse.

But she was already hurrying toward Jasper, who was now lying on the ground with Lady Bethany kneeling over him, her handkerchief pressed to the spreading red stain on his shoulder. She looked up at Marissa when she reached them, but although her face was pale, her voice was calm. "I believe we require a doctor."

Jasper groaned, his eyes rolling up, and Lady Bethany opened her reticule, reaching inside for her smelling salts, and waved the bottle expertly beneath his nose.

Just then Valentine arrived back, panting from his run, and began to shrug off his jacket. "Did he get away?" Marissa asked, although the answer was obvious.

"Yes. He had his horse tethered in the trees over the hill."

He handed his jacket to Marissa without a word and pulled his white linen shirt over his head, folding it into a thick pad, and proceeded to press it to his friend's bleeding wound.

It occurred to Marissa that she should avert her eyes, but she didn't seem able to. A very strange thing was happening to her. As Valentine bent over Jasper, the broad and delectable expanse of his naked back and shoulders was quite the most exciting thing she had seen in her life thus far. The muscles in his biceps bunched as he pressed down, his untidy hair fell forward over his brow, while—dear Lord—his skintight riding breeches clung to his buttocks and the long, strong muscles of his thighs.

"Where is he?" Jasper's voice brought her back to herself. His eyes were open and he was staring wildly around. "Von Hautt was here, Kent. He was right here."

"He got away. Keep still, will you?"

"Blast him."

"What did he say to you, Jasper? What did you say to him to make him act so rashly?"

"I called him a swine and a thief and told him I'd have him locked up."

"That would do it then," Valentine said dryly.

"We need to get Lord Jasper to a doctor," Lady Bethany repeated loudly. "You can have this discussion later."

"Ahem." The sound of the vicar clearing his throat behind her made Marissa jump violently, and she wondered if he'd noticed her avid interest in Valentine's flesh. "There's a doctor in the village," he said helpfully. "He's retired now but he still takes urgent cases. I'll show you the way, if you like?"

Valentine sprang into action. He lifted the groaning Jasper in his arms and placed him into the carriage, his head resting in Lady Bethany's lap. The vicar squeezed in beside them and Valentine set his own foot on the step, ready to take control of the horses. And then he stopped and looked down.

Marissa, standing with his jacket still in her arms, gazed up at him mutely. She didn't mean to do it but she couldn't help it. Her eyes dropped from his, skimming over his chest and the golden matt of hair that stretched from his nipples and down over his flat belly to the fastening of his breeches.

Dear Lord, they really were tight, and there was a prominent bulge between his thighs.

His body was nothing like hers. The thought of finding out just how different was making her feel quite flushed and dizzy, and when he spoke she had to ask him to repeat himself.

"My jacket, Marissa."

She handed it to him but didn't immediately let go, so they stood, joined by the jacket between them.

His hair was darker against the blue sky, his eyes bluer, and she felt her knees growing wobbly as blood rushed into places she'd never felt it rush before. Her breasts grew heavy and sensitive, and between her legs the flesh ached, while her breath quickened in her throat.

"Do you want to squeeze into the carriage?" he said.

She shook her head. "I'll w-walk, I think."

"Do you think you can manage the horses then?"

"Of course. Yes, I'll bring the horses."

He took the jacket and slipped it on, but his eyes stayed on hers and his jaw tensed, and Marissa knew without doubt that he read everything she was feeling. Then he was whipping up the horses and the carriage moved away down the lane toward the village.

Marissa stood a moment and watched them go. Her heart was beating hard and she still felt shaky around the knees. She took a deep breath and then another, wondering what on earth had possessed her to ogle him so blatantly. The question as to whether or not she was fast had been answered well and truly. At least, that was what Valentine must think her.

Well, it was too late now to turn time back. Later, she would deal with the consequences of her actions.

The horses were tethered to the churchyard fence, but as she took a step toward them, she heard the sound of another horse approaching from over the crest of the hill.

Baron Von Hautt had returned and he was coming toward her. She could hardly believe it. She was certain her mouth fell open. He drew up his mount opposite her in the lane, earth scattering around him, his long coat flapping about him like giant wings.

He was looking at her. His eyes were light, but not the glorious blue of Valentine's, rather they were pale and chilly. With his gray hair and youngish face he was striking, and yet his looks left her cold. And afraid.

Von Hautt's mouth twitched into a half smile and he nodded at her. "You are every bit as beautiful as I believed you to be when I saw you through the window at Abbey Thorne Manor," he said.

"How dare you spy on me!"

"Oh I dare," he said in that cold voice. "I dare a great deal."

For an awful moment she thought he was going to urge his mount closer and she wondered if she should turn and run to the safety of the church. But he must have seen the panic in her eyes because he laughed.

"Do not fear, I will not hurt you. Not yet. I mean to save you for last."

The next moment he'd wrenched his mount around and galloped off, down the hill toward the village. Shocked, shaking, Marissa ran a few steps after him, and saw him take a sharp turn to the left, away from the coaching inn, where the others had gone, and vanish between a row of cottages.

Chapter 7

Valentine carried Jasper into the inn and up the creaking staircase, into a chamber above. By the time the doctor arrived at the vicar's behest, his friend was lying on the bed, pale and in pain, but awake. Perhaps he would be better unconscious, Valentine thought with a grimace, as the doctor opened his bag and took out some sharp-looking instruments.

"The bullet is still lodged in his shoulder," he announced, slipping on a pair of glasses. "I will need to remove it and dress the wound."

Lady Bethany moved closer and took Jasper's hand firmly in hers. That was when Valentine decided he was no longer required, and made a hasty exit, closing the door behind him. It wasn't that he was afraid of the sight of blood, it was just that he preferred not to see too much of it. Especially when that blood belonged to one of his closest and oldest friends.

A servant hurried by, giving him an odd look. Self-consciously, Valentine pulled his jacket tighter across his bare chest and buttoned it. His shirt was still upstairs with Jasper but he was unlikely to be wearing it again, considering the state of it. He used it as a bandage because there was nothing else, never thinking twice, until he'd seen Marissa.

The image of her was suddenly right there in front of him and he knew it wasn't possible he could have mistaken the look on her face. Valentine groaned and rubbed a hand over his eyes, shaking his head. Just because Vanessa had shuddered at his merest touch didn't mean all women were the same . . . did it?

Marissa's gaze on him had been like liquid fire, singeing his skin, lapping his body, burning him. He'd felt his cock jutting out like a prize stallion. Valentine never lost control of his passions, but in that moment he'd honestly wondered if he was about to spill in front of her. She had done that. The carnal force they were generating between them had done that.

God help him if he ever actually touched her bare skin. He'd probably self-combust. They'd find his body smoldering away and never know why.

The thought was humorous in a black sort of way, and he grinned as he continued down the creaky stairs and out through the door. But his smile vanished when the first person he saw was the source of his physical discomfort. Marissa had arrived with the two horses. A hostler was just helping her down from the saddle to the cobbles—there was a flash of stockinged calf above her riding boots. Safely on the ground, she shook out the skirt of her riding habit and reached up to adjust her hat, brushing back the veil that had fallen over one eye.

Valentine stood and admired her pale skin and dark hair, allowing his gaze to follow the trim curve of her waist and the voluptuous swell of her bosom in the tight emerald green jacket. Already he could feel her effect on him beginning to take hold, and he had to give himself a stern talking-to before he felt able to approach her with the required decorum.

"Miss Rotherhild," he called in a hearty voice that sounded horribly false even to his own ears.

She jumped like a frightened filly and looked at him with huge dark eyes and it was only then he knew something was very wrong.

He reached her in several strides and took her arm in a firm grip. As he thought, she was trembling. He wanted to hold her, to wrap his arms tight about her and draw her into his body, where he knew she fitted so well. If they hadn't been in such a public place he may well have done so.

As if she'd read his mind she stepped away, putting space between them, clearly making an effort to regain her usual calm. "He came back," she said.

"He?" Valentine growled, hoping she didn't mean who he thought she meant.

"Baron Von Hautt. He came back after you had gone."

His anger and frustration were difficult to contain. He made a sound in his throat, took a step away and then spun around and came back again. "I should never have left you there alone," he said with a low, intense fury.

"You couldn't have known—"

"I should have waited for you."

"Lord Jasper needed help."

He fixed her with a compelling look. "Did he hurt you, Marissa?"

She shook her head and a lock of her dark hair tumbled onto her cheek. "He frightened me, that's all."

He glowered at her, although it wasn't Marissa he was upset with and she seemed to know that.

"What are we going to do now?" she said after a moment.

"That depends on Jasper," he answered her more moderately. "He may have to remain here until the doctor thinks it's safe to move him. You and I and Lady Bethany can of course return to Abbey Thorne Manor, but while we're here I'd like to visit the ruins of Montfitchet Castle and talk with this Mr. Jensen, the local historian."

"No, the baron mustn't stop you from doing what you came to do, Valentine," she said with approval. She took a couple of steps toward the inn, her silk skirts rustling. She looked back at him over her shoulder. "Will we see how Lord Jasper and my grandmother are managing?"

He followed after her without another word.

The doctor had finished his operation and dressed the wound in clean bandages and was arranging for some restorative medicines to be prepared by the local apothecary and brought to the inn. The last remnants of the messy business of removing the bullet were being tidied away, and Lady Bethany looked up with a relieved smile when she saw her granddaughter.

Marissa went to take her outstretched hand, giving the patient a sympathetic grimace.

"Poor Lord Jasper," she said. "Are you in a great deal of pain?"

"Not so much, thank you, my dear. The doctor tells me I will live to make a full recovery."

"And you, Grandmamma?"

Lady Bethany's smile grew thin. "If I'd known when I agreed to accompany you to a weekend house party, Marissa, that it would be this exciting I may have reconsidered. Perhaps next time you could confine yourself to playing whist and charades, my dear, instead of gallivanting about all over the countryside after roses and Prussian barons."

Marissa bent to kiss her cheek. "Come now, Grandmamma, you have to admit this is much more fun than standing on windswept hillsides admiring ferns and mosses?" Even as she said it she wondered whether she was trying to soothe Lady Bethany's ruffled nerves or whether she actually was enjoying herself.

"I am not admitting to anything." But Lady Bethany's eyes sparkled.

"I wish I had got my hands on Von Hautt," Jasper muttered. "This is all his fault."

Lady Bethany's expression hardened alarmingly. "Next time he turns up you will let me deal with him, Jasper. I find a nice sharp hatpin does the trick very nicely."

The two men looked at her in astonishment—with a hefty dollop of admiration in Jasper's case—while Marissa stifled a giggle.

"Lord Kent still wants to see the ruins of Montfitchet Castle," she said, when she was able.

"I will rest here until you are done," Jasper declared. "The doctor says I should be able to travel back to Abbey Thorne Manor if there is no more bleeding from the wound."

"Did you want to come with us, Grandmamma?"

"I think I will stay here, too," Lady Bethany replied, fixing her dark gaze on Valentine. "I trust you will take care of my granddaughter, Kent."

Valentine hesitated. Marissa could guess the reason. It wasn't that he didn't intend to take care of her, but rather because he would have preferred she remain here at the inn, out of the way. Perhaps she should save him the awkwardness and feign a headache? But Marissa had no intention of making life easier for Valentine.

Besides, she had to prove to herself that she was perfectly capable of being in his company without behaving like the wayward heroine in a dreadful penny novel.

"Indeed I will take good care of her, Lady Bethany," he said smoothly, and gave a little bow. "Unless she prefers to rest here . . . ?"

Marissa dashed his hopes. "I'm not at all tired, thank you."

"My granddaughter has never been one of those feeble young ladies who cannot walk more than a few steps without catching breath. I blame tightlacing," Lady Bethany said. "Once at Brighton Pavilion I remember I was—"

"We will leave you now, Grandmamma, and Lord Jasper," Marissa spoke hastily, before her grandmother's risqué story could progress any further. "Come, Lord Kent, we have a rose to find."

All that remained of lonely Montfitchet Castle was a crumbling stone tower surrounded by a sea of long grass. A wild rose rambled through what had once been a narrow window, but although Valentine examined it closely he knew at once it was just a common dog rose, the single petalled flower a pale shade of pink and not the exquisite cup of golden petals he had read and dreamed about.

"No luck?" Marissa said.

"If the Crusader's Rose was ever here then it is long gone."

"At least we know Baron Von Hautt has not found it, either."

"Yet," he muttered.

"Do you know," Marissa said, "this is nothing like my father's expeditions. Are your rose hunts always this exciting, Valentine?"

"Actually they are normally very leisurely affairs. It is only since you arrived that things have heated up."

The word was a mistake. It reminded him of what else was heating up every time he glanced in her direction.

"I think we should return to the inn," he said gruffly, but as he moved away one of the whiplike stems of the thorny dog rose caught across his sleeve and the back of his jacket. He tried to shrug himself free but the thorns were too sharp and too tenacious; he was effectively their prisoner.

Marissa, seeing his dilemma, tried to pry the

thorns loose, only to stop with a cry as one of the hooks dug deep into the pad of her thumb, despite her glove.

"Let me see."

Valentine reached for her hand, his fingers closing around hers, just as he remembered he shouldn't risk touching her. But it was too late. Slowly, like someone unwrapping a forbidden birthday treat, he unfastened the single delicate button at her wrist and gently drew off her glove. Her hand was soft and her skin unblemished apart from a smear of blood on her thumb. He bent to examine the wound, playing for time. The bead of red swelled against her white flesh where the thorn had dug deep.

"I—I don't think the thorn broke off," she said, her voice little more than a whisper. "Valentine?"

The veins on her wrist were visible through her pale skin, and he could feel the beat of her pulse beneath his fingers. He felt dizzy, as if he'd drunk too much, but it wasn't alcohol making his head spin. It was her, Marissa Rotherhild.

Before he considered consequences—indeed his brain had little to do with it—he lifted her hand to his mouth and ran his tongue delicately across the injury, the taste of her blood clean and salty.

His eyes met hers and the intense eroticism of the moment held them spellbound.

Her lashes swept down to hide whatever she was feeling, but he felt the involuntary trembling of her fingers in his, and knew she was as affected as he. "You will think me—" she began, but didn't finish.

"What will I think you?" he murmured, his voice deep and husky. She was closer than a moment ago, the scent of her filling his senses. Although her dark hair was pinned up beneath her hat, he could see some curls ready to tumble down. He wanted to tug them loose and bury his face in their warm darkness.

Gently she withdrew her hand from his. She took a step back, stumbling, putting space between them.

Was he frightening her? Valentine felt a wave of doubt crash over him. Could he have misread her? Was what he'd thought of as an intense attraction actually terror and disgust, the same emotions Vanessa had felt whenever he came close to her? The old poison seeped stealthily into his heart and mind and certainty turned to doubt.

You are no better than a beast, Valentine. I cannot bear your touch or your kisses.

No amount of patience or declarations of love had changed her opinion, and in the end they were bitter strangers living underneath the one roof. But always in the depths of his heart he'd wondered if perhaps Vanessa was right and he was beastly. A man beyond love.

"The rose thorns will tear your jacket," Marissa said. Her voice saved him from further memories of the past. "You'd better take it off."

He gave a grateful nod. It was only as he reached to flick open the buttons and shrug himself out of the garment that he recalled he was no longer wearing his shirt.

He stood, uncertain whether to proceed. "Miss Rotherhild," he said, uncomfortably, "I am naked. You may wish to turn your back."

She blinked at him, but there was no disgust in her face. Her expression was gentle, a little dazed, and the smile that curled her lips teased his senses in a way that was exceedingly dangerous.

"Oh, I—I don't think that will be necessary, Lord Kent."

A ripple of lust curled in his stomach. There it was in her face, that same sense of a storm brewing that he'd seen outside the church. Slowly Valentine slipped one arm out of his jacket. Her gaze widened and her hand went involuntarily to her lips. She stood perfectly still as he began to remove his other arm from its sleeve.

In other circumstances he may have found it amusing, ridiculous, this deliberate disrobing in front of an innocent young lady. But there was nothing funny about what he was feeling. And Marissa . . . well, if he could believe what he was reading in her face she found his actions utterly compelling.

Valentine knew he was no Adonis, and yet the way she was eating him up with her eyes made him feel like a god. A master of sensuality. In a heartbeat he'd been released from the misery of his marriage to Vanessa, his shackles broken.

She took a step toward him, reaching out her hand, only to pause uncertainly. "I have a great need to . . . That is, may I touch you?" she spoke earnestly.

"Yes," he growled, aching for her fingers on his nakedness.

She pressed her palm to his chest, waiting a beat, and then slid it down and over his breast bone. He shivered. She put her other hand on him, then remembering her glove, quickly unbuttoned it and drew it off, before replacing her hands—her skin against his. His chest was rising and falling heavily with his breath as she stroked her palms over his shoulders and down the muscles of his arms, then back again. Once more he had to resort to squeezing his hands into fists to stop himself from grabbing hold of her. She brushed her fingertip over his rigid nipples and examined the wiry strands of hair growing around them. She leaned closer, as if she was a botanist examining some rare specimen, and her warm breath teased his flesh. An image flashed into his mind of her mouth closing over his cock.

"Marissa," he groaned, the sound of a man in great pain. It had been so long since he had a woman, any woman, and this woman was exceptional.

Her eyes flew to his, dark and aglow. Her cheeks were flushed. She gave a shaken smile. "Valentine?"

Doubts still flickered at the edges of his senses, but he could no longer mistake what he saw in her face. *Desire.* She wanted him almost as much as he wanted her.

What would it be like to kiss her lips? When he was a younger man he'd had a strong lusty streak. There'd been ladies, lots of them, and he'd taken his fill. And then he'd married Vanessa and all that had changed—he'd changed. He wanted to be that young and lusty man again.

He took a step, caught her in his arms, and drew her clumsily against him. Her skirts caught in the long grass and she fell forward. He caught her, losing his own balance, and sat down hard on the ground, narrowly missing some scattered pieces of Montfitchet Castle. Marissa sprawled in his lap.

He gave a gasp of laughter. "Not quite with my old finesse," he said, his heart thumping. But at least she was where he wanted her.

However it seemed she wasn't where *she* wanted to be. Marissa climbed awkwardly to her knees, tugging her skirts out of the way, straddling his thighs and kneeling above him. She touched his cheek, the gentlest of touches. Her hat was crooked, barely attached to her hair, and he reached up and removed it, bowling it through the long grass. Heavy strands of her hair, dark as midnight, tumbled down.

"Marissa," he said, "may I kiss you?"

Her dark eyes were serious. "Yes, Valentine. You may."

He leaned forward. Nothing mattered but the here and now, and any control he'd imagined he still had was shattered to bits as he took the warm soft wonder of her mouth with his.

Chapter 8

He was kissing her. Marissa was aware of how soft his lips were and yet how firm, as they moved over hers. He seemed to know what he was doing and she wound her arms around his neck. As if it was the most natural thing in the world, her fingers tugged at the wiry curls of hair that grew at his nape. He bent his head and began to press his open mouth to her throat, making her hot and trembly, and when her head fell back helplessly, he kissed the scant bit of bare flesh that showed above her bodice.

Pleasure brought goose bumps to her skin, and when he rested one hand in the hollow of her waist she was certain she could feel his touch burning like a hot coal through her clothing. His other hand was gathering up her tangled locks of hair and when he buried his face in the heavy mass, groaning with pleasure, she felt a tremor of passion ripple through her.

He lifted his head slightly, and she saw that his eyes were closed. She bent to kiss his eyelids, and then his lips, feeling his breath mingling with hers. It was like a dream, except it was too vividly real to be part of a dream. Marissa felt as if she was taking her first steps in some unexplored Amazonian jungle, a place no one had ever been before, and she was full of trepidation and excitement, but she had no intention of stopping or turning back.

Now he was kissing her more deeply, his arms tightening their grip about her body. She made a sound but it wasn't a protest, and then she was pressing closer to him, too. She couldn't seem to get enough of him. Her hands slid over his shoulder blades, down to the moving muscles of his back. Her nails were long enough to scrape gently against his skin, and he gasped, nuzzling against her throat.

He lifted his head and looked at her, his eyes so brilliant she felt like blinking.

"I want . . ." he began, but then couldn't seem to finish it.

"What do you want?" she said shakily.

He reached up and rested his fingers on the tiny pearl buttons that ran down the front of her bodice, holding it modestly in place. Marissa could feel a tingle in her breasts; they felt almost painful. She nodded her head jerkily, eagerly, and watched, holding her breath, as he began to unfasten the tiny buttons, one by one.

Her tight corset cut in under her bosom and had the effect of pushing her breasts up, while her chemise covered her to the neckline of her riding jacket. Once he had opened her bodice to the waist, he slid his fingers under one of the chemise straps and tugged it down over her shoulder. The swell of her breast was exposed to his gaze, her nipple peaking dark red and swollen. He took his time looking while she waited, hardly able to bear it. And then he stroked his finger over her, down, down, brushing over her hard nipple, and back again.

Marissa jumped at the contact on such a sensitive point, but she made no move to stop him. He smiled, and swooping forward, took her in his mouth.

She cried out. She couldn't help it. The hot wetness of his tongue and his mouth against her aching breast was pleasure almost beyond bearing. She cupped his head in her hands, unconsciously holding him to her.

Perhaps you should stop him now, said a voice in her head. But the voice was faint, and easily ignored.

He was exploring her other breast, and giving it the same treatment. The ache in her breasts was intense, but so was the throbbing between her legs. And it was worse because although she knew a little of what it meant to have connection with a man, she didn't know the full details. Or perhaps it was just as well she didn't know, because then she might throw him back on the ground and put her knowledge into practice.

She squirmed on his lap, trying to relieve the need growing inside her, and felt him hard against her stockinged thigh, like a rod of iron. Was this the bulge she'd seen in his breeches earlier? Surprised, curious, she reached down beneath the folds of her skirts and closed her hand about him.

He jerked like a man shot and she felt the rod in her hand twitch. She tightened her grip and he caught his breath, his teeth digging into his bottom lip. He reached down, fumbling his way through her skirts, and covered her hand with his.

"Valentine?" she whispered, confused, afraid

she'd done something wrong.

He seemed to recognize her emotions. "Your hand on me makes me feel good," he said bluntly. "Too good."

She wasn't certain what he meant, but she understood enough. She loosened her grip but did not let go entirely.

"May I touch you there, Valentine?" she said seriously.

He gave a shaken laugh. "Not right now, Marissa. But I am going to touch you, because I think you want me to, don't you?"

"I—"

"I promise if you don't like it then I'll stop."

She hesitated, but he must have taken that for a yes, because she felt his hand on her thigh, sliding up over her warm bare flesh and finding the lacy edge of her pantaloons.

You are not behaving like a respectable and well-brought-up young lady, the voice in her head told her.

No, but if I don't practice my feminine wiles then how will I be able to use them with any accomplishment?

The voice had nothing to say to that.

Or maybe she'd stopped listening, because now his fingers had found the opening between the legs of her pantaloons and slid inside. At the first brush of his fingers over the swollen, damp folds of her flesh she whimpered. Then he touched her again, more firmly, finding a particularly sensitive place and exploring it with a thoroughness that made her tremble and gasp.

"If I had time," he said, as he stroked her, "I would

use my tongue."

"Your tongue? How . . ." she moaned.

He smiled.

After a moment she said, "I feel—I feel . . ."

He pressed the heel of his hand against her, sliding his fingers inside, and a bolt of such pleasure went through her she arched upward, her body rigid, unable to speak or breathe. A moment later waves of warm release washed over her, and she collapsed against him, breathing hard against his bare shoulder.

He was murmuring endearments, but she hardly heard him. As soon as the intense feeling of pleasure began to fade the voice in her head was back, and it wasn't saying anything nice.

"What must you think of me?" she said to Valentine, her voice stiff and formal, and out of place after what had just happened.

He lifted her face and smoothed back her hair, gazing into her eyes, no doubt reading the turmoil within them. "I think you are the most beautiful thing I've seen in years. But you are an innocent, Marissa. This isn't what your grandmother meant when she told me to take care of you."

"Valentine, I assure you I do not expect you to take blame for what just happened. I am quite capable—"

But he wouldn't allow her to finish. She could see the self-disgust in the twist of his mouth. "You are no compliant widow or Covent Garden slut. You are an innocent young lady from a respectable family. You are my brother's . . . friend." His gaze dropped from hers and he sighed.

George. She'd forgotten all about George. How could she do that? How could the man she loved and wanted to marry slip her mind so conveniently?

Nevertheless she had been in full possession of her senses when she made the decision to cavort with Valentine, even if those senses had led her seriously astray.

"I liked what we did," she said. "You asked me and I said yes. There's no need to apologize. We are equally to blame."

"Nevertheless . . ."

She climbed off him and began to button up her bodice, feeling hot and flushed, her fingers trembling. "This was between you and me," she said gruffly, "and has nothing to do with anyone else. We will not mention it ever again."

He snorted. "That just shows how innocent you are."

"Oh rot!" she burst out, her eyes flashing with anger.

"My behavior is more than reprehensible," he went on, rising to his feet and standing over her. "I deserve to be flogged."

She stared at him a moment and then she began to laugh. His reaction was such a contrast to a moment ago, from one extreme to the other. Her laughter only seemed to antagonize him and angrily he untangled his coat, before pulling it back on.

"I think when you have considered the matter you will see that the only option left open to us is for me to ask—"

"Don't you dare!" she burst out. "Don't you dare

propose to me!"

He stared at her, openmouthed.

"I don't want to marry you," she said in a low, shaking voice. "We'd both be miserable, forced into an intolerable situation. We'd end up hating each other. Besides, I would refuse you, so don't even bother putting the question."

"Marissa—"

"No." She was searching around for her hat.

He reached down and picked it up and presented it to her with a formal bow.

"Thank you. I am returning to the inn now. I think you should finish your business with Mr. Jensen, and then we can all ride back to Abbey Thorne Manor."

"When your grandmother hears what has happened—"

She sighed, and then she smiled. Then she came up to him, stood on her toes, and kissed his lips, gently, without any trace of their earlier passion. "Don't be so foolish, Valentine."

And then she walked away.

Marissa could feel his eyes on her, puzzled, angry, probably wishing he could strangle her and hide her body in the long grass. Everything was a mess, but she could hardly blame Valentine for that. She had played a big part in the wild encounter they'd just shared.

She needed time to think, to order her scattered thoughts, and to work out exactly what she was going to do to make things right.

Chapter 9

Moodily, Valentine watched her go. She appeared to be unaffected by what they'd just done. The fact that his body was still agonizingly hard didn't help. He'd given her a climax she wouldn't soon forget—he'd wager the first she'd ever had—and now he had to suffer in solitary frustration.

Well, it was his fault. He didn't blame her for what had happened. He'd let her innocent dimpled smiles and her clear dark gaze, not to mention her luscious figure, confuse and bamboozle him, and before he knew it he was in too deep. And then, despite it being the very last thing he wanted, he'd done the only thing an honorable gentleman could do. He'd gritted his teeth and put his own feelings to one side and had been about to propose to her.

She'd refused him.

He supposed he should be relieved he had been rejected. Instead he was uneasy and not a little depressed. In their world, marriage was really the only option in such circumstances, unless one was a complete bounder, but despite her lack of experience, she'd rejected any thought of marrying him. And that could only be because the thought of tying herself to him was so appalling she'd rather be ruined than contemplate it.

You are a beast, Valentine.

He shoved his hands into his pockets and mooched through the long grass toward his tethered horse.

One thing he knew for sure, if she asked him if she could touch him again he was definitely going to say no!

By the time Valentine returned to the inn Marissa was settled calmly in the room with Jasper and Lady Bethany. He glanced at her, noting her serene expression, and that her hair was once more neatly fastened up beneath her hat. In every way she was the perfectly innocent young lady. In fact, if he hadn't seen her with his own eyes, half-naked and gasping with the pleasure he was giving her, he wouldn't have believed it.

The beautiful minx.

Jasper was explaining how the local constable had visited them for an explanation of the shooting at the church, and Valentine forced himself to concentrate. He found if he turned his back slightly to Marissa and couldn't see her then it was easier to put her out of his mind. Jasper went on to say he'd had no choice but to tell the truth, the vicar knew anyway, but it seemed as if there was little that could be done unless Von Hautt was found.

"Not much chance of that," Valentine said. "He's vanished back into whatever bolt-hole he came out of."

He then gave them a shortened version of his visit to Mr. Jensen, and what the local historian was able to tell him.

"The Montfitchets died out in the sixteenth century and the castle was sold. Eventually it was abandoned."

"So no good news," Jasper muttered, sinking back against his pillows with a dispirited air.

"There was one thing. Jensen knew another of the names on the list. Henry Fortescue. The Fortescues still live in the village of Magna Midcombe . . . in some form or another."

"That sounds very mysterious," Lady Bethany said.

"Well, Mr. Jensen did warn me they are no longer of the same social station as they once were."

"And Von Hautt?" Jasper demanded. "Has he seen anything of him?"

"No sign of him, yet. But I did warn Jensen to keep this new information to himself. Besides, now the constable is looking for him he'll be afraid to show his face in Montfitchet again."

"Baron Von Hautt doesn't seem to be afraid of much," Marissa said thoughtfully.

Valentine met her eyes and she stared back, a faint flush in her cheeks. He was glad when there was no return of his wild, reckless lust. Perhaps he had given himself such a fright that he was already cured? He hoped so. He knew one thing for certain, he was going to stick to his roses from now on and leave women to his brother, George.

But that didn't mean he couldn't unsettle the

lovely Marissa, just a little, in revenge for the pain she'd caused him.

"I expect Miss Rotherhild has told you about the ruins of the castle," he said, with a glance at Lady Bethany.

"Only that the Crusader's Rose was not there," the older lady answered. "Is there anything else to tell?"

He hesitated, then lifted an eyebrow at Marissa. "*Was* there anything else, Miss Rotherhild?"

A spark lit her eyes but she dropped her eyelids to hide it before he could decide whether she was angry or afraid. "No, nothing else. Unless *you* can think of something, my lord?"

Was she daring him to tell? To ruin her reputation in front of her grandmother and Jasper? He would never do it, of course, but the fact that she would risk it said much of her character. Marissa was a gambler, masquerading beneath the façade of a respectable young lady.

Satisfied he had her measure, Valentine turned back to his friend, examining his features closely for signs of pain, but although Jasper appeared a little pale and drawn, his eyes were clear and alert. "Are you able to travel, Jasper?"

"Yes, of course, old boy. As long as you take it slowly, I'll be more than happy to return to Abbey Thorne Manor and the ministrations of Morris and your excellent Mrs. Beaumaris."

Valentine went to arrange the carriage. In the end it was necessary to bolster Jasper with rugs and blankets and pillows, to prevent him from being jolted about too much, and Lady Bethany sat with him to keep a watch over him. Valentine drove the carriage and Marissa rode her horse, while Valentine's mount was fixed behind the carriage.

But, as usual when it came to Marissa, nothing went as he'd expected. Instead of riding timidly beside him, she rode some way in front, and he found his treacherous gaze fixed on the sway of her hips beneath her skirts, or the bounce of her jaunty hat atop her dark curls. For a time he struggled, and succeeded, in keeping his mind focused on what Jasper and Lady Bethany were saying, but then his thoughts would drift again. All too soon he was re-membering the moment in the long grass when Ma-rissa had reached down and closed her hand around his cock. Her warm fingers squeezing, while his face was buried in her lush flesh, in her scent, and she was rising above him like a pagan goddess . . .

A tremble started in his belly and traveled all the way up to his throat, causing him to catch his breath and tighten his hands involuntarily on the reins. The next thing he knew the carriage came to a violent and jerky stop.

"I say, Kent!" Jasper cried out in complaint.

"Why are we stopping?" Lady Bethany demanded, her hat over one eye as she tried to return the cush-ions to their proper positions around Jasper.

Marissa had trotted back to join them. "Is there a problem?" she inquired anxiously.

"No, I . . . It was nothing." Valentine's voice was rigid and he couldn't meet her eyes. "My apologies, Jasper."

"Well . . . no harm done, Kent," Jasper said in a puzzled tone. "Just don't do it again, eh, old boy?"

"Can we get on?" Lady Bethany said impatiently.

Marissa moved to one side to let him pass and Valentine set the horses in motion again. This time he meant to keep his eyes to the front, but his gaze wasn't as obedient as he'd hoped. It fastened on her riding boot, and then her trim stocking-covered calf, quickly skimming over the folds of her green riding habit and up, to her gloved hands resting lightly on the reins, and came to a stop on the tiny pearl buttons that enclosed her bodice. Before he could stop himself, he was remembering her breasts under his hands, and his tongue sweeping over her nipples before drawing their succulent sweetness into his mouth.

One of her hands rose and pressed to her throat, and as he met her eyes, Valentine realized she knew exactly what he was thinking.

Because she was thinking it, too.

Marissa Rotherhild was disturbing his peace of mind by simply being here. What madness had made him want to bring her on his quest to find the rose? And how was he going to keep his hands off her delectable person next time they were alone? It was an impossible situation and it couldn't go on.

Valentine was going to have to find some way to send her back to London, and the sooner the better.

By the time Marissa reached the manor she was more than grateful to climb the stairs to her room and close the door. She needed to think and it was difficult when Valentine was glaring at her back, as she was certain he'd done all the way from Montfitchet.

Did he blame her for what had happened between them at Montfitchet? She thought it more likely he was cross with himself because he'd lacked the will-power to resist her, and was then forced into a mar-riage proposal. Just as she was cross with herself for the same reason.

And confused. And guilty.

She'd come here to hunt George, after all, not fall in lust with his brother.

And yet she could not deny those moments with Valentine had been wonderfully exciting, empow-ering, and special. She wanted more. Like one of those laudanum addicts she'd always despised, she couldn't stop at one draught.

With a groan she tossed her hat onto her bed and sat down to remove her riding boots, throwing first one and then the other across the room, hoping the violence would release some of her pent-up emotion.

Marissa could honestly say she'd never done any-thing like she did today at Montfitchet. And she'd never felt such a thrilling, dark pleasure as she had when Valentine kissed her and touched her. Her hand rested lightly on her breast, remembering. She'd never thought of herself as a sensual woman, but Valentine had shown her the truth. Was it awful to admit she wanted more? And there was more, she was certain of it, a great deal more he could teach her about herself and physical pleasure. Wasn't that what husband hunting was all about?

But he's the wrong man!

It was all very well her friends from Miss Deben-ham's urging her to use her feminine wiles, but what would they think when they discovered she'd used them on the wrong man? And while she was using them she'd not given dear George a single thought.

"It's all his fault for not being here," she mut-tered, and then jumped when there was a rap on her door.

"Marissa?" Her grandmother entered, looking about the chamber suspiciously. "Were you speak-ing to someone?"

"No, Grandmamma. Only myself." Marissa was glad to be interrupted.

Lady Bethany had changed from her traveling dress into something less restrictive, wrapping a cashmere shawl around her shoulders. With her hair loosened, softening the lines of her face, she looked younger and strangely vulnerable.

"How is Lord Jasper?" Marissa asked, as her grandmother came to sit beside her on the bed.

"Sleeping, and hopefully no worse for his experi-ence." She hesitated, fiddling with the rings on her fingers. "What do you think of him, my dear?"

"I think him a very nice man," Marissa said promptly. "Much nicer than Mr. Garfield."

Lady Bethany waved her hand impatiently at the mention of her previous beau. "Garfield is gone and forgotten." Another pause, more fiddling with her rings. "He is a little younger than me, you know."

"Is he?"

"Ten years," Lady Bethany said heavily.

"But you are so very youthful in your ways,

Grandmamma," Marissa assured her. "Everyone says so."

Her grandmother brightened. "I am, aren't I?"

"An older man would have trouble keeping up with you."

"I do believe you're right."

Marissa placed her hand on her grandmother's. "But then again . . . You don't think it is a little soon to be considering Lord Jasper in such an . . . an intimate light, Grandmamma?"

Lady Bethany's thin eyebrows climbed. "Not at all. I always know the moment I meet someone whether I want them as a lover and a friend. I am a very good judge of character, my dear."

"Yes, Grandmamma," Marissa replied, trying not to be shocked, but the vision of her grandmamma welcoming Lord Jasper into her boudoir was almost more than she could manage.

"And at my age there isn't time to dilly-dally," her grandmother added. Her eyes narrowed. "What happened between you and Kent, Marissa? He was like a sulky schoolboy when you came back from the castle ruins."

Marissa avoided that sharp gaze. "Nothing happened, Grandmamma. He was disappointed he didn't find his rose, that is all."

"Hmm, well I don't believe you. I suppose you'll tell me the truth when you're ready." She rose to her feet and made for the door. "Now I am going to take a little nap before dinner."

Marissa breathed a sigh of relief as the door closed, aware she had got off lightly. If Lady Bethany hadn't been busy with her own concerns about Lord

Jasper she would never have given up so easily, and her probing was always needle sharp.

Marissa flopped back onto the bed and closed her eyes. She felt as if she was one step away from disaster, and at the same time she knew how simple it would be to take that step. Her body tingled with memories of Valentine's smile, his touch, the way his breath warmed her skin. It was all wrong, so very wrong, and yet it felt so very right.

Her eyes sprang open.

Could she? Dare she? It would serve him right, of course, and it might also help her to develop those skills she was only just beginning to realize she possessed. He'd proposed to her despite obviously hating the idea of marrying her. It was logical that no gentleman who would propose to her against his will would harm her—such an action would be against his code—therefore she was perfectly safe.

But just in case, her grandmother and Jasper would be there to act as chaperones.

Marissa smiled. As her grandmother said, more or less, life was too short to dilly-dally.

Chapter 10

Marissa dressed carefully for dinner. She was not greatly enamored of the pale pinks and pastels and debutante's white that young women were expected to wear in society. The colors that suited her were the more striking reds and purples and royal blues, as well as her favorite emerald green. For this evening she had chosen a dark rose silk trimmed with knots of ribbon and lace.

The current fashion was for evening necklines to be low and off the shoulders, and Marissa's was almost indelicately so, although a lace fall helped to disguise the fact she was baring so much flesh. The sleeves were mere scraps of cloth, clinging to her upper arms, while the narrow waist emphasized her hourglass figure, before the dress flared out in a great many yards of cloth. She wore her pearl drop earrings and matching necklace, a gift from her grandmother five years ago, on her eighteenth birthday, and the maid servant assigned to her by Morris had been more than competent when it came to dressing her glossy dark hair in a myriad of curls and braids, with ringlets caught up and cascading from a jeweled comb.

The dress had been designed and packed with George in mind, but George wasn't here, and it was of Valentine she was thinking as she made her way down the stairs in her matching rose satin slippers.

Morris was waiting for her in the hall.

"Miss Rotherhild. Your grandmother advised cook that she will be taking her meal with Lord Jasper, in his sickroom."

"Oh." Marissa was taken aback. This wasn't part of her plan. Suddenly thrown into confusion, she wondered if she should offer to take her own meal on a tray in her room. But before she could suggest it Morris spoke again.

"I'm to let you know that Lord Kent is still expecting you to join him for dinner. He has asked that it be served in the yellow salon. It is less formal than the dining room, and in the circumstances seemed more appropriate to the occasion."

Did less formal mean more intimate? Marissa wondered.

"Shall I show you the way, Miss Rotherhild?" Morris inquired, his face expressionless, as still she hesitated.

"Yes, thank you, Morris."

As she followed Morris's sedate pace, Marissa tried to tell herself that she would have to deal with Valentine in private sometime, and it was best to get it over with. She'd worn the red dress thinking she'd be dining under the safety of her grandmother's beady eyes, which would enable her to tease him and flirt and hone her skills, but without any fear of repercussions. In other words, she could play with fire without being burned. Now they were to be alone. What if he proposed to her again in that depressing way? Her brow wrinkled. More likely he'd want to send her back to London as quickly as possible, and then what would become of her plans concerning George?

Well, she wouldn't go. This was supposed to be a house party and he was the host. It would be extreme bad manners to order the guests to leave. No, she was not leaving. Not until she'd accomplished what she'd come for.

In the yellow salon a small dining table and two chairs had been placed in the center of the room, where a candelabra threw a soft pool of light, leaving the remainder of the room in shadows.

Indeed, it was so shadowy that Marissa didn't realize Valentine was waiting for her until he rose from an armchair by the window, a glass in his hand.

"Miss Rotherhild. As Morris will have told you, Lady Bethany has decided to dine upstairs with Jasper. I thought it more practical for us to eat here. I hope this arrangement is acceptable to you?"

He spoke with scrupulous politeness and Marissa answered just as formally. "Yes, thank you, Lord Kent, it is perfectly acceptable to me."

As he walked into the candlelight she noticed he wasn't smiling, and in fact there was a troubled look in his eyes to go with the straight line of his mouth. She wondered, cravenly, whether she was doing the right thing. But it was too late. She wasn't going to change her mind now. So she would just have to set about changing his.

Morris cleared his throat, and Marissa noticed

with amusement the slightly despairing glance he cast over his master's evening wear. She made her own inspection. A fitted black jacket, as was the fashion, smooth across his broad shoulders; his white silk shirt was spotless and the frills attached to the front were smartly pressed, as were the cuffs; black trousers accentuating his long legs; his necktie . . . Ah, there was the problem. Instead of tying it about his throat, Valentine had left the white strip of cloth hanging loose, as if he had slipped it around his neck and then forgotten to do it up. Or just couldn't be bothered.

Morris cleared his throat again and raised a hand to indicate his own immaculately tied necktie. Valentine's brows came down in a warning frown.

"Morris, you sound as if you have a cold."

Morris's jowls quivered in defeat. "Do you wish the meal served at once, my lord?"

"Yes, I do, thank you, Morris."

Morris turned away a broken man, and closed the door behind him.

Valentine drew out one of the chairs for Marissa and she took her place with a polite smile and waited for him to take his.

"I didn't realize my grandmother was dining upstairs," she said, hurriedly filling the silence. "I saw her earlier and she didn't mention it."

"If you are concerned at the propriety of our dining alone together, Miss Rotherhild, be assured that I did ask Lady Bethany's permission and she had no objections."

He'd asked her grandmother's permission? If she'd ever believed Valentine to be a libertine or a gentleman with evil seduction in mind then his words would have set her mind at ease.

"I have dined in stranger situations than this, Lord Kent," she said briskly. "On one of my parents' expeditions we ate in an underground cave and then spent the night there, waiting for the weather to clear." She paused, ready to enlarge on her story if he gave her the least encouragement.

But although he smiled in polite acknowledgement he did not respond, and Marissa knew with a sinking heart that her fears had been well-founded. He was going to send her away—well *try* to. The silence between them grew longer, and when he finally began to speak it sounded to her as if his words were rehearsed.

"Actually, I am glad we have this moment alone, Miss Rotherhild. I wanted to talk to you privately." He looked at her, the expression in his eyes hidden in the reflection of the candlelight.

Marissa tried to smile. "I think we should discuss the Crusader's Rose and how you are going to approach the next part of your search—"

Thankfully, at that moment Morris arrived with servants bearing food. The soup was placed on the table, the wine was poured, and all too soon they were alone again. Marissa took up her spoon, wondering how she was going to eat anything when her stomach was squirming with nerves.

"How serious are you about George?"

She was so surprised she almost dropped her spoon. Opposite her, Valentine was ignoring his soup, a wineglass in his hand. He looked tense but other than that she could not read him.

She shook her head, feeling the sway of her pearl earrings. "I'm not sure what you mean."

"You know exactly what I mean, Marissa," he retorted.

"We seem to have a great many things in common," she said primly.

"For instance, family members who are engaged in boring botanical pursuits? Yes, I see," he said dryly. He picked up his spoon then put it down again. "Let me be blunt, Marissa. George has never touched you as I touched you?"

"What—what a shocking question!" she exclaimed. "Hardly the question of a gentleman."

"I think we've established I am no gentleman."

"I disagree. I think you are the epitome of a gentleman."

"Answer the question," he growled.

"Then, no, he hasn't." She lifted her chin, meeting his eyes without flinching. "The only man who has ever touched me like that is you."

He was studying her face, reading her, and whatever he saw seemed to satisfy him. "Good," he said.

Good? Why was that good?

Marissa waited for him to speak again and make all clear to her, but it seemed that he had finished because he began to eat his soup. After a moment, so did she. The silence grew heavy, uncomfortable, and she was glad when Morris returned with the servants and more plates. She hoped he would linger and began a conversation about recipes and whether Mrs. Beaumaris used white or black pepper.

But Valentine put a stop to that.

"Morris, bring the dessert, would you, and leave it on the sideboard. We can serve ourselves."

Morris bowed and a moment later he was back, carrying out his instructions with muted efficiency. "Is that all, my lord?"

"Yes, thank you, Morris. Give my congratulations to Mrs. Beaumaris on a splendid meal, and then take yourselves off to bed. No need to wait up."

"Mrs. Beaumaris will be pleased to know you enjoyed her efforts, my lord. Goodnight, my lord. Goodnight, Miss Rotherhild." Another bow and the door to the yellow salon closed with an air of finality.

"This looks delicious," Marissa said quickly. "You have a fine cook in Mrs. Beaumaris, Lord Kent."

He said nothing but she felt his gaze on her, considering.

"My parents are so rarely at home we find it difficult to keep good cooks—the last one complained she had nothing to do. I remember, when I was younger I longed for a normal life. To sit down at the table and be asked questions about my day rather than listen to details of the next expedition to find new varieties of my parents' favorite plants."

She sounded woebegone, Marissa realized, but it was too late to withdraw her words.

"Were you a lonely child, Marissa?" His voice was low and deep. Intimate. Marissa felt a shiver run over her skin as if he'd reached out and caressed her.

"I . . . Sometimes. But my grandmother was there. Well, sometimes she was busy with her own affairs, so I couldn't always be sure of her undivided attention. But I remember my eleventh birthday," she said, smiling. "She went to a great deal of effort, to make up for my tenth birthday, and arranged for a barge on the Thames. It was decorated with ribbons and flowers, and there was food and music, and Grandmamma's Bohemian friends fussed over me and made me feel very special."

Valentine was smiling back, but he wore a puzzled expression. "You have had a most unusual upbringing, Marissa. Perhaps that is why you are such an innocent when it comes to the male sex."

She answered him coolly. "You are mistaken, I—"

He interrupted. "Why was your tenth birthday a disappointment?"

Marissa hesitated, irritated with herself for giving so much away. "What makes you think it was?" she hedged.

"You said that on your eleventh birthday your grandmother went to a great deal of effort to make up for your tenth birthday. Why?"

Marissa sipped her wine to gain time, but he was still waiting when she'd finished, so she told him. "I had asked my friends to come to my party. There was going to be a cake and games. But my parents forgot—something else had come up to claim their attention—and when my friends arrived nothing was prepared, nothing was ready. It was . . . embarrassing, mainly. Painful. I pretended it didn't matter, but I could see they felt sorry for me, and that was horrible."

He said nothing and she was grateful he didn't offer meaningless platitudes. The memory was still an uncomfortable one, like a stone in one's shoe. She couldn't believe she'd mentioned it at all—she never did normally—and decided it must be her anxiety in his presence that had caused her to say far more about herself than she'd meant to.

"On my own tenth birthday," he began, sipping his wine and gazing across the room as though he was seeing into the past, "my mother had just died."

Marissa felt an ache in her heart for the little boy he must have been, but she did not think he would want gushing sympathy any more than she did. "Was she ill for a long time?"

"She was always ill." He grimaced. "That sounds callous, but it is true. I'm afraid that, although I missed the fact I no longer had someone I could call mother, I rarely grieved for her. She wasn't involved in my upbringing in any way, and apart from an occasional visit to her boudoir, always dim and smelling of eau de cologne, I was kept from her. I was told my boisterous ways made her head ache."

"And then she died."

"Yes. I used to overhear the servants whispering that it was George who finished her off—she died soon after his birth—but I didn't blame him."

"Was your father often away?"

"While Bony was locked up on Elba, he had more time to be with us, but then Bony escaped and there was the showdown at Waterloo, and afterward he was dead, too. George and I were alone, apart from a collection of elderly aunts to fuss over us. I was glad when I was old enough to take over my own affairs, and George."

"Yes, I can see you would be. But it is different for

a man. He is expected to be independent. Whereas women are to be cosseted and cared for, and any decisions about their lives are made for them by their parents or the menfolk in their lives. At least, that seems to be the belief held by a large part of our society."

"But not by you?"

"Definitely not by me."

His mouth curled up in a mocking smile, the sort of male smile Marissa found particularly annoying. "You know there is a good reason for that belief," he said. "Women are unworldly and they need men to guide them through the pitfalls that await them beyond their front doors."

"What rot—"

"Look at your own behavior, Marissa. Do you know how dangerous it is? There are bad men out there who would hurt you without a moment's thought and believe your behavior gave them the right to do so."

He was sounding so prim and proper, she wanted to scream. Or laugh in his face. But she schooled her expression into one of polite interest.

"I am only telling you this for your own good," he finished, a little clumsily, and sat back in his chair as though he'd just performed an unpleasant but necessary task.

He was treating her like a silly child and she'd had enough of it. Marissa knew her own mind; she had done for years. And even if she didn't she wouldn't ask someone else to tell her what to do. If he wished to play the man of the world to her innocent then he deserved to be taught a lesson.

"Actually, Valentine," Marissa said, picking up her wineglass and taking another sip, "that is the very thing I was intending to speak to you about."

"Oh?" His eyes narrowed. "Bad men?"

"About how to conduct myself safely in the sort of situation I happened to find myself in today. I mean, if it wasn't you I was with, if it was someone else. For instance . . . Baron Von Hautt."

"What has Von Hautt got to do with it?" he said sharply, his brows lowering.

"Well . . . he did say I was beautiful."

He seemed to be speechless, but not for long. "He said what!"

"Today, when I saw him outside the church. He said I was beautiful, and then he said he wouldn't hurt me. Not yet. You can see why I might consider that some sort of threat to my person. What if he captured me somehow and carried me deep into the woods and threw me down onto a soft bank of grass, and then undressed me and himself and—"

"Marissa, stop, please." Valentine set down his glass with a thud and stared at her, while she gave him one of her wide-eyed innocent looks. "I will not let Von Hautt do anything of the sort to you, you can be certain of that."

"That is all very well, Valentine, but what if you're not around to protect me?"

He sighed, glanced down at their meal. "Have you finished? I find my appetite quite gone."

"Of course." She rose promptly and followed him over to the two armchairs by the windows. The shadows were deeper here, but that was good. It would make it easier for her to play the role she had chosen to play.

"Tell me what should I watch out for?" she asked him, leaning forward in her chair. "I mean, in case a man wishes to seduce me and in my cloistered innocence I don't immediately understand his intentions?"

The words sounded ridiculous to her own ears but Valentine didn't appear to notice. He cleared his throat uncomfortably. "Well, he may try to persuade you to be alone with him."

"Do you mean like we're alone?"

"Yes." He frowned. "Only this is quite different."

"And what might he do when we're alone?" She wrinkled her brow. "Perhaps you should show me exactly what you do mean, Valentine?"

He was still staring at her and now his gaze dropped to her décolletage, her rounded flesh straining against the deep rose of the cloth. A muscle twitched in his cheek, and Marissa knew with complete certainty that she had been right to pack this dress for George.

It was a shame he wasn't here to see it.

Chapter 11

Valentine felt as if a bolt struck him low in the belly, traveling like wildfire throughout his body. His head swam, his heart began to thud heavily. This was a degree of lust, of need, he had never felt before. With her pale flesh falling out of that delicious dress and her dark curls caressing her neck, she was like something from a midnight fantasy.

And, oh God, he wanted her.

"Would he touch me, do you think?" she said in that same dreamy voice. "Like you touched me?"

He tried to cool himself down but her words brought images to his fevered mind that only raised his temperature higher. "Marissa," he groaned, "stop."

"Would he kiss me, do you think?" She slid forward on the edge of her chair, closer to him. He could feel the warmth of her body and smell her scent. "Like you kissed me, Valentine?"

Her lips were only a fraction of an inch from his. So near he could taste them. Valentine struggled to gain control of himself, trying to remember all the reasons he'd sworn he would stay away from the minx. He was winning, or he thought he was, and then she slipped down onto her knees on the floor, her hands resting on top of his thighs, and smiled up at him.

Her dark eyes were wide, guileless, but there was a laughing sparkle deep within. Her dimple peeped out, teasing him. And that was when he realized it was all pretense. He'd been treating her like an innocent ingénue so she was playing the part.

She must have seen something in his expression warning her he'd seen through her act, because she went to withdraw her hands. Quick as a flash he grasped them tightly with his, holding her prisoner.

"Oh no you don't, minx," he said. "You asked me to show you what a man like Von Hautt would do to you and I'm going to show you. It's the least I can do after your performance just now."

Her lashes swept down and she stopped struggling.

He closed the distance between them, taking her mouth deeply, completely. She made a sound but surprised him by not pulling away. He didn't plan to be gentle. He was going to show her the worst of mankind.

At least that was his plan.

But the warm delight of her mouth was already blurring the lines between punishment and pleasure. Valentine slid his tongue between her lips, deepening the kiss. She froze and then, dash it, she did the same to him. He groaned, but didn't stop. It wasn't until he felt her tugging at his grip on her hands that he was able to control himself enough to draw back.

"Valentine," she said, and her voice was breathless. "Please."

He felt ashamed, and for a moment he was back with Vanessa. "My apologies, Marissa. I got carried away."

"I don't want you to apologize. I want to touch you."

He went still. Why did those words of hers affect him so? Because they made him feel wanted and desired, emotions he'd forgotten over the years?

"Is that what you'd say to Von Hautt?" he said huskily, trying to regain control. "Have some sense, Marissa!"

"I am sensible," she replied calmly. "I always have been sensible. But right now I wish I wasn't. Right now I refuse to be sensible!"

He began to protest, but she placed her fingertip against his lips. And then she leaned forward and pressed her lips to his.

"I trust you," she whispered.

"Well, you shouldn't," he growled, and showed her why.

She was hot, her skin on fire, as if the passion he'd lit was burning through her from the inside. She was struggling for breath, probably because of her corset and other fiendish feminine devices. He cupped her breast through the dress, feeling her soft flesh, the hard nub of her nipple butting against his palm and seeming to beg for his mouth. He wanted to oblige. He wanted to take her now, on the Turkish rug. His body was begging him to give it release after so long without a woman.

But Valentine knew he wasn't going to do that.

This was neither the time nor the place, and he was not the man to initiate Marissa into such pleasures, although no doubt she would argue about that as she did everything else.

"Please," she gasped, "can you do what you did before? Can you touch me . . . ?"

For a moment his head went fuzzy. His hand even moved toward her skirts, but he stopped himself. If he touched her then it would only be a short step to taking her on the rug.

With grim purpose he set her away from him.

For a moment she sat among the folds of her rose red dress. A lock of her hair had fallen over one eye, her cheeks were flushed and her mouth was swollen from his. At first she looked at him expectantly, and then, when he made no move to join her, in bewilderment. Her gaze dropped to the bulge in his pants.

"You want me, Valentine," she said huskily. "I have learned that much already."

"Oh yes," he growled, "I want you, you minx. I don't deny it."

"Then why . . . ?" she wailed.

"Because I have no intention of taking a virgin on the salon floor."

She turned her face away. "I suppose that is a reasonable answer," she said quietly. Then, with a sideways glance and a little smile, "Is there somewhere else you prefer?"

"This isn't a joke, Marissa! Despite your wild and passionate behavior, you are an innocent and if I took advantage of that for my own pleasure I would be the worse sort of rake."

She looked down at her hands, clasped in her lap, and then sighed and pushed her hair out of her eyes. She climbed to her feet, slowly, despondently, and shook her skirts to straighten them. When she looked at him again he saw, with genuine horror, that there were tears sparkling in her eyes.

"I wish you wouldn't treat me like a silly child," she said. "I do know my own mind. I am twenty-three years of age and have been an independent woman for a great many of those years now—I've had to be."

Valentine hardened his heart; it was the only way to withstand her. "If you want an affaire, Marissa, there must be a great many men in London willing to oblige you. Why come all the way to Abbey Thorne Manor and pick on me? Or were you planning to ask George?"

She gave him one of her direct looks. "George," she repeated, and sighed. "George was my first choice . . . is still my first choice. Are you going to tell him about—about this?"

"Of course," he mocked. Then, at her gasp of dismay, "No, I'm not going to tell George! I'm not such a beast as that."

But you are a beast, Valentine.

"Thank you," she said quietly. "You know that neither of us planned this thing that is happening between us. Neither of us is able to control it."

"Speak for yourself," he said in a hard voice. "I am perfectly able to control myself."

She wrinkled her brow irritably. "Oh?"

He ignored her. "I agree we are laboring under a strong physical attraction, but it will soon fade and then you will be amazed you ever considered me a candidate for something so precious as your virginity."

She was watching him, listening to his words, but if he'd expected her to argue or pout and stamp her foot like a child, he was wrong. Marissa was no child. She replied in a way that was honest and touching, though he refused to allow himself to be swayed.

"I have never felt this—this . . . I don't even know what to call it. Mating attraction? I want to understand it; I want to wallow in it—take a deep breath and dive in. I am a little out of control, I think, and for someone like me, who is always in control, that is terrifying. And exhilarating. Both at the same time."

Valentine made another effort to warn her of the perils of her behavior. "You make conversation like a Bohemian. Beware of what you say and who you say it to."

Her chin was up and she looked as regal as a queen . . . only far more touchable. "My grandmother is a Bohemian so I learned at an early age to say what I mean."

"Tell me you are not intending to follow your grandmother's way of life?" he said. "Your father would never allow it, surely?"

She laughed. "There you go again, thinking I do not know my own mind and must have a man to tell it to me. My father has said he doesn't care if I marry or not. I think on the whole he would prefer I didn't because then I could help him catalogue his papers and keep his library tidy. My mother wants to see me happy. They are somewhat Bohemian, too, you see."

"Marissa," he growled, "you are driving me to madness."

"My grandmother has lived a very happy life. She has given herself up to pleasure."

"Dear God, I am in the presence of a madwoman. Is that what you intend to do? Give yourself up to pleasure?"

She blinked at him, startled. "I suppose, in a way, I do."

He closed his eyes in genuine pain. When he opened them again she was smiling in a manner that made him extremely nervous. "What are you thinking?" he asked suspiciously.

"I was wondering whether you were about to offer to initiate me into the world of pleasure, Valentine."

He gave her a hard look and her smile grew, the dimple peeping out in her cheek.

"Don't worry, Valentine, I won't force you to do anything you don't want to."

He scowled at her and refused to answer.

She waited a moment, and then said, "Goodnight, Valentine, I will see you in the morning," and turned away, her skirts rustling about her.

"Dash it," he muttered, as the door closed. He poured himself another brandy, despite knowing he'd had enough. The silence of the empty room weighed dark and heavily upon him. It was as if her presence had made it lighter and airier and it was only now she was gone that he realized the fact.

She was like no other woman he'd ever known and he knew he'd never meet another who could match her. He was besotted with her and despite all the problems he could see looming over him he couldn't bring himself to drive her away.

Valentine set down his half-full glass. He should go to bed and sleep it off, the brandy and Marissa. One thing was for certain, he had no intention of making the same mistake he'd made last time, when he married Vanessa in a warm haze of romantic dreams and woke up with cold, harsh reality. Whatever madness Marissa was trying to inflict upon him must be fought and defeated, because whatever she said this was all her fault. Until she arrived on his doorstep he'd been perfectly happy with his life.

And he refused to consider any alternative views.

It wasn't until he was in bed and drifting into sleep that he remembered George. Marissa had made it clear—or as clear as anything she said could be—that George was her reason for being at Abbey Thorne Manor. Did she believe herself in love with George? Was he the man she hoped to initiate her into a life of pleasure?

Valentine was no expert on relationships, far from it, but he was fairly sure Marissa and George were not going to be a fairy-tale couple. They were too different and George would treat her carelessly and not like the treasure she so obviously was.

"Dash it!"

With a groan he put the pillow over his head and tried to sleep.

Eventually he did sleep, but it seemed only a moment later that he was sitting bolt upright, staring into the darkness. Voices were coming from downstairs. A door banged shut. In his half-awake state he thought it was Baron Von Hautt come for Marissa, come to carry her out into the woods and undress her.

His eyes sprang open and his heart began to thud. Valentine was just about to leap to her rescue when he realized one of the voices he could hear was Morris's.

Clambering out of bed, he pulled on his robe and made his way to the landing. There was a candelabra on the table, the wavering light picking out the scene in the hall below. Morris, dapper even in his night robe and nightcap, was helping a man remove his traveling coat, fair hair glittering with raindrops.

"Will I wake Lord Kent, sir?"

"No, no, Morris. Best leave it till the morning. He might be in a better mood then."

Valentine began to make his way down the stairs. "I doubt it," he said, and had the satisfaction of seeing his brother start. "Where have you been, George? And what the devil do you mean by it?"

George met his arrival at the bottom of the stairs with a handshake and a warm smile. "Valentine."

Valentine tried to maintain his anger but it was already dissipating into a sort of grumpy irritability. George always had that effect on him; he could never stay truly cross with him for very long. Now he sighed and led his brother into the library. Morris followed them, lighting first the candles and then the fire in the grate.

"Well, George?" Valentine demanded, determined to get an answer. "Where have you been?"

"Here and there," his brother said airily, thanking Morris as he sank down by the fire and warmed his hands.

"Miss Rotherhild was understandably concerned when she arrived and you weren't here to greet her," Valentine went on, watching George's face intently. He wasn't disappointed. George grimaced and his eyes held a trace of guilt, but only for a moment.

"Marissa? I did remember to tell Morris about her, Valentine. I'm sorry if you were put out. Is she still here or did you insult her and send her fleeing from the ogre, back to London?"

It was Valentine's turn to feel guilty as he remembered exactly what he and Marissa had been doing. "She is still here," he said, sitting down opposite his brother. "Why? Did you hope she'd be gone?"

George grinned. "Good God no! She's a dear girl, don't you think? I'm looking forward to seeing her."

Valentine tried to read his face and failed. "What is she to you?" he asked bluntly. "I haven't a clue what you're up to and I wish you'd tell me."

"I'm not up to anything," George said, with his innocent look. "And Marissa and I have a great deal in common."

"So she's told me," Valentine muttered.

"Well why ask me then?"

"You've never mentioned her before."

George grinned. "Do you fancy her yourself, brother? I should warn you she has an aversion to anyone who dabbles in botanical matters. You'd have to give up your rose."

"I heard it was by dabbling in such matters that

you made Miss Rotherhild's acquaintance, George. What were you doing attending botanical meetings? It seems very unlike you."

George sighed. "I'll only tell you if you promise not to tell her."

"On my honor," Valentine said dryly.

"I was passing and I happened to see her entering the building." George's expression took on a dreaminess that sharpened his brother's interest. "She really is a goddess, isn't she? So I followed her in and pretended to be one of the crowd. They were thrilled to have me, I can tell you, when they knew I was your brother!"

Thankfully Valentine didn't have to answer, as Morris had reentered the room carrying a tray. George perked up at the sight of it. "Ah, Mrs. Beaumaris's delicious fare. I tell you, I'm starving! Thank you, Morris. Valentine, I intend to kidnap Mrs. Beaumaris and take her back to London with me. You don't realize how lucky you are."

"And you're changing the subject," Valentine retorted, nodding his own thanks to Morris.

George shrugged, and began piling his plate with an assortment from the tray Morris had brought in. "I lost track of time. You know me, I'm easily distracted. There was a boxing match and then I met some friends and was invited to join a shooting party and before I knew it . . ."

Valentine leaned back in his chair, watching his brother eat. He wanted to berate him, play the stern elder brother, but he couldn't drag up the necessary emotion. The truth was he was very fond of his younger brother, and there wasn't any harm done, was there? In fact, George not being here had meant Valentine had Marissa all to himself, and despite all his doubts concerning her, he had enjoyed her company immensely. He'd felt more alive than he'd felt for a very long time.

So instead of telling George off he began to talk about the letter from Bonnie and their father's army papers and the new direction the quest for the Crusader's Rose was taking.

George listened intently. "Baron Von Hautt actually shot Jasper?" he said, shocked. "The man has quite clearly lost his mind."

"I've had the servants keep a watch for him around Abbey Thorne, but so far no one has seen him again. But we need to take care, George. Whatever is driving Von Hautt is so strong he is willing to kill for it."

"I think I will come with you to Magna Midcombe tomorrow," George said. "Jasper will be of no use, even if he could travel, and Marissa should not come, either, if it's dangerous."

Valentine gave a short laugh.

"What?" George demanded, smiling inquiringly.

"If you think Marissa Rotherhild is going to be stopped by the threat of danger then you don't know her at all."

George's gaze sharpened, searching his, but the next moment he was stretching and yawning, saying he'd better get to bed if he was going to be up bright and early in the morning. "Goodnight brother," he said, as he left the room.

Valentine stayed where he was, casting a baleful eye over the crumbs and mess George had left behind him, so typical of his brother. But still he smiled as he took up the candelabra and followed George upstairs. He felt troubled and he knew the reason wasn't George or Von Hautt, well not entirely. Marissa was the source of his inner turmoil and he still wasn't certain how he was going to deal with it.

Chapter 12

Marissa opened one eye as the maid brought her tea and briskly threw back the curtains. She hadn't slept well, tossing and turning, her body reacting to the bedcovering as if they were made of Hessian and not the finest linen, while the ache deep inside her reminded her that this time she'd had no release from her newly awakened desire. Was it possible to give herself that release by her own machinations? She thought it probably was but she didn't make the attempt.

Because it wasn't simply release she wanted, but release with Valentine. Valentine's hands and lips on her body, and hers on him; Valentine wonderfully warm and naked, the passion between them rising and unstoppable.

And it *was* unstoppable. No matter how she tried to be her usual sensible self she couldn't seem to find her way back to the person she'd been before she met Valentine.

Now, remembering their conversation of the night before, she couldn't help but smile. Valentine had seemed so shocked when she spoke of her grandmother's Bohemian outlook on life, and so angry with her plain speaking, but she had a sense he was using his shock and anger to disguise his other feelings for her. He was a gentleman and the idea of compromising her was anathema to him, but worse than that was the fear of being trapped into a marriage he didn't want.

Marissa wondered what his wife had been like and why things had gone so very wrong between them. Perhaps Lady Bethany could ask Jasper . . .

"Mr. George came home and—"

The maid had been chattering away in the background and until now Marissa hadn't been paying attention.

"I beg your pardon?" She blinked, propping herself up against the pillows.

"Mr. George came home late last night," the maid said.

"George? You mean the Honorable George Kent?"

"Yes, miss, that's right. He's been off with some of his friends. Lord Kent took him into the library and tore strips off him . . . at least that's what Mrs. Beaumaris is saying below stairs."

George was here! What a relief. Now, finally, she could begin her husband hunting in earnest.

But, oddly, it wasn't relief she was feeling, only more agitation. George and Valentine under the one roof was going to be difficult for her to handle. How was she going to concentrate on George when Valentine was clouding her senses?

Marissa sipped her tea, holding the cup in both hands.

But this was what she wanted, wasn't it? For

George to come? Of course there was the question of where he'd been all this time and what he'd been up to, but she supposed she couldn't be too cross with him, in the circumstances. George, as she well knew, lived for the moment and conveniently forgot engagements that interfered with his current pleasure. She told herself she accepted his idiosyncrasies, just as he did hers.

Then why did she feel so out of sorts?

Eventually Marissa gave up trying to come up with an answer and went to find her grandmother. She found Lady Bethany propped up on her pillows, a frilly nightcap on her head and a woolen shawl about her shoulders.

"Did you hear the rumpus in the night?" she said before Marissa could get a word out. "Evidently George arrived and he and his brother had a tiff. I could hear voices but I couldn't understand what they were saying, and I am too old to go creeping downstairs to listen at doors."

"I should think not!"

Lady Bethany smiled. "I would have done so when I was your age, my dear. Especially if I knew the argument intimately concerned me, and one of the parties arguing was the sort of man who made my pulse race and my—"

"Grandmamma, stop it."

"But, my dear, I thought George was your particular beau?"

"He's my friend," Marissa replied, her cheeks beginning to feel hot under her grandmother's penetrating gaze.

"Have you found someone who's more to your

taste?" Lady Bethany gave a wicked chuckle. "You can tell me, Marissa. I'm the soul of discretion."

Marissa ignored that. "Are you coming down to breakfast, Grandmamma?"

"I think I will lie in this morning—I feel quite weary from all the excitement yesterday."

She didn't look weary, her eyes were far too bright, but Marissa tried to be charitable, reminding herself that Lady Bethany was an old lady of sixty. Besides, she was very fond of her wicked grandmother. She leaned forward to kiss her cheek and her grandmother reached to clasp her hand, holding her close so that she could look searchingly into Marissa's eyes.

"I know you have your secrets, my dear, and I wouldn't ask you to divulge them. But do take care. For the sake of one who loves you dearly?"

"Grandmamma—"

"I gave up on giving advice when my daughter married your father, Marissa. He was the last person I would have expected to make her happy, and yet they have been very happy. I know it is important to follow your heart's desires—I have done so myself, numerous times—but it is possible to mistake desire for love—I have done that, too."

"What are you saying, Grandmamma?"

Lady Bethany smiled. "I am saying that sometimes it is better to try on a new hat and see if you like it, rather than taking it home and finding it isn't what you really wanted."

"I am not buying a new hat," Marissa said, bewildered.

"No, of course not." The wicked sparkle lit her

eyes. "I will speak frankly then, Marissa. It is better to spend an afternoon in bed with a man and discover if he's really the one you want to spend your life with, rather than marry him and find yourself a prisoner of unhappiness. Now you are shocked!"

"No, I—I don't think so. Are you giving me permission to ruin my reputation, Grandmamma?"

"If it saves you a lifetime of misery with the wrong man? By all means."

Marissa wasn't sure whether to laugh or cry. Only her grandmother could say such a shocking thing and make perfect sense.

"Thank you, Grandmamma," she said softly.

Lady Bethany patted her cheek. "Good girl. Now off you go to breakfast. And if you love me, please say nothing of this to your parents."

"Of course not."

They smiled at each other in perfect understanding.

George saw her first, and strode across the breakfast room to clasp her hands warmly in his. "I am sorry, Marissa. I hope you'll forgive me for my thoughtlessness in not being here to greet you? Although my brother tells me that what I did was utterly *un*forgivable."

He was as handsome and affable as ever, his expression a mixture of good humor and apology, as if like an overindulged child he fully expected to be forgiven his transgressions.

Her waspish thought surprised her and she glanced at Valentine, as if afraid he'd read her mind. But Valentine was pretending to ignore them and drinking his coffee. She noticed that his jacket was rumpled, but he'd tied his necktie today and his hair was brushed, although it was long enough to fall into his eyes as he bent his head to sip from his cup.

Her fingers itched to push it back. She had a sudden image of herself, sitting on his lap and kissing his lips in between feeding him pieces of buttered toast.

Sharp tingles of desire reminded her of her fragile state and she took a deep breath, concentrating on George.

"I did wonder where you were when I arrived," she said in a voice that strove to be calm but sounded peevish. "What if you'd been kidnapped by Baron Von Hautt? How would we know? Perhaps it would do you good if I did refuse to forgive you, George."

George glanced at her sideways, not expecting her to react like she did. He was used to instant forgiveness and smiling understanding. In chastened silence he pulled out a chair opposite his brother and waited until she was settled before returning to his own seat.

"Would you pay the ransom to get me back?" His eyes were sparkling although his voice strove to be contrite.

"No," Valentine replied shortly.

George looked crestfallen.

"Of course we would," Marissa said, her heart softening just as it always did.

George laughed and began to spread marmalade on a slice of toast. "I'm glad someone is on my side. I knew I could rely on you, Marissa."

"This isn't a matter of sides," Valentine said mildly. "One day you're going to have to grow up, George, and think of others rather than yourself."

George appeared crestfallen but as before he soon rallied; he could never be serious for long. Marissa watched them as their banter continued, amused by what was clearly a habit of long standing. Despite his stern demeanor it was obvious to her that Valentine was very fond of his younger brother, and it was equally clear that the feeling was returned by George.

"I have apologized to Marissa for abandoning her to my ogre of a brother," George said. "You do forgive me, don't you, Marissa?"

"Of course, George. I have been well taken care of."

But not as well as I would like.

Suddenly, as if he was aware of her thoughts, Valentine looked directly at her. His blue eyes blazed. She felt scorched. Almost instantly they both looked away.

Shocked and breathless, Marissa's hands were trembling as she pushed aside the remains of her breakfast. Just one look and she was reduced to a quivering wreck. How could this have happened to sensible Marissa Rotherhild in so short a time? It was as if Valentine had scrambled her brains with his kisses. What she needed to do was to start kissing George and then, surely, she'd soon forget his brother?

She had her grandmother's permission to spend an afternoon in bed. Wasn't that what Lady Bethany had said? To try a man on like a new hat to see if he suited? What would Valentine say if she told him that?

A nervous giggle threatened to escape her, and she pressed her napkin to her lips and lowered her eyes.

It was a relief when George stood up and declared he was ready to go to Magna Midcombe. "Are we riding? I fancy a good gallop," he said, rubbing his hands together in anticipation.

Valentine finished his coffee and also rose to his feet. This time when he met Marissa's eyes his expression was coolly polite. "Do you still wish to accompany us, Miss Rotherhild? It may be dangerous if Von Hautt makes an appearance."

"Of course I am coming with you," she said, surprised he would even ask.

The brothers shared a look she didn't understand, but before she could quiz them on it, George came to possess himself of her arm.

"Who would have thought we'd ever go on a botanical expedition together?" he said with mock horror. "Don't tell any of my friends, Marissa. I'll never live it down."

Marissa smiled but she wasn't as amused as she expected to be. His casual dismissal of what was actually becoming quite an adventure irritated her. "Perhaps you need to change your friends," she said.

George laughed as if she'd made a joke—perhaps he thought she had—and she let it go. Now was not the time to start an argument with the man she intended to marry.

* * *

Valentine decided on the smaller carriage for himself and Marissa, while George rode on horseback. George pretended to complain, demanding to know why his brother had suddenly become one of those boring old country gentlemen who preferred to rattle along in comfort rather than reaching their destination as quickly as possible.

"There's no hurry, is there?" Valentine retorted. "Magna Midcombe isn't going anywhere, George."

George had never been a particularly deep thinker. Life didn't, in his opinion, require lots of contemplation to be enjoyable. Quite the opposite in fact. But even he could see there was something going on with his brother.

Valentine had insisted on taking the carriage and more or less insisted that Marissa ride with him, at his side. He'd expected her to argue, to demand she ride with George, but she'd seemed deep in her own thoughts and hadn't said a word of complaint. There was definitely some tension between them; it had been obvious at the breakfast table.

George considered what he should do about it.

He glanced back at the carriage. Marissa was holding her parasol up to the sun, swaying with the movement of the carriage, and trying not to let her eyes close. George found himself wondering, tongue in cheek, if her weariness was due to a wild night of passion with Valentine. But he knew his brother too well. Valentine was so wary when it came to repeating his mistake with Vanessa that he would resist even a woman as beautiful as Marissa.

Vanessa had been a poisonous bitch who made his

brother's life a complete misery. Who could blame him for avoiding even the possibility of making the same mistake again?

"Is that as fast as that dashed thing can go?" he called out. "We'll never get to Magna Midcombe."

Marissa smiled back, more like herself. "Do you have an urgent appointment somewhere, George?"

Was there a sting in her question? George wondered. Was she still upset about him neglecting her? But Marissa wasn't the sort to hold a grudge. "Not at all," he said. "I intend to spend the entire afternoon being the perfect host."

At the time he meant it sincerely, but he didn't know then that there was a boxing match on in Magna Midcombe he just had to see . . . .

Chapter 13

Magna Midcombe had once been the site of an abbey. The Fortescues were very pious and therefore benefactors of the abbey, so when Henry VIII, mad with love for Anne Boleyn, decided to turn his back on the Pope and close the religious houses, they argued against it, and for their troubles they lost everything. According to a Miss Johnson, a local spinster who collected local history, all that now remained of the Fortescue estate was a meadow attached to an old mill.

"The family are long gone, of course," she said. "But I can direct you to the mill."

The former Fortescue estate was a little way beyond the village. The mill was neglected and forlorn, the wheel seized up in its pond, while the surrounding meadow was full of flowers, their colorful faces peeping over the long grass.

George, observing the pretty scene from his mount, said, "You should have brought a picnic basket, Valentine. Mrs. Beaumaris always packs the best picnics."

"Hungry again, George," his brother mocked. "I'm afraid I had more important things on my mind."

"What could be more important than a picnic on a summer's day?" George retorted. "Well, it just so happens I had the forethought to ask Mrs. Beaumaris for a picnic basket. It's tucked into the back of the carriage."

Valentine gave him a suspicious look. "Indeed?"

"Someone has to remember to play the host," George said smugly. "Women appreciate a man with a thoughtful nature."

While George was collecting the basket, Valentine handed Marissa down from the carriage, and they stood surveying the scene.

"What will we do now?" Marissa used her parasol to shade her face from the sun, but already she could feel perspiration trickling down her back. The air was still and hot, not a breath of wind stirring.

"Eat the picnic that George so *thoughtfully* brought," Valentine said.

"No, I mean . . ."

"I know what you mean. I'll take a look around but I doubt I'll find anything. If the Crusader's Rose was here then it's long gone. We'll just have to move on to the next name on the list, and hope for better." He looked at her, as if waiting for something. "You haven't told me that there's a chance I may never find the rose, that I should prepare myself for failure."

Marissa gave him a puzzled glance. "I wouldn't say anything so spineless."

His mouth curled into a reluctant smile. "No, I don't believe you would."

George arrived with the basket and a rug to lay out on the grass. He wandered over toward the mill and the shade thrown by the old building. Here he shook out the rug, setting it by the pond where the water was deep and green, beams of sunlight barely penetrating the surface, while insects darted above. At any moment, thought Marissa, a woman's hand might rise up from the depths, clutching a gleaming sword.

The thought made her smile.

"Mrs. Beaumaris has outdone herself." As they made themselves comfortable, George was investigating the contents of the picnic basket. "There's cold roast lamb, lobster salad, cherry tart . . . and a bottle of champagne!" He began to wrestle with the cork.

"What are you thinking?"

Marissa turned and found Valentine watching her from beneath his lashes. He was resting on his side, his long body stretched out on the rug and propped up by an elbow. He was twisting a blade of grass between his fingers, and one of his legs was bent at the knee, the cloth stretched over the thickness of his thigh. His jacket had fallen open and she could see the muscles of his chest beneath the thin linen shirt.

It was impossible not to remember him half-naked, his mouth hot on hers, as she sank down onto his lap and his fingers stroked her most secret places.

Marissa felt a tremor run through her, and beneath her skirts she squeezed her thighs tightly together, trying to ease the ache that was centered between them. Somehow, when George handed her a glass of champagne, she managed to thank him in a calm voice, as if her skin were not feverish and her thoughts full of wicked, unladylike longings.

"To us!" he announced.

She smiled and took a sip. The liquid was cool and delicious and this time her delight was unfeigned. "To us."

Valentine gulped some of the champagne, but he was still waiting for her to answer his question.

"I was thinking this could be the watery place where King Arthur commanded Excalibur to be thrown, when he lay dying."

"Romantic fairy tales?" he said, brushing his hair out of his eyes and frowning at her. "I thought you were a woman of intellect and reason."

Marissa took another sip of her champagne. "I am. But I also believe that we do not understand everything in our world and therefore we should keep our minds open to the possibilities."

Valentine grunted a noncommittal answer. He emptied his glass and glowered at the sunny meadow surrounding them. He seemed to be following his own thoughts, and after a moment he said, "Can Abbey Thorne really be the only manor surviving from the days of the Crusader's Rose? I would never have believed it."

"I don't think you realize how lucky you are," she said quietly. "You live in a place that has been in your family for centuries, surrounded by the belongings and memories of generations. Abbey Thorne Manor belongs to you, but you also belong to it. My family has kept very little of the past. My father says he doesn't believe in the burdens of history, and although in some ways that may be a good thing, in others it means we are like plants without our roots in the soil. We do not belong to anything or anyone."

She hadn't meant to say so much on a subject that was painful to her, but her tongue had run away with her—or perhaps it was the excellent champagne.

"This does look good," she said, beginning to fill a plate from the picnic basket. "And I am famished."

"Mrs. Beaumaris always sent me back to school with a jolly good feast," George said, eyeing his own plate with pleasure. He glanced up at her. "Didn't you attend some finishing school or other, Marissa?"

"Miss Debenham's Finishing School," she said with a reminiscent smile.

"I thought your parents weren't interested in the social niceties?" Valentine interrupted, digging his fork into the lobster salad.

"My grandmother is, however."

"Do Bohemians value etiquette and manners? Don't they prefer to live their lives outside the strictures of society?"

Marissa smiled in the face of his suspicion. "Not all of them, Lord Kent. My grandmother has always been very keen on etiquette and manners."

And giving herself up to pleasure, she almost added, stopping herself in time. It didn't matter, though. Valentine read her unspoken words in her eyes and something in his own flashed like a sapphire in the sun. "Pleasure" seemed to be occupying both their minds to a dangerous degree.

After he'd finished eating Valentine went off to

search the meadow for his own personal treasure, while George lay back replete and closed his eyes. Marissa observed the play of light on the water of the pond, or amused herself watching the family of swallows who had made their home in the roof of the mill. The parents flitted back and forth, finding morsels to bring back to their noisy and hungry babies.

"What is this about Bohemians?" George murmured, opening one eye to look at her.

"Your brother brought the subject up, you should ask him."

"You don't seem at all intimidated by him, Marissa. Women sometimes are. They either try too hard to please him or make excuses to leave."

"He's a clever and interesting man," she said uncomfortably.

"And you say what you feel, Marissa. Valentine appreciates women who say what they feel."

"Does he?"

She turned to look across to the other side of the meadow, where the man in question was standing, head bent, the sunlight turning strands of his hair to gold. Perhaps there was something wistful in her gaze, although she tried hard not to let it show, because George reached out to give her hand a brotherly pat.

"We are friends, aren't we, Marissa? You've forgiven me for abandoning you?"

"Of course I have," she said. "And yes, we are friends, George."

"You know, I only have your best interests at heart."

Puzzled now, Marissa sat up straighter. "Whatever do you mean, George?"

But he had jumped to his feet and was standing over her, a silhouette against the sun that was beginning to eat into their patch of shade. "You may not have noticed, but there was a poster fixed to the door of the inn in Magna Midcombe."

"Do you mean that poster of the dreadful boxing match you were staring at while your brother was trying to find out about the Fortescues?"

"Ah, but you only say that because you don't understand the finer points of boxing. One of the combatants happens to be the Dorking Destroyer."

"Good heavens."

"The match begins in . . ." He took out his pocket watch and perused it. "In twenty minutes."

Marissa shaded her eyes and looked up at him, waiting for what she knew was about to come next.

"Marissa?"

"Yes, George?"

"Would you be very disappointed if I returned to Magna Midcombe and left you in Valentine's care?"

"Oh, George. How can you give up such a lovely day to watch a brutal, sweaty boxing match?"

Laughter gleamed in his eyes. "I knew you'd understand."

"I don't understand at all, but if you must go then I won't stop you."

He rested his hand on her shoulder and gave it a squeeze. "I'll probably stay for a round or two of drinks with the locals and then toddle off home later. So don't worry about waiting for me."

"George . . . !" she protested.

But he only grinned at her and strode across to his horse. With a wave of his hand, he kicked the animal into a fast trot and set off toward the gate, and the road to Magna Midcombe.

Chapter 14

S elf-centered, self-indulgent, irresponsible . . ."
Marissa muttered to herself as she cast her gaze
around the meadow, searching for Valentine. This
time she found him stooping to peer into a thicket
of weeds. As she watched he straightened, and
she saw his head turn sharply as George galloped
by, no doubt in response to George's shout. For a
moment he gazed after his brother's receding figure,
and then he spun around to face Marissa. She felt
her heart begin to beat faster as, with long, urgent
strides, he started to make his way through the tall
grass toward her.

"He's gone to a boxing match in Magna Midcombe," she said, when he was close enough to hear
her, and before he could speak himself. "He said
he'd make his own way home afterward."

Valentine looked startled, and then his brows
drew down and his expression changed to suspicion. "He's up to something," he said. "Do you think
he's up to something?"

"He's your brother. Surely you know him well
enough to answer that question yourself."

"I do, and he's up to something," he repeated with certainty.

Marissa unfurled her parasol; the shade was almost gone now. She glanced at the pond, and wondered if the water was as cool as it looked. It would be heavenly to dip her feet into those green depths.

Well, why not?

She set down the parasol and began to take off her shoes.

"He didn't mention any boxing match to me," Valentine said thoughtfully. "Did he say anything to . . . ?" His voice trailed off.

Marissa set her shoes neatly to one side and, drawing her skirt and petticoats over her knees, she began to untie the ribbons that held up her fine white stockings.

"What are you doing?" Valentine demanded in hushed tones.

"I'm taking off my shoes and stockings," she replied calmly.

She peeled one stocking down over her calf, and then slipped it off her foot. Her toes felt much cooler already and she wriggled them with pleasure before beginning to remove the second stocking. Once that was disposed of, Marissa climbed to her feet and, lifting her heavy skirts, picked her way to the very edge of the pond.

Cautiously she sat down on the bank and dipped her toes in the water. It was deliciously cool, bringing goose bumps to her skin. She sighed, submerging her ankles and then a good six inches of leg, careful to hold her clothing out of the way.

She glanced sideways at Valentine. He was standing, watching her. "You should join me. It's very soothing on such a hot day."

"I haven't dipped my feet in the water since I was a child," he said, as if she was suggesting something immoral.

Marissa laughed. "Then it's time you did."

Valentine glowered at her for a moment, and then suddenly he seemed to give in. He sat down beside her, tugging off first one boot and then the other one, before yanking off his stockings with flattering speed. He proceeded to roll up his trouser legs before he lowered his feet into the water.

"Must be deep to be so cold," he said, slightly breathless.

She smiled at him and after a moment he smiled back. His eyes played over her mouth, and she felt her inner warmth returning, prickling her skin beneath her clothing, and making her breasts feel heavy and sensitive.

Impulsively she reached down to cup her hand in the water, lifting it to trickle over her throat. The cold liquid ran over and beneath the tight bodice of her dress. Relief was immediate, and she shuddered, and then laughed, turning back to Valentine. His face was flushed, and he was following the trickle of water with rapt attention.

Marissa reached down for more water, but this time she trickled it over Valentine's throat, where his necktie was now undone, and the top of his shirt was unfastened.

He captured her hand. His eyes gleamed. "Minx," he growled, and lifting her wet fingers to his mouth, kissed them.

This time it was Valentine who scooped up the water in his hands, allowing it to escape through his fingers and onto her skin, soaking her bodice. Then he used his tongue to follow the trail as far as he could. With gentle hands he cupped her breasts, fondling, until she began to breathe quickly, her eyes half-closed with pleasure. She swayed, dizzy, and suddenly she was slipping. Falling. With a squeak she began to slide down the steep bank and into the pond.

Valentine grabbed at her hands and gripped them tightly in his. Slowly, inexorably, he pulled her back up the bank and into his arms. They fell backward onto the ground together, cradled by the soft grass, their hearts beating hard.

"Valentine," she whispered, reaching with a trembling hand to stroke his cheek and then brush his hair away from his eyes. He sighed and closed his eyes, and growing bolder, she bent to nuzzle the hollow of his throat, breathing in the masculine aroma she found so exciting.

She planned to explore further but Valentine had other ideas.

He clasped her in his arms and rolled her over, so that she was now beneath him, trapped under his weight and bulk. There was a moment when Marissa wondered whether she should be afraid—and she might have been afraid if it was any other man—but instead of fear she was filled with a sense of security. As if instinctively she knew that with Valentine she was perfectly safe.

His thighs were pressing to hers, and she wrapped her bare feet around his legs, at the same time wrapping her arms around his neck. Valentine bent his head and began to kiss her lips with a slow thoroughness that soon had her swooning.

His hand was on her hip, and then he was bundling up her skirt in determined folds, until he found what he was seeking. His fingers brushed against the flesh of her thigh. He found the ribbons that held her pantaloons in place, and proceeded to untie them.

"Take off your jacket," she gasped, tugging at the garment.

He did, with her help, but a moment later he won the battle of her underwear and she felt the waist sag and begin to slip. With a grin, he edged his body downward.

"Valentine?" she cried, breathlessly.

But he had disappeared under her voluminous skirts and petticoats. His hands clasped her thighs, pressing them inexorably apart, and his warm breath teased her sensitive skin. A tremor ran through her, all sensation centering on the building ache at her core. His fingertip brushed against her and she whimpered, wriggling, but he held her still, blowing against her. He touched her again, more pressure this time, and she squirmed and moaned.

"Oh!"

"Be patient, Marissa," he said, his voice far away.

Above her the hot blue sky was vast and beneath her the earth was warm and alive. She tried to do as he said and be patient, but her legs were trembling and she arched against his hand as he continued to tease her without giving her the release she urgently craved.

"Valentine . . ." she wailed, and then to her shocked amazement she felt the brush of his tongue. A wave of pleasure quickly followed and she cried out, hands clutching at the grass either side of her, her heels digging into the earth.

After a long moment she lifted her head. He was resting against her, smiling up at her with a particularly male expression. "That wasn't something we learned about at Miss Debenham's," she said huskily.

"I haven't finished yet," he retorted.

"But—"

For the next several minutes Marissa was put through an agony of passion and impatience, as Valentine lathed her swollen flesh with his tongue, licking and sucking, bringing her closer and closer to a new peak of pleasure only to deny it to her. She begged him. She tried to grasp hold of him and force him to concentrate on where she wanted him. But he eluded her, forcing her to his slower pace.

And then, when he finally gave her what she wanted, Marissa reached a degree of ecstasy she'd never dreamed of. She lay limp and replete, unable to utter a single word, as he flung himself down beside her, chest heaving.

Dazedly, Marissa wondered if this was what her grandmother had meant by trying on a "hat" before buying it, and whether there could be any doubt that this "hat" was exactly the one she wanted.

But that couldn't be. George was the hat she'd set her heart on. Surely he would be just as good or—or better? The odd thing was, Marissa didn't want to kiss George or allow him the liberties Valentine had just taken. The very thought of lying here with George was somehow . . . wrong.

She wished she could talk to Valentine about it, but that was impossible. Everything felt so complicated. She preferred to lie here, limp and contented, beneath the summer blue sky, and wait for the future to sort out itself.

She was smiling, that irrepressible dimple playing in her cheek. Valentine had never seen anything more beautiful than her lying like a wanton in the meadow grass, her hair falling in curls about her, her eyes half-closed and her pink mouth smiling. But his body was hard and throbbing and the knowledge that she'd offered herself to him and yet he had to resist her was driving him to the edge of insanity.

"You really are a most unusual girl," he said, unable to disguise his irritability. "I don't know anyone else like you. Don't you feel the slightest bit concerned for what we've just done?"

Marissa brushed aside a blade of grass that was tickling her cheek, and turned her face toward his. "No, I don't. Does that mean I'm a Bohemian, like my grandmother? I rather think I must be. Thank you, Valentine, for showing me how pleasurable such a life can be. You are a wonderful teacher."

She always had an answer for everything. He was frustrated, not just physically but emotionally, intellectually . . . He was beginning to understand that he didn't want to lose her to George, or anyone else for that matter. But at the same time he didn't want to become entangled in another marriage.

"Is that all you care about, Marissa? A pleasurable life?"

"It is certainly better than kneeling on the damp ground searching for lichens. Don't you agree?" She reached forward to brush his hair out of his eyes and he let her, the intimacy of the action filling him with joy.

"If I am your teacher," he said, and paused, his thoughts becoming muddled and rather dark. "When you've learned all you can from me, will you find other men?"

What he asked was truly shocking to his own ears, but Marissa didn't appear to be shocked. She stretched and yawned, like a cat after it has had its fill, and smiled at him, that dimple peeping out again.

"Are you tired of me already?" she asked.

He felt his stomach clench with some violent emotion that he didn't fully understand, nor did he want to. His voice was harsh and tight, the words hard to get past the constriction in his throat. "Don't you think you may be hurt by other men, Marissa? Taken advantage of? Not everyone is as scrupulous as I am. Not everyone who calls himself a 'gentleman' is deserving of the title."

She sighed as if his questions were beginning to annoy her, and sat up, straightening her clothing with irritable little tugs. "You did not answer me. Are you tired of me already? Do you *want* me to find another man, Valentine?"

"No," he growled. "You know I don't, minx."

"Then I won't." He couldn't see her expression. She'd bent forward to draw on her stockings and

shoes, and her hair had fallen forward to hide her
face. Valentine wondered what it was he wanted her
say. He'd already made it clear he had no wish to
remarry. What could he possibly have to offer her to
keep her by his side while he continued his search
for the Crusader's Rose?

Pleasure.

The word reverberated in his mind, shaking him
to the core. He could offer her pleasure and all the
different ways of seeking and finding it. She'd already spoken of him as her teacher, hadn't she? In
his younger days, before Vanessa, he'd been utterly
enamored with women and he'd gained a great deal
of knowledge. Just because he'd been a monk since
Vanessa died didn't mean he'd forgotten those les-
sons. Oh, he may be a little rusty, but it would soon
return to him.

The real question was whether he could control
himself, whether he could prevent himself from
unleashing all his pent-up passion on Miss Marissa
Rotherhild, taking her virginity, and catapulting
himself and her into forced wedlock. After what
they'd done so far, deflowering her was perhaps a
technicality, but to Valentine it was the point beyond
which he must not go.

"I can show you how to find more pleasure," he
said at last.

"Valentine, what do you mean?" she said, looking
up, her eyes questioning.

"Let me be your mentor, your teacher. If you
really want to live a Bohemian life then let me show
you how."

She seemed to be considering his offer. "No attachments? I will not hold you to such a proposal if at any time you wish to stop, and you will not try to keep me by your side if I decide to go?"

Somehow he managed an indifferent shrug, although the voice inside his head was screaming at him to tell her he had no intention of allowing her to go off and place herself in the power of any other man but himself, and how could she even ask it of him.

She took his shrug as an affirmative. After a moment she nodded briskly. "Very well, Valentine." She held out her hand toward him, and he grasped her fingers, holding them swallowed within his far bigger hand. She felt small and fragile, something to be protected, but Valentine knew Marissa Rotherhild did not consider herself either small or fragile, and she was certainly very much used to looking after herself.

"One more thing," he said. "You must remain at Abbey Thorne Manor for the time being and join me in my search for the Crusader's Rose."

She wrinkled her nose.

"Come, Marissa, you will enjoy it," he assured her.

"Very well. I will stay and help you. For now."

They began to pack up the picnic and put things away. The sun was still warm but it was definitely sinking lower in the sky. Time to return to Abbey Thorne Manor. Valentine wondered what Marissa expected from him now. He would have to give his next move some thought. He'd promised to give her pleasure so he must give her pleasure, and in a way that would keep her by his side.

Chapter 15

George finished his ale with a sigh of contentment, looking around the smoky little room of the tavern. It was crowded with bare-knuckle boxing enthusiasts like himself, and they were all enjoying discussing the fights they'd seen on Magna Midcombe green today.

Unfortunately the Dorking Destroyer had been knocked out after fifteen minutes and refused to rejoin the fray, but it didn't matter in the end. They had a new hero, and George had been the first to raise his tankard to the Midcombe Mauler.

Now he looked into the bottom of his tankard and hesitated. Did he have time for another before he set off for home, or should he go before it began to grow dark? Surely he'd still reach Abbey Thorne Manor before the long summer evening turned to night even if he lingered another ten minutes?

George was just getting to his feet when he saw someone he recognized moving toward the doorway.

At first he doubted his own eyes, because what would Baron Von Hautt be doing here in the Magna Midcombe tavern? He must be mistaken. But as the man reached the doorway he turned and looked straight at George, and he knew with a chill in his blood that he wasn't mistaken. The gray hair and youthful face, those icy blue eyes. It was Von Hautt all right.

He stumbled to his feet, almost knocking over his chair, apologizing as he shoved through the crowd in pursuit of the Prussian. It didn't occur to him to wonder why Von Hautt would be showing himself like this. He felt no sense of anxiety or danger, only an urgent need not to allow the man to escape him.

George reached the door and burst out into the warm, calm evening. He stood, taking gulps of air, trying to clear his head. The village street was empty . . . or was it? Something caught his eye and he turned just in time to see Von Hautt vanishing around a corner. With a grin of triumph, George hurried after him.

Had Von Hautt come to Magna Midcombe to find what remained of the Fortescues? Well, he was going to have to explain himself to George. Maybe, George thought, he could capture the Prussian and take him back to Abbey Thorne Manor and hand him over to Valentine and Jasper. Wouldn't that make their eyes pop!

He turned the corner, full of confidence, and his heart leaped into his throat. Von Hautt was standing right in front of him, a big grin on his face.

"Ah, it is the little brother," he said cheerfully. "How are you, little brother George?"

George stopped himself from taking a step back—just. "What do you want?" he said, in his best imitation of Valentine's growl. "What are you doing following us about?"

Von Hautt didn't bother to answer. His strange pale eyes were searching George's face, and then he shook his head in mock despair. "You have been drinking," he said. "The only way to find the Crusader's Rose is to reject all such crass temptations. Your brother knows that. You should ask him what he has given up in his quest for the prize."

"You know nothing about my brother!" George shouted, but the chill in his blood was back again. This man was dangerous and all of a sudden he was wondering why he'd followed him out here. Alone.

"I know a great deal about your brother," Von Hautt said in a voice as cold as snow.

"Then you'll know he doesn't want you following him around and shooting his friends," George retorted.

"His friend deserved to be shot." He dismissed the incident.

George opened his mouth, closed it again. His sense that this man was unpredictable and dangerous was growing, and any dreams he'd had of capturing him were gone. All he wanted to do now was to get away from him in one piece.

"Valentine will not find the rose in Magna Midcombe," Von Hautt said with a sneer. "Unless he believes it is hidden under Miss Rotherhild's skirts." He smirked. "She is a very beautiful woman."

"What has Miss Rotherhild to do with you?" George shouted. "Have you been spying? You damned filthy coward . . ." Rage overcame self-preservation and he tried to grasp the other man's shirtfront, meaning to shake him like a dog. But Von Hautt was too quick for him, or perhaps George was more affected than he thought by the amount of ale he'd imbibed.

The man loomed over him, those icy blue eyes staring into his. "It will be *I* who finds the rose," he said softly, "and you will all be very sorry that you turned your backs on me and my mother."

He was gone.

George swallowed, leaning back against the brick wall and trying not to sag to the ground. The fellow was completely bonkers. He made no sense at all. But that didn't mean he was any less dangerous.

George straightened up. He needed to get home to Abbey Thorne Manor and talk to Valentine. Turning, he made his way back to the tavern. One more drink, he thought. He deserved another ale after what he'd just been through. Yes, a drink to bolster his spirits. And then he'd fetch his horse from the stable and go home.

Chapter 16

Dinner at Abbey Thorne Manor was a leisurely affair. Lord Jasper and Lady Bethany looked as if they'd been drinking the elixir of life, their faces content and glowing in the candlelight. Marissa wondered what they'd been up to while she was in Magna Midcombe, but she didn't ask. Even when a besotted Jasper lifted her grandmother's hand and placed a kiss on it, she thought it best to pretend not to notice Things between them must have reached a new level of intimacy to be so open in their affections. Valentine also politely ignored the obvious, although she saw him giving his friend a quizzical look.

He was also ignoring Marissa and she was beginning to wonder if she'd imagined the intimacies they'd shared. Had Valentine really offered to teach her about pleasure? And had she really agreed?

"Did you know that Lady B was an artist, Kent?" Jasper demanded.

"Indeed I did not," Valentine said evenly. "What sort of artist?"

"I paint," Lady Bethany replied with a little smile.

"My daughter and son-in-law wanted someone to make a record of their discoveries, so I have been painting pictures of plants ever since."

"You must ask her to immortalize the Crusader's Rose when you find it!" Jasper seemed unable to keep the grin off his face.

"Of course. *When* I find it."

The meal finished, Jasper and Lady Bethany went to take a turn about the garden. Marissa wasn't sure if she wanted time alone with Valentine—she needed time to compose herself—but he excused himself, telling her he had some estate business to deal with and that his land manager awaited him. So Marissa enjoyed a rare moment alone, pretending to read one of the novels she found in the bookcase.

In reality she was pondering her situation.

She'd set her sights on George but she'd be a fool not to realize by now that it wasn't thoughts of George keeping her awake at night. Every inch of her being called to Valentine and when he made his offer to her she'd known it was right to accept. She may well be following a path that would lead her astray but nevertheless she had to do it. She had to discover for once and for all whether Valentine was the man for her.

"Are you tired?"

His voice startled her; she hadn't heard him enter. He was standing in the doorway and she didn't know how long he'd been watching her.

"A little. Why?"

"I had planned a little game, but if you prefer we can leave it until tomorrow."

Something wicked in his eyes caught her attention. A warmth spread through her limbs, and she felt languid in a way that had nothing to do with feeling tired. Marissa laid her book aside. "What little game do you have in mind?"

With a smile, Valentine closed the door behind him and came to join her. "I have been remembering an incident that happened when I was a green youth of eighteen, first exploring London. I've never forgotten it."

"How intriguing." Marissa gave him an encouraging smile.

He sat down and, reaching into his pocket, took out a pair of dice. "I went to a gaming club—not my first, but this one was rather different. I wasn't greatly interested in gaming even then, but some friend or other persuaded me that this club really must be visited at least once if you were to begin to shrug off your country dust and think of yourself as a urbane gentleman of the world."

"And what was so different about this gaming club?"

"There was an area at the back, a room in which guests could play the game of their choice, while others were allowed to watch through a series of discreet and very narrow windows."

"But who were they and why would they want to watch?" Marissa said, and only realized she'd been naïve when he laughed softly.

"Shall we call them interested spectators?" His blue eyes warmed as he watched her attempting to understand. "Perhaps you will better comprehend if I tell you that the night I visited the club there was a game going on between a gentleman and a lady. They were both masked and she was wearing a dress cut so low I found myself holding my breath in the fear—or should I say the hope?—that her bosom would tumble out of it."

Marissa raised an eyebrow. "So the gentleman and lady were in the room and the rest of you were watching them. What exactly were they doing?"

"They were throwing dice."

"That sounds innocent enough."

"Ah, but whoever lost had to remove an item of clothing." He grinned at the memory. "The spectators were agog, the tension was palpable, and yet the two of them acted as if they were entirely alone even though they must have known they weren't."

"Whoever lost the throw of the dice had to remove an item?" she said slowly. "Did they end up, eh, naked?"

His reminiscent smile grew wicked. "Oh yes."

Marissa waited for him to elaborate and when he didn't she asked with an impatient note, "And then what happened?"

Valentine made her wait a moment more. "Not what we hoped. He lifted her up in his arms and carried her into a farther room, unfortunately one without windows, and shut the door."

Marissa imagined the scene; she'd discovered she had a rather vivid imagination when it came to risqué detail. The idea of undressing, slowly, in front of dozens of watching eyes should have horrified her, and indeed if it was actually happening she was sure she would hate it, but to pretend was different. She pictured the room, Valentine and herself opposite each other, the atmosphere tense with expectation and the knowledge that soon they would consummate their growing desire. Consummate it fully and completely, as they were yet to do . . . .

His fingers brushed her cheek, breaking the spell. "What are you thinking, minx?"

"I am wondering why you are telling me this story. And why," she looked down at the dice he was rolling in his hand, "you have those dice."

"Come, come, Marissa, you know why."

"And this is the game you wish to play?"

"This is the game I wish to play with you."

She glanced toward the door.

"I locked it," he said promptly, "and left instructions we are not to be disturbed."

"My grandmother and Lord Jasper?"

"Gone to bed, I am told, also with instructions not to be disturbed."

"And George?"

"Not back yet. No doubt he is enjoying rubbing shoulders with the Magna Midcombe folk and partaking of the local ale. Don't worry about George."

Marissa gave a little shiver, a frisson of excitement, and rose to her feet. She approached the small card table where Valentine was waiting and allowed him to draw out a chair for her, calmly arranging her skirts about her as she sat.

"Is this part of your promise to show me about pleasure?" she said, clasping her hands before her and watching his face.

But instead of answering her he said, "Here are the rules. There must be no touching, not until the game is over."

"No touching?" she cried, unable to keep the disappointment out of her voice. For Marissa, the act of touching his skin was a pleasure in itself.

He smiled and threw the dice. They landed on four and two. "Now your turn," he said softly, gathering them up again and handing them to her.

Marissa held the dice tight in her hand, feeling the excitement growing inside her. She couldn't decide whether she wanted to win or lose, but when she threw and the numbers were revealed—a three and a two—her disappointment made her realize what her true wishes were.

"I lost," she said, raising her eyes questioningly to his.

His triumphant smile made her shiver again. "And I won."

"Does that mean I—"

"Wait, I haven't finished explaining the rules of the game. The winner of each throw must choose the item of clothing the loser must remove. Otherwise, minx, I suspect you will take off a single shoe or a ribbon, and then the game will go on for far too long."

"I suspect you're right," Marissa said. "Nevertheless I am a little anxious to know what you are going to choose for me to remove."

He took his time deciding. His gaze traveled leisurely over her, increasing her tension, until she felt quite light-headed.

"Your jewelry," he spoke at last.

She reached up to touch her necklace, feeling the pearls warm beneath her fingers. "Which piece of my jewelry?"

"All of it. Jewelry counts as one item."

"Oh?" She considered arguing but decided to save it until the game had progressed further. Slowly, Marissa began to remove her necklace. She placed the pearls on the table and then added her earrings and her two rings, finally unclipping her bracelet and setting it down on top of the pile.

She'd expected him to ask her to take off an item of her clothing, and been relieved, though slightly confused, by his choice. But now, without her jewelry, she felt uncomfortable and strangely naked, as if she was improperly dressed. It made her understand just how important a woman's jewel box was as part of her imaginary armor, adding to her self-confidence when she appeared before others.

Valentine met her eyes, then let his gaze take in the nakedness of her neck and earlobes and hands. "Thank you," was all he said, as he picked up the dice and threw again.

The numbers were six and a one. Marissa threw a five and a four, and breathed a sigh of relief. "Me this time," she said, a lilt of anticipation in her voice.

She tapped a fingertip to her chin, pretending to deliberate, but she'd already decided what she was going to ask him to remove. From the first moment she'd seen Valentine without his shirt she'd been struck by the sheer beauty of his body. She wanted him naked as soon as possible.

"Your jacket."

He made no comment, merely removing the item

and dropping it on the floor beside him. His shirt was silk and her fingers itched to caress it, but that was against the rules of the game, and she turned back to the dice with a renewed determination to win.

But it was Valentine who won the next two throws.

First, he asked her to take off her shoes and, second, to remove her pins and the ebony comb that was holding up her hair. She set her evening slippers on the floor beside her chair and then reached up to begin dismantling her hair. Without the comb the long tresses fell heavily about her shoulders, curling against her back and the low décolletage of her violet silk evening dress, and with each pin she removed her hair became wilder.

Instinctively he stretched out his hand, as if to capture a tress of dark hair, but stopped himself, clenching his fingers into a fist before drawing it back. "No touching," he said, reminding them both. "Not yet."

Her breath caught in her throat. "Not yet? What if I want you to touch me?"

"Touching means you forfeit the game. Are you prepared to do that at this early stage? Do you want to lose, Marissa?"

"No, I want to win." She spoke with conviction. Yes, she wanted to win. She wanted Valentine in her power, naked before her.

His eyes delved into hers. "I want to win, too," he said.

Marissa won the next four throws. First she had him take off his silk shirt, so that his skin gleamed in the candlelight, while the muscular curves and hollows of his body bunched and rippled every time he moved. Then she had him remove his neck cloth, because it ruined the effect dangling about his neck all on its own. Thirdly she asked for him to take off his shoes and then, lastly, his belt. She planned to get rid of the trousers on the next throw, but her run of luck ran out and this time Valentine won.

"Your dress," he said with satisfaction, and sat back and folded his arms, as if preparing for the ensuing show.

Marissa laughed at him, disguising her anxiety as best she could. She'd never undressed before a man and although this was Valentine, the man she'd already shared a great deal with, it was far more nerve-wracking than she'd imagined.

To begin with there were the hooks at the back. After struggling with them inelegantly for several moments she gave up. "You will have to help me," she said. "Surely it won't count as touching if you only touch the hooks and the cloth and not my skin?"

He bowed his head in acquiescence.

Marissa went around the table and stood with her back to him, and waited as she felt the tug of the hooks being released. The dress began to loosen about her, and she put up her hand to prevent it slipping down over her bosom to her waist. When he'd done she turned to face him.

It was difficult to read his expression. He was keeping himself very much under control. Suddenly she knew she wanted to see his will crumble. She wanted to see him vulnerable. That was what winning meant to her. Having Valentine in the palm of her hand.

She allowed the cloth to slide through her hands, slowly, uncovering the lacy top of her chemise where it cupped her breasts. The evening dress caught at her waist, and she bent to release the ties, aware that doing so meant he could see the full swell of her bosom. The dress slithered to her feet, and calmly she stepped out of it, returning to her chair in her petticoats and undergarments and her stockinged feet.

Marissa won the next throw and was finally able to watch him stand and unbutton his trousers. He pushed them down over his trim hips and muscular thighs. Much to her disappointment, he was wearing a tight-fitting undergarment, but as it really was very tight she soon reconciled herself.

Valentine won after that, and Marissa removed her petticoats after a great deal of argument as to whether they constituted one item of clothing or three. In the end he won, and she removed all three. As she sat down opposite him, she was flushed from the argument and very conscious of her half-naked state. Although in fact she wasn't really naked; her bloomers covered her down to the knee and from there her stockings covered her to her toes. Her chemise and stays were another barrier to his gaze, despite her shoulders and arms being naked, and her breasts pushed up to make the décolletage of her evening dress more daring.

He took his time admiring her. "You are beautiful," he said, his voice low and husky.

"So are you," she teased, her gaze admiring his torso. "Can't I touch you, just a little, Valentine?"

But he shook his head and handed her the dice.

Marissa won next and ordered him to remove his stockings. She was tempted to go straight for the undergarment but decided it would be too peculiar to see him naked with his stockings still on.

Valentine won twice after that, and Marissa removed her own stockings, peeling them slowly over her calves and dropping them to the floor, then her stays, which were a struggle that left her breathless and hot, although much less restricted. Only the chemise retained her modesty.

"Do you still think you are going to win?" he demanded, eyes glittering, the dice ready in his hand. "This game requires more skill than you think, minx."

"It is a simple game of chance," she retorted, watching his hand as he allowed the dice fall and rattle across the tabletop.

A one and a two.

With a little smile, Marissa picked up the dice and held them a moment tightly in her palm, before letting them fall. She could hardly believe her eyes. A one and a one! Her gaze lifted to his, and saw the bright flare of triumph.

Again he took his time while she shifted about uncomfortably.

"The chemise," he said.

She reached to the small buttons and paused.

"Do you want to default?" he said.

"And allow you to win? Never!"

Slowly she began to unbutton the front of the garment, aware that with every inch her breasts were revealed to his gaze. She slipped one of the shoulder straps down, and then the other, allowing the chemise to slide to her waist, then wriggling it over her hips and thighs, reaching down to tug it away and drop it on the growing pile of clothing beside the table. When she straightened, her arms were crossed over her breasts, hiding her nakedness, while only the bloomers covered her lower body.

"No hiding," he reprimanded her huskily. "That's against the rules."

"How do I know you're not making up the rules as we go along?" she retorted breathlessly.

"Unfold your arms, Marissa."

His gaze was compelling, his voice commanding, but neither would have made Marissa capitulate if she didn't want to. Because the truth was, she wanted him to see her naked. She felt beautiful beneath his gaze. She wanted his eyes on her.

Marissa unfolded her arms. He drew in a sharp breath, taking in the sight. It was as if she could feel him touching her, brushing against her skin, causing her to give a little shiver. Her breasts felt full and heavy, her nipples aching and dark with excitement.

He groaned aloud. "Beautiful . . ."

Her stomach went hollow. She drank him in, sitting there in the candlelight, so masculine, so handsome. She almost stood and flung herself into his arms, but then she remembered that if she touched him then he would win, so she stopped herself. Because it was important to her that she win this tug of war, almost as if to win was an omen of things to come.

"Your turn," she said, her voice sounding unlike her own. "Roll the dice, Valentine."

He hesitated, as if this moment was important to him, too, and then he picked up the dice and lifted his closed hand to his lips as though to give himself luck. This time he didn't draw out the process, but threw quickly.

A five and a three.

Marissa gathered them up and into her palm. She rolled them across the table, aware of his warm naked skin so near to hers, the quick rise and fall of his chest.

A five and a five.

She had won.

He groaned and stood up, fumbling at the buttons on his undergarment. Her gaze took in the bulge between his thighs, as he rolled the cloth over his hips and down his thighs. His cock was jutting out from his body, and as she looked it quivered as if it had a life of its own. She wanted to touch him, feel him, discover all there was to know about him. He shoved the garment down to his feet and kicked it aside, and a moment later she was reaching out to close her fingers around him.

"Oh, Marissa," he whispered, the words barely coherent. He covered her hand with his and she felt him shaking.

"Can I touch you?" she said, but she was already doing so, unable to stop herself any longer. "I want to touch you, Valentine."

"I'll spend in your hand," he groaned.

"Can I do that to you?" she said, eyes bright as she looked up at him. "I want you to lose control, Valentine."

She saw the sudden flare of passion in his face. He caught her upper arms and dragged her against his chest, and his mouth came down hard on hers. He was kissing her as if he wanted to swallow her up, his tongue in her mouth, his lips covering hers. Her breasts were jammed against his chest, and the abrasion of his hair and her nipples made her squirm, gasping. Clasping her buttocks in his palms, he drew her hard against him, and she felt his cock settle in the niche between her thighs.

Marissa squeaked. Pleasure threatened to overflow, trembling on the brink, and she moved against him, the friction edging her toward the desired peak.

In their efforts to get closer he lifted her higher and she shifted the angle of her hips, and suddenly he slid inside the slick, tight sheath of her body. Surprise stopped them. Panting, Valentine looked down into her eyes, his own startled. She licked her lips and pushed against him, feeling him enter her another inch, filling her in a way that was new and exciting.

"Marissa, I can't," he groaned. "I won't take your virginity."

"I want you to," she said quietly. Reaching down, she clasped her hand about the root of him. "And you want to. Please, Valentine. If it is what we both want . . ."

He bent his head and took her nipple into his mouth, drawing on it while Marissa's head fell back and she gasped. Her body arched toward him, only her fingers clutching his shoulders and his hands on her buttocks keeping her on her feet.

Such sweet pleasure. Couldn't he see how perfect they were together? That it was meant to be? Marissa's thoughts were barely lucid as his hand slid between her thighs, and his fingers dove into her slick core. She cried out as the climax took her, shuddering in his arms, beyond all thought now.

When at last she came to herself, he was sitting on the chair with her gathered into his arms, holding her close, his chin resting on top of her head.

"Valentine?" she managed.

"Hush."

"No, I want you to—"

"I want to teach you about pleasure."

"But I want you to be my lover!"

"I am your lover."

"No, you're not. Not completely. Not properly."

She stood up on shaking legs, angry and tearful, and began to gather up her clothing, pulling it on as best she could. And all the while she spoke in a trembling, angry voice she hardly recognized.

"I don't want you to protect me. I don't need your protection when it comes to my virginity. It is mine to give and I give it to you. Don't you see that? I'm not some silly young thing who doesn't understand what she's doing, I've never been that sort of woman. I make my own decisions, Valentine, and I want you to respect them."

She reached the door and turned the key. Her hair was in her eyes but there was no time to tidy it. She thrust it back over her shoulder and stared back at him, where he remained in the chair, watching her, expressionless.

"I don't understand," she said, her lips trembling, and then she was outside, the door was closed, and she was hurrying through the silent house to her bedchamber, tears already pouring down her cheeks.

Chapter 17

Valentine stood alone in the darkness. The night air was meant to cool his blood—or so he'd hoped when he stepped out here into the inner courtyard—but so far there'd been little relief. Above him the sky was ablaze with stars and the scent of the night-perfumed plants in the walled garden threatened to make him swoon.

Or was that the memory of Marissa wanton in his arms?

His body began to throb again and he gritted his teeth. This was madness. He was suffering. And yet he could not seem to stop himself. Despite his doubts about his own capacity as a lover and a man—Vanessa's legacy—he felt remade when he was with Marissa. The way she gazed at him, the way she made him feel, was like a healing draught.

And now he'd arranged matters so that he could keep her by his side, at least for the foreseeable future.

But he wasn't healed completely—the scars were still there.

An owl called from the gatehouse. He turned to follow it, a black shape against the sky, as it flew through the arched gateway and over the stone bridge that spanned the moat and disappeared into the park. Valentine wondered if Baron Von Hautt was out there, spying, and then dismissed the thought. What was the point now they both had the list? One thing Valentine knew with cold, hard certainty; he would never let Von Hautt beat him to the Crusader's Rose.

And what about Marissa? his inner voice mocked. *Will you protect her just as fervently?*

He knew in his heart that he would.

She was good and beautiful and honorable, everything he could ask for in a woman, but she was also set against the life he led, with his obsession with roses and his library full of dusty botanical tomes. Her childhood had driven her to look for another life. And then there was George. Valentine felt a twinge of guilt, but he suppressed it. George had had his chance and he'd preferred a boxing match to wooing Marissa.

Is that what I'm doing? Wooing her?

Out in the park the owl called again—perhaps it had a mate—and then there was silence. Suddenly the whole world felt empty and he was very much alone. Was this how he would feel without Marissa? Or would he be able to lose himself once more in his search for his rose, burying his emotions and pretending he didn't care? Would his feelings for her turn out to be an illusion, an infatuation, and like a summer cold would pass as swiftly as they had come.

"I'm not good enough for her," he said aloud.

"No matter what she thinks now, I'll never be good enough for her. How can we be happy?"

It was what he'd learned from Vanessa and now the words were like a well-worn path in his head. It did not occur to him to question them.

With a sigh he lifted his face to the stars, then turned to go inside, and ran straight into a figure standing a mere yard away from him.

"What the hell . . ." Valentine began, struggling with the loose-limbed body clinging to him. The overpowering smell of ale engulfed him and he swore again, pushing George hard. His brother fell into the privet hedge, struggling to escape its scratchy clutches.

"No—no n-need to be like that," he slurred.

"What are you doing here?" Valentine said furiously. "And in that state?"

George had got himself back on his feet and was peering at his brother in the starlight. "Who w-were you talkin' to?" he demanded. "Thesh no one here."

"I was talking to myself, if it's any of your business." Valentine strode off through the walled garden, but George followed him, stumbling every now and then and muttering curses.

"I—I was in Ma-agna Mi'combe," he said at last, catching Valentine's sleeve and attaching himself to it, trying to stay upright.

After trying to shake himself free, Valentine gave up and let his brother use him as a crutch as they made their unsteady way to the door and into the lamplit manor. Somehow he pulled George up the stairs after him, into the long gallery.

Moonlight washed through the windows, illuminating the family portraits gazing down upon them, generations of de Fevres and Kents and everything in between. Usually Valentine was inured to the faces, not even seeing them, but now he remembered Marissa's words about how lucky he was and how the past mattered, and he viewed them in a new light.

He could give Marissa that stability, that sense of belonging. He could make her Lady Kent and carry on the family line for another generation. And just as all these people had lived and loved and wept within the walls of Abbey Thorne Manor, then so would they. Well, live and love, hopefully, with less of the weeping.

"You're at it again." George was digging a finger into his chest, pressing it painfully through his clothing. "Talkin' to yourself."

Valentine frowned—he hadn't been aware of speaking his thoughts aloud.

"Firsh sign, you know," George announced wisely.

"Of what?" Valentine muttered, as he moved toward the library.

"Insan-insan . . . madness."

George had followed him and he shoved his brother none too gently down into one of the leather chairs. George sprang up again like a jack-in-a-box.

Valentine poured himself a drink, uncomfortable with the events that had taken place in here only a short while ago—Marissa's face, lifted to his, the tears in her eyes as she fought against what she perceived as his rejection of her most precious gift.

"I have something to tell you," George said importantly.

"And what is that?"

"I saw Von Hautt." His pronunciation of the name left much to be desired. "In Mi'combe. I came to tell you. Important."

"You saw Von Hautt in Magna Midcombe?"

"I juss said so, didn' I?" George waved his arms furiously, and lost his balance, stumbling backward and falling into the chair. He went on as if nothing had happened. "Rode home as quick—quick . . . as fass as I could."

"With a stop off at the tavern, George." Valentine frowned. "We need to sober you up so that you can tell me about Von Hautt."

The process took time. Morris was woken and dragged from his warm bed to make some of his special coffee—a brew he'd perfected when Valentine was young and prone to experimenting with the family wine cellar.

"This takes me back," Valentine said, holding George's nose while Morris poured the coffee into his unwilling mouth. "Remember the days before the inestimable Mrs. Beaumaris came to cook for us permanently?"

Morris shuddered, his jowls trembling. "I never claimed to be a cook, my lord."

"You did your best, Morris. And you were rather better than some of those who declared they *were* food experts."

Morris looked pleased with his praise.

"Morrish has been with us for . . . for years . . ."

George spluttered. "Time he retired to a nice lil' place and put hish feet up."

"I suppose that day is coming, sir," Morris admitted, "and sooner than I like to think."

"Oh." Valentine looked surprised. "I do hope not yet, Morris."

"So do I, my lord. Now come on, Mr. George, drink up," Morris said heartily, pouring more coffee into the protesting George. Valentine turned back to the task at hand.

Eventually, between the two of them, they sobered George sufficiently so that he was able to tell Valentine what Von Hautt had said to him in Magna Midcombe.

"But that makes no sense," Valentine said crossly.

"Made no sense to me, but that was what he said."

"I know nothing of his family, and as for his mother . . . how could we turn our backs on a woman we don't even know?"

"The man is clearly loopy." George shrugged, then gave a jaw-breaking yawn.

Valentine stared into space, considering the puzzle his brother had presented to him. The trouble was that Von Hautt, while clearly mentally unstable, believed that what he said to George was the truth. The truth as he saw it. And if Von Hautt thought Valentine or his father had caused some ill to befall his mother, then it just might explain his obsession to be the first to find the Crusader's Rose.

"Revenge? Is that what this is all about?" Valentine said. "Von Hautt wants to hurt me because he thinks I hurt his mother?"

"There was something else." George looked uncomfortable.

Valentine sighed. "What else?"

"He said something about you searching for the rose beneath Marissa's . . . well, her skirts." Swiftly he glanced at Valentine and away again. "I don't think we need to talk about that."

"No, I don't think we do," Valentine said, his face taut with anger.

George thought a minute more, then seemed to remember something else. "I was meaning to ask you: What is it you've given up for the rose? Von Hautt told me I was a weakling for taking an ale or two, and that I should be keeping myself pure for the rose. I should give up ale for the rose, like you have. Or some such guff. What did he mean by that, Valentine?"

Valentine considered the question. "I think he's drawing allusions to the knights of old, King Arthur and his knights of the Round Table."

"Lancelot and so on? What have they got to do with anything?"

"When they went on a quest they believed that to be worthy of the prize they must be pure. Pure of heart and mind and body. They would make vows to forgo worldly things until their quest was complete."

George thought about that, and then his eyes narrowed. "Bloody hell, Valentine, please tell me you're not trying to be Lancelot?"

"Don't be stupid, George. I'm no Lancelot. I don't know if that's what Von Hautt is talking about and from the sound of it you probably don't, either."

They made their way to bed at last, and Valentine found himself in a far more optimistic mood than he'd been in earlier, when he stood outside in the courtyard and listened to the owl. Determination and confidence buoyed him up, as he strode along the corridor to his bedchamber. He was on a quest to find his rose and he would not fail. He could not fail.

At least when it came to this he was confident and sure of his abilities. A pity he could not feel the same way about Marissa.

Chapter 18

By the time Marissa arrived in the breakfast room the following morning, Valentine, Jasper, and her grandmother were already there and were involved in a spirited conversation. Marissa hadn't slept well and the last thing she needed was loud voices, but she smiled when Lady Bethany paused to wish her good morning and then, for good measure, complimented Jasper on his return to the breakfast table, before sitting down and pouring herself a much-needed cup of hot tea.

After a sip or two of the restorative, Marissa was feeling strong enough to glance surreptitiously at the far end of the table, where Valentine was ensconced. Even that brief glimpse of his face was enough to make her heart begin to rattle in her chest. Memories of the evening before took hold of her mind, causing all manner of dangerous emotions.

She hadn't meant to end their lovemaking in such a way, with her storming from the room in tears. They had played such an exciting, erotic game, and when he held her naked in his arms she'd felt the thrill and joy of being with the man she wanted

above all others. And she *did* want him. She could
no longer deny it. The feelings she was experiencing
for Valentine were deep and real. Which was why
she was so upset when he refused to accept the gift
of her virginity.

He was acting the gentleman, refusing to ruin her,
but Marissa didn't believe him. She sensed there was
far more to his behavior than he was letting on. But
if he wouldn't tell her the truth then what could she
do? As she'd lain in bed, tossing and turning, she'd
wondered whether Valentine's response to her could
be due to his unhappy marriage. Was he determined
not to make the same mistake again?

"Valentine has received a message from his friend
in London. The medieval scholar." Jasper was leaning toward her with a smile. "He has given us a little
more information on the list of names." He turned
to his friend. "Tell Miss Rotherhild what he said,
Kent."

Valentine finished his sausage and set down his
knife and fork, dabbing at his mouth with his napkin
and avoiding her eyes. "We know now where the
three remaining families on the list lived, and it just
so happens that the Prideauxes are quite close to
Abbey Thorne Manor." He dropped the napkin carelessly beside his plate and reached for the coffeepot.
"We could be there and back in two hours, and I was
trying to persuade Jasper and Lady B that they are
fit for the journey."

He was speaking to her so offhandedly, refusing
to look at her, as if they were distant acquaintances
rather than almost-lovers. No, not even distant
acquaintances, more like someone he didn't like

very much and was wishing to the far side of the county.

"Really?" Marissa spread marmalade on her toast, concentrating on playing a similar role. "So are you going rose hunting today, Lord Jasper?"

Jasper looked down at his arm, still awkwardly encased in a sling. "I wish I could say yes, but I fear my arm isn't up to it just yet. I'd only be a burden to the fitter members of the party. I rather think it would be better if I stayed here and awaited the news on your return."

Lady Bethany bestowed a sympathetic smile upon him. "Then I am determined to remain with you, Jasper, and keep you company. I'm certain Kent and Marissa can manage perfectly well on their own."

"Of course we can," Marissa said, sounding far more certain than she felt, but she was dashed if she was going to hide in her room and refuse to go with him. If he could play this game of pretending she meant nothing to him, then she would play it, too. Last night she'd discovered she was good at playing games.

Valentine downed his coffee and rose to his feet. "Then I will meet you at the stables in half an hour, Miss Rotherhild," he said brusquely, and he strode from the room.

"Good luck, old chap!" Jasper called after him, but Valentine barely acknowledged him.

Marissa, toast in one hand, teacup in the other, felt a wave of depression.

"Whatever is up with Kent?" Jasper said in an undertone to Lady Bethany. "He's like a frog in a rainstorm, twitching and hopping all over the place."

Lady Bethany laughed. "I can't imagine," she said, her gaze sliding to Marissa. "Do you know what is wrong with him, my dear?"

"No, Grandmamma, I don't," she replied. "And I am not at all sure I want to."

By the time Marissa had changed into her emerald green riding habit and hurried back downstairs the clock was showing she had taken more than her allotted half an hour. She found Valentine outside, marching impatiently up and down in his riding boots, breeches, and jacket.

"Ah, there you are!" he said, his head snapping up. "Come on, let's go."

Marissa quickened her steps, trying to catch up to him. "I didn't realize it was so urgent," she grumbled, further annoyed by his high-handed behavior.

"Of course it's urgent, Marissa. Von Hautt is probably already on his way. He's known every move we've made so far. Why should it be any different this time?" He stopped and turned to face her so abruptly that she almost ran into him. "George saw Von Hautt in Magna Midcombe."

Her eyes grew round.

"He came home last night. Late," he added, his eyes holding hers, their meaning clear. *Late, so he didn't see us together.* "Von Hautt stopped him at Magna Midcombe, threatened him, and said some things George found rather puzzling. He also knew about . . . well, he knew things he shouldn't have known. Things he could only know if he had a very good source of information inside Abbey Thorne Manor."

"So he really does have a spy here?"

"Yes, I rather think he must."

"Then he'll know about the letter? And where we are going today?"

"Which brings us back to why we're in a hurry, Marissa." His smile was warm, as if last night had never happened, but she still didn't trust him.

To her surprise she was presented with a mount very unlike the sluggish animal she'd ridden to Montfitchet. Restless, nervous, and well-bred, this creature would test her abilities. Evidently Valentine had come to the conclusion that Marissa was a more capable rider than he'd given her credit for, and she relished the chance to show him his confidence was not misplaced. Before long they were galloping across the bridge that spanned the moat, and through the park.

"Did your London friend discover anything more about the Prideaux family?" she asked, while they paused to allow a farmer to drive his sheep across the road from one field to another.

"Yes, he did. He wrote that the last female Prideaux married a Longhurst, but they continued to reside at the Prideaux manor. The manor is called Canthorpe, and it is still there—more or less. This is the best chance, the most likely chance, we have of finding the rose, Marissa."

That would explain his restless excitement. And she hoped he would find his rose, she really did. But, if he did find the rose today, then what would become of her? A sense of loss filled her, but her feelings were more complicated. She'd come here on a husband hunting expedition and ended up with the wrong man. If Valentine found his rose and turned his back on her, she would be left with nothing.

Not that she cared about returning home a spinster. She'd rather be alone than marry the wrong man—that was what hunting the right husband was all about. But she was beginning to believe that the wrong man was in fact the right man, the man she should have been hunting all along.

"You're very quiet," Valentine said.

Marissa was too proud to want him to see the true state of her emotions. As far as Valentine was concerned she was a woman of the world, a woman who planned to lead a free and unfettered Bohemian life. If he discovered that she was actually longing for a cozy hearth, husband and children, then he'd probably ride off at top speed. She suspected his opinions on domestic bliss were grim to say the least.

Marissa couldn't bear him to pity her or avoid her.

So she smiled and played her part and said, "I was thinking about your quest, Valentine. If the rose is at Canthorpe and you find it . . ."

The change of subject worked. He was soon too involved in discussing his quest to notice her introspection. All she needed to do was nod understandingly, smile occasionally, and return to her own thoughts.

But she was wrong. Valentine was more observant than she'd imagined.

"Marissa? Marissa!"

She blinked at him, trying to remember what he'd been saying, but something in her eyes must have given her away. His own gaze sharpened and when he spoke it was in that stiff, autocratic manner.

"What is it? You're miles away. You're thinking about last night, aren't you?"

"No, I'm not. I'd forgotten all about it."

They both fell silent again. For her part Marissa was busy pretending not to care.

"Last night—" he began.

"You must live your life as you see fit," she interrupted airily.

"Last night—"

"That was the agreement we made, remember? Neither of us are bound by the other. No recriminations, no explanations."

"Stop it!" he said in a deep, shaken voice.

Surprised, she finally looked at him and saw that he was angry. *Really* angry. For a moment she was at a loss. Should she continue with her chosen role or open her heart to him? But anyway it didn't matter because he was the one doing the talking.

"Do you really believe a word of that stuff you spout at me? I know you're upset over last night. You've convinced yourself that I don't really want you, that I'm the sort of cad who plays games with innocents."

"Now you're being silly," she managed but her voice shook and he wasn't convinced.

"If you think I'm going to allow you to go off and throw yourself at some . . . some bloody bounder then you are seriously array in the head, my girl," he growled.

"But you agreed—"

"*I never agreed.* No gentleman would agree to allow a lady to ruin herself, no matter what she thought she wanted. Last night you accused me of treating you as if you didn't know your own mind. Of not understanding you. But do you understand me, Marissa? If you did then you'd know I could never allow you to run off and join the demimonde."

"*Allow me?* You don't own me," she said in a low, trembling voice. "We are not married, Valentine."

"Not yet!" he roared.

She blinked. She was finding it difficult to understand what was going on in his head, but one thing was for certain, it wasn't what she'd thought was going on. Did he want to marry her after all? And was that because he genuinely wanted to spend his life with her, or because he wanted to protect her like the proper gentleman he was?

She tried to clear her head. If the latter was his reason then it wasn't enough. It wasn't ever going to be enough. And she'd rather leave right now and go and live her life in Yell, collecting specimens for her father, than marry a man who asked her out of obligation. Wasn't that why the Husband Hunters Club was formed in the first place? As a protest against such recipes for misery?

It was Valentine who broke the silence.

"Marissa," he said, and his chest rose and fell heavily, his expression taut and tense, as if he was laboring under an enormous strain. "I have spent years on the quest of the Crusader's Rose and that's all that's mattered to me. Now a beautiful, desirable woman has suddenly arrived in my life. Forgive me if I'm less than coherent."

She watched him warily, not sure whether he was telling her something she wanted to hear.

"Valentine," she began, feeling her way as cautiously as a cat across a floor of tacks. "When I was attending Miss Debenham's Finishing School some friends and I formed a special, eh, club. You could say it was rather like your quest to find the rose, only our quest was to find something, eh, different. When I came to Abbey Thorne Manor my own quest was uppermost in my mind."

He made an impatient gesture with his hand. "Marissa, I don't believe you want to be a Bohemian like your grandmother."

"I'm trying to explain," she said, attempting to remain calm when she felt like screaming. "Perhaps if you listened for a change you would understand."

They glared at each other, and then Marissa felt the tension ease, and with it came an urge to laugh. At the same moment Valentine's mouth twitched and he gave a chuckle.

"Perhaps we should continue this conversation after we've been to Canthorpe," he suggested. "When we can give it our full attention."

"Yes, perhaps we should," she agreed, softly.

"We are clearly at cross purposes, minx."

"Yes." She sighed.

They had been climbing a gently sloping hill and now they reached the top. The scene spread out before them was quite breathtakingly delightful, with the cottages of the village gathered neatly about a spired church, and the green fields surrounding them.

"How lovely," Marissa declared. "It looks perfect."

"It would be perfect if I found the rose," he said.

He turned to her, and his eyes lingered on hers, a spark deep within them. Just by looking at her he made her feel flushed and alive, and very much aware of herself as a woman.

"Marissa." Reaching out he took her gloved hand, his fingers enfolding hers. Despite their misunderstandings, she felt as if they were in complete harmony. Just for a moment. Perfect companions.

A moment later the feeling was gone, and Valentine was urging his mount into a gallop as he rode down the slope toward the fulfillment of his dream.

There was nothing Marissa could do but follow him.

Chapter 19

Canthorpe, the home of the Longhurst family, was beyond the church and hidden within a grove of splendid old trees. Even to Marissa's untrained eyes the sprawling manor was a mingling of varying styles and time periods, evolving and growing over the years as it passed from generation to generation. It appeared to be well cared for, the paintwork was fresh and there were no missing bricks or broken tiles. A formal garden ran along the terrace in front of the house, with bushes clipped into topiary balls and spiraling twists.

There was no sign of any roses.

"There is a more promising garden at the rear of the house," Valentine assured Marissa when she mentioned her concerns. "Morris knows of Canthorpe. He told me Lady Longhurst is renowned for her floral arrangements using roses, picked directly from her own rose garden."

"What would we do without Morris?" Marissa said with a smile.

They were led into a sitting room which Marissa personally thought far too full of bows and ruchings and clashing floral designs, while the maid who'd admitted them to the house went off to ask if Her Ladyship was receiving visitors.

They waited in a silence broken only by Valentine's restless tapping on the mantelpiece as he stood by the hearth. After several moments the door opened and Lady Longhurst made her entrance, pausing a moment on the threshold, as if she were accustomed to being admired.

It was understandable.

She was one of the most beautiful women Marissa had ever seen. Almost as beautiful as her best friend and fellow member of the Husband Hunters Club, Olivia Monteith. With her blond hair softly dressed, ringlets falling to her nape from a clasp on her crown, and her elegant but understated blue dress with white lace trimmings, Lady Longhurst could have been posing for a portrait called The Wealthy Country Lady at Home.

"Lord Kent?" the fair vision spoke in a well-modulated voice. She moved with single-minded purpose toward Valentine, ignoring Marissa.

He took the hand she held out to him, bowing elegantly over it. "Lady Longhurst, how do you do?"

As she gazed up at him with pale blue eyes, Marissa was surprised to see that Lady Longhurst, standing now in the cruel light from the windows, was a great deal older than she'd first appeared. The fine lines about her eyes and the faint sagging of the skin about her throat and jaw were a clear sign she'd never see forty again.

"How strange we are neighbors and yet we've

never met?" Lady Longhurst said with a quizzical little smile.

"I am not a great one for socializing," Valentine replied.

"That's a great pity. We will have to do something about that, my lord."

When their gazing into each other's eyes seemed to have gone on for far too long, Marissa stepped forward and held out her own hand. "Lady Longhurst? I am Miss Rotherhild. How do you do?"

Lady Longhurst's eyebrows lifted in surprise—to introduce oneself was a social faux pas. She took Marissa's hand with care, as if it might bite, her sly sideways glance at Valentine seeming to invite him to join her in appalled amusement.

Marissa also gave Valentine a glance but hers was far from ambiguous. "Perhaps you should tell Lady Longhurst what we're doing here, Lord Kent?" she suggested meaningfully.

"Yes. Of course. Hum, Lady Longhurst, we are here to find a rose," he began.

"A rose?" She clapped her hands together like a child. "But I am famous for my roses!"

"Then you will understand," he said, and proceeded to explain the story of the Crusader's Rose.

After a few sentences, Lady Longhurst gestured for them to be seated, and arranged herself gracefully on a sofa. She was watching him intently as he spoke; indeed, thought Marissa, hanging on his every word. And while this was obviously flattering, and most men would be flattered, Valentine seemed far more intent on his story than his audience.

When he finished, Lady Longhurst sighed and placed a hand on her breast, blinking her pale eyes as if the emotion was too great for her. "I am quite overwhelmed," she gushed. "And you believe the rose is here? At Canthorpe? In *my* garden, Lord Kent?"

"I very much hope so, Lady Longhurst."

"Then you must look at once," she declared, rising lightly to her feet. "And I will come with you."

Pleased at her enthusiastic response, Valentine jumped up after her, and disappeared through the sitting room door. Marissa sighed and also followed, only to run into him as he hastily returned to the sitting room. The pleasant shock of his big body against hers shook her momentarily, and then he clasped her elbows, steadying her, as he stepped back.

"Sorry," he said gruffly. "I'm like a boy today, thinking only of my quest and—"

Before Marissa could answer him, Lady Longhurst was calling out, "Lord Kent? The roses are this way!"

Valentine spun around and went striding in her direction, but this time he remembered to keep a firm grip on Marissa's arm.

"We can reach the rose garden through the conservatory," Lady Longhurst said when they reached her, and led them into a well-lit saloon with glass doors, which she proceeded to open.

The warm, heady scent of earth and vegetation was suddenly very strong, as if they'd stepped into an Amazonian jungle. Marissa couldn't help but

stare at some of the stranger plants, with their twisting root tendrils and huge flat leaves and faintly
alarming flowers. Her parents would be entranced
in such a place—they would probably refuse to
leave—but Valentine barely gave the contents of the
conservatory a glance. His mind was on the roses—
his rose—and when Marissa was prone to linger,
his hand tightened on her arm and he hurried her
out through some more doors and into the garden
proper.

"This is more like it," he growled, as he gazed
over a sea of lush, well-tended bushes.

To Marissa's startled eyes there were roses of
every imaginable color, as well as every size and
habit. They climbed, they drooped, they sprawled in
huge bushes, or were upright and neatly trimmed.
Instinctively she bent to press her face to a pink cup
of soft petals with yellow stamens, breathing deeply
of the heady perfume.

"Oh, how lovely," she whispered. "What is this
one called?"

"One of the *Albas*. 'Celestial,' I believe." Valentine
dismissed it with a single glance.

He began to make his way down the rows of
plants, searching, occasionally pausing but never for
long. Marissa watched him, torn between wanting
him to find his rose and selfishly wanting him not
to find it just yet. But she never really believed he
wouldn't find it, with so many roses to choose from,
because surely it must be here, somewhere? It *must*
be here, she told herself.

Lady Longhurst was trotting along after him.

Marissa could see her mouth opening and shutting as she chatted away, her breathless voice too low to carry. It was possible Valentine was ignoring her, but Marissa was of the opinion he was so involved in his search he simply didn't notice. Perhaps Lady Longhurst was of the same opinion, and not being a woman who was used to being ignored, she chose to do something about it. The next time Valentine paused to inspect one of the bushes, she tucked her hand into his arm, giving him a smile when he started with surprise. When he moved on, she continued to cling to him, refusing to take second place to her roses.

After a few steps Valentine turned his head, searching around, and it occurred to Marissa that he was looking for her. His gaze, across several rows of plants, was so beseeching she almost laughed aloud. Valentine, her Valentine, was not interested in the flattering attentions of the beautiful Lady Longhurst. He was only interested in finding his rose.

And her.

Valentine could feel Her Ladyship's soft breast brushing against his biceps. At first he thought it must be accidental, but when he looked down her pale eyes were staring up at him and he was startled to find them full of the sort of invitation he had no intention of accepting.

For the first time it occurred to him that Lady Longhurst was far more interested in him than the roses. He looked up, searching for Marissa, and saw her standing alone on the far side of the garden, watching him. She was surrounded by roses of

every color, adrift in their perfume, and he wanted
. . . he wanted . . .

Valentine felt his body tense with need as he
imagined taking her in his arms and rolling her
naked in a bed of rose petals. He wanted her with
a desperation that was making him irritable and ill.
Feverishly he reminded himself that if the rose was
here, now, then his quest would be over. He'd be a
hero, a celebrity, and it would be the perfect moment
to claim her as he longed to.

And Marissa would be dazzled by his fame, too
dazzled to see him as he really was. Staid, boring,
and a beast.

He glanced at Lady Longhurst, still attached like
a leech to his side, wishing he could shake her free.
She must have thought the glance, and his introspection, was all for her, because she gave him a mean-
ingful little smile, her eyelashes fluttering.

"Lord Kent, I am a little light-headed," she murmured, leaning on him heavily. "I wonder if you
might escort me back to the house?"

There was a seat some steps away, set in a bower
dripping with white roses. Valentine led her in its
direction, gently but firmly peeling her fingers from
his arm, and sitting her down.

"Rest a moment, Lady Longhurst. I must continue
my search." He stepped away from her, smiling to
take the sting out of his rejection.

Her mouth hung open in shocked surprise.
Quickly she snapped it closed, turning her face from
him. "Very well," she said stiffly. "Search for your
rose. I will try not to faint until you are done."

Valentine felt a pang of guilt, but a moment later

it was gone, when Lady Longhurst shot a vicious glance across the garden at Marissa, who was working her way along the row of roses, stopping to smell each and every one.

He set off again. He tried not to grow disillusioned and disappointed, but as the number of roses to be searched grew smaller and smaller, it was difficult to keep his hopes up. The garden, though beautiful, did not hold what he was looking for. Eventually he reached the last row and the last rose, and stood a moment, asking himself if he'd missed something, if he'd inadvertently bypassed the Crusader's Rose.

But he knew he hadn't.

His hands tightened into fists at his side. "Are these the only roses you have, Lady Longhurst?" he called to her, the desperation plain in his voice.

Lady Longhurst shrugged, not trying to hide her irritation. "There are some wilder species in the woods," she admitted, pointing toward a wooden gate that led into a wilderness section of the garden.

It seemed unlikely *his* rose would be there but he couldn't leave without making certain. Just in case.

A small, warm and familiar hand slipped into his and squeezed. Marissa's calm and sensible voice said, "Let's look then. We can't give up yet."

Valentine nodded jerkily, swallowing down his sense of failure.

"Come with me." Lady Longhurst was on her feet again, looking anything but faint, a flush in her cheeks and a sting in her smile.

For the next hour they tramped through woodlands and peered into grottos and arbors, where statues of scantily clothed nymphs and horse-legged satyrs lurked in the shadows. Although Valentine tried to keep his hopes up, he'd already accepted the Crusader's Rose wasn't at Canthorpe and his sense of failure weighed him down.

Somehow Lady Longhurst had hold of his arm again, and Marissa trailed dejectedly behind them as they made their way back through the rustic wooden gate.

"You could always stay a little longer," Her Ladyship said in a voice meant just for him. "There may be places I have forgotten and will only remember later, when you are gone. Lord Longhurst is in London, and I am sadly lonely, so you will not be intruding." The last sentence was spoken with a trace of desperation.

"I am not sure—"

"Miss Rotherhild, too, of course," she added hastily, with a wave of her hand to include Marissa. "I'm sure I can find something for her to do while we are busy."

Her Ladyship was propositioning him. He couldn't pretend otherwise, although good manners insisted he try. The strange thing was, his discomfort was laced with a growing sense of masculine pride. First Marissa and now Lady Longhurst wanted him. Was Vanessa wrong about his physical attractiveness?

He smiled.

Lady Longhurst, taking this as encouragement, clutched on to him, her voice rising in pitch. "My gardener is a modern man. I fear he does not appreciate the older style of rose. He has replaced a great many of the original plants with more modern varieties."

"That is a great pity," Valentine said, his smile gone.

"Oh, don't give up. There may still be hope," she went on. "What about this rose, Lord Kent?"

"No." Valentine dismissed her offering with a brief glance.

"Or this one?"

"Unfortunately, no, Lady Longhurst. You don't seem to understand that the rose I am seeking is unique. I cannot substitute it with another at a—a whim. It is like . . . like the woman one loves—no other will do."

She blinked, as if tears were in her eyes, but he noted they were perfectly clear. Suddenly he was tired of her games and her "modern" garden. He wanted to leave. He wanted to ride home with Marissa by his side. He wanted to . . . to . . .

Valentine almost groaned aloud. He'd been longing to claim Marissa, like Richard de Fevre coming home from the Crusades claimed his wife, like Lancelot claimed Guinevere. Triumphantly push himself deep inside her and gaze into her eyes as he made her his for now and forever. But he hadn't found the rose. He wasn't famous or a catch, the sort of man a beautiful woman might regard with pride.

He was the same Valentine Kent he'd always been, and the knowledge was turning his temper ragged.

"The rose I'm seeking is not here, Lady Longhurst," he said stiffly.

"Oh." She shrugged and smiled. "Why not stay anyway?"

"I don't think so. But I do thank you for your generosity in allowing us to see your garden."

"But you will take some refreshments?"

She sounded a little desperate, as if she was afraid of being on her own, making it difficult to refuse. So they sat politely, making conversation, until eventually it was possible to escape.

"Oh, Lord Kent," Marissa said breathlessly as she rode at his side, the village and Canthorpe receding behind them. "Look at this rose, surely it will do?" She sounded uncannily like Lady Longhurst.

He frowned down at her. "That is not kind."

"Perhaps you can stay and help me prepare for bed? I find myself all thumbs today," she added, with the nearest thing to a leer he'd ever seen on her face.

Despite his low spirits Valentine chuckled.

"What a dreadful woman." Marissa was herself again as she gave a shudder.

"I would have liked her a great deal more if I could have found my rose in her garden."

"I'm sorry you didn't find the rose," she said gently, "I really am, Valentine. But just imagine if you had found it at Canthorpe? You'd never be able to escape Her Ladyship's advances."

"I found it rather flattering," he retorted with a smug smile.

Marissa gave an unladylike snort.

"I'm not that sort of man."

Marissa stared at him as if she'd misheard. "The sort of man who what?"

Valentine shifted awkwardly in his saddle. "The sort of man women pursue."

"Do you really believe that?" She sounded bemused, her dark eyes searching his.

Valentine knew there was no escaping this conversation. The time had come. Reluctantly he drew his horse to a halt and turned to face her.

Chapter 20

Marissa had never seen him look so serious. There was clearly something heavy weighing on his mind. Something other than the rose. She didn't for a moment believe what he'd said about his attractiveness to women. Valentine was the most charismatic man she'd ever met. No, whatever he was going to say must be serious indeed for him to be regarding her in such a stern manner.

He's going to ask you to leave.

No matter how she tried to ignore them, the words repeated over and over in her head, taunting her.

Valentine dismounted and came to help her down, his hands firm and warm about her waist. She had to stop herself from melting into him, drawing back as soon as her feet touched the ground. There was a fallen log within the glade, looking almost as if Lady Longhurst's gardener had arranged it himself. Marissa sat down, fussing with her skirts, while she waited anxiously for him to say whatever it was he intended to say.

He took his time tethering the horses, then took off his hat and slapped it against his thigh, before finally approaching her. Resting a boot on the log beside her, he began to twist his hat in his hands, staring into the distance. And all the while she said nothing, waiting, her sense of dread growing.

"I suppose I have to go back in time," he said. His gaze brushed hers briefly. "When my father died at Waterloo I decided I would take on his job of finding the Crusader's Rose and restoring it to the family. It seemed important, a task I could make my life's work. I know you find that ridiculous, Marissa. You've made it very clear what you think about botanical pursuits."

"I did think that, yes," she agreed.

"*Did* think it?"

His eyes searched hers, looking for something, but when he didn't find it and she didn't oblige him by answering his question, he gave up and sat himself down on the log beside her. With his elbows resting on his knees and his head bent, he continued to fidget with his hat.

"I've realized just recently—when George was talking about Von Hautt—that I had a romantic idea of my quest for the rose. That it made me like one of the knights of the Round Table. Brave and honorable. Von Hautt said something similar, but I have grown up and he obviously hasn't." He gave a short laugh. "As I grew older I began to see my quest for what it was—the important restoration of an ancient rose—a piece of history that would otherwise be lost to the world, and my family in particular. While I sought the rose I learned more about roses in general, and now I am somewhat of an expert in the field."

"You are the leading expert in the field."

He gave a wry smile.

Marissa, feeling that something more was required of her, said, "Go on."

"That is the thing. I am an expert, well-known to others in my field of expertise, but my life is spent in solitude. I am not an exciting character. The past few days are the most exciting I have ever spent where roses are concerned, and that's mainly because of you, Marissa."

"It has been most enjoyable," she agreed.

"But this has been an anomaly. I live a staid and insular life, rarely does something out of the ordinary happen. I am busy with my studies and my correspondence. Sometimes I lose track of time. I rarely accept invitations. I rarely travel to London, and when I do it is to visit libraries or museums, never to socialize with my peers."

He was watching her closely but Marissa didn't know what he expected. Cries of shock and horror? Surely he realized her own life had been more or less the same as his, before she was sent off to Miss Debenham's Finishing School?

He ran a distracted hand through his hair. "Marissa, are you listening to me? Are you hearing what I'm saying?"

She rested her cheek against his shoulder, feeling the warmth and strength of his body. "I'm listening," she said. She turned her nose into the cloth of his jacket, breathing in his scent, then stretched up to nuzzle his jaw, enjoying the masculine scratch of whiskers.

He turned his head, blindly seeking with his lips

for hers, and they kissed. Lightly at first, a mere touching of flesh to flesh, and then deeper, more passionately, as the ever-present desire took hold.

Marissa forgot to breathe. Her skin was hot, her body melting, and she wanted him so much. She wanted to be able to touch him every morning and smile at him across the breakfast table, to soothe him when he was upset and to laugh with him when he was happy. She wanted children with his eyes, and the years to stretch on, both of them growing old together at Abbey Thorne Manor.

A moment later she was floundering, trying to keep her balance. He'd stood up so abruptly she was left reeling. Catching her breath, she clung to the log, staring up at him as he loomed over her, his chest rising and falling heavily.

"No!" he burst out, an agony of regret in his face and voice.

"Valentine?" she whispered, bewildered and hurt and now very frightened.

She didn't understand. Valentine had hoped, coward that he was, that she would catch on without him having to spell it out. That she would guess his meaning and . . . And what? Walk away? Agree with him and display horror at the very idea of joining her life to his?

The truth was he wanted Marissa to disagree.

He rubbed his hands down his face and when he looked at her again he could see he'd frightened her. No wonder. She probably thought he'd lost his mind.

"I'm sorry." He dropped to his knees and wrapped

her in his arms. For a moment she was stiff and un-responsive, but gradually she slipped her own arms about his neck and rested her cheek against his, and he felt her body soften in that sweet, trusting way he was so worried he was going to lose forever.

He tilted her face up and kissed her. Then kissed her again, deeply and intensely, showing her how much he desired her with tongue and lips and teeth. Soon she was kissing him back, his rejection for-gotten, and when he placed his hand on her thigh through the layers of her clothing, she made no objection.

She was on fire, eager to experience all he could give her, not at all shy about letting him know how she was feeling. He loved that about her. He didn't believe in his heart there was another woman like her in all the world.

Valentine groaned, then couldn't speak at all when she slid her hand down his body, cupping the bulge in his breeches.

He'd forgot why he'd brought her here. Rational thought caught flame and turned to ashes. He forgot everything but the need to be inside her, part of her, deep in the pleasure of making love with this woman.

His hands slid under her skirts, seeking her soft, warm flesh. She pressed against him as he opened her thighs, brushing aside the soft cloth of her bloomers and slipping his hand into the opening to touch her slick, swollen folds.

"Yes," she breathed. "Please, Valentine, this time."

Yes, he thought wildly. Yes, he would take her. She

wanted it and so did he. What did it matter about the future? It was nothing, it meant nothing. Only the present had any importance.

Somehow his breeches were open, and he was lifting her toward him. Her hands tugged his buttocks, drawing him closer, but he didn't need any urging. He wanted her with a single-minded desperation he'd never known before. The head of his cock brushed her soft flesh and she whimpered.

He tightened the muscles of his buttocks and thighs, preparing to push himself deep inside her, aching for the sheer bliss of being sheathed within her beautiful body.

Now, he thought. *Now!*

But even as he began his thrust forward he was slowing, then stopping. His taut muscles went to jelly, and wearily he dropped his brow against her hair. His body was shaking with the effort it had taken to deny himself something he thought he wanted with all his heart and all his being.

"Valentine?" she wailed, squirming against him.

A chuckle forced its way through the lump in his throat.

"Valentine!" She was distraught, her hands thumping on his chest, and tugging at his arms and shoulders. "You're laughing. Why are you laughing?"

He felt light-headed. He wanted her so much but he couldn't do it. He couldn't do it and he knew why. But when he looked down into Marissa's flushed, worried face he knew he wasn't going to tell her the truth, not entirely.

"You are a vibrant and beautiful woman. You deserve someone young and untarnished, someone who isn't set in his ways."

Her eyes widened. "But you do want me. I know you do."

"Oh, I want you. I also know that I will not take away your chance to change your mind, no matter how much you think you want me to."

Wanting her could lead them into very murky waters. There wasn't always a happy ever after. That was something he knew and she didn't, not yet.

Now there were tears in her eyes. She reached up to touch his face, her palms sliding to cup his lean cheeks. "Valentine, I appreciate your care of me, really I do, but there is no need. I thought we understood each other on that. Don't you believe me?"

"You deserve better than me. I'm afraid I could never make you happy," he said.

She sighed. Her lips trembled and she bit into them to make them stop. "You are a very stubborn man."

"Another of my myriad faults," he replied with a shaky laugh.

"Oh, you have a great many," she agreed with a lopsided smile. "Can—can you hold me? If you do not think it will compromise my spotless reputation."

He pulled her into his arms, holding her tightly and forcing back the heat of the passion that remained lurking just beneath the surface. *This is enough for now,* he thought, and almost convinced himself into believing it.

"Valentine, I am going to make you change your mind," she said, her voice muffled against his jacket. "I haven't given up, you know."

"Now who's being stubborn," he said.

He would give her time to realize how unsuitable a prospect he was for her, and eventually she *would* realize it. But he already knew the truth. He'd seen it, clear as day, when he was on the verge of irrevocably making her his. The future, spread before him. And he'd been afraid.

Marriage, domestic life, children . . . he'd be committed to the lot. But what if the past repeated itself? What if the misery of his life with Vanessa returned? He had survived once but this time, with Marissa . . . Marissa, the woman he was beginning to love with a single-minded passion. No, he didn't think he could bear it if one day she turned to look at him as if he was a beast.

He would be utterly destroyed. There would be no way back.

How could he take the chance?

But even as he made his decision there was an odd ache in his chest, an agonizing sense of loss. He wondered what was worse, committing himself to Marissa and taking the chance of destroying her life and his sanity, or living the rest of time without her.

Chapter 21

It seemed as if Marissa had barely closed her eyes and fallen asleep, after an evening filling in Lady Bethany and Jasper on the search at Canthorpe, while inwardly obsessing over the problem of Valentine's pigheadedness. She was woken by knocking on the front door and a loud shout for entry. Then more voices began shouting and doors slamming, all with an increasing sense of urgency.

Marissa sat up in her bed, hair in her eyes, and stumbled out barefoot, searching for her robe. She'd been dreaming of being wrapped in Valentine's arms, and now it was a shock to find herself alone in the darkness. Ever since he'd spoken to her about his concerns she'd felt as if she was in limbo, knowing he wanted her as much as she wanted him, but unable to convince him to take the final step.

She thought there was probably an element of self-preservation in his behavior. He'd been through one bitter experience and was shy of facing another. Marissa couldn't blame him for that, but she wished he would just throw all his doubts aside.

But if he did that he wouldn't be Valentine, would he?

By now she'd wrapped her robe over her nightgown, and made her way out to the landing. Leaning against the balustrade, she peered down into the
hall. Lamplight wavered, showing Morris standing
shivering in his nightgown and his nightcap, while
Valentine, in hastily donned breeches and a crumpled shirt, questioned a disheveled-looking young
man who shuffled his boots as he gave his answers.

"Lady Longhurst begs you come, my lord," Marissa heard him say. "She's beside herself, she is. Hy-
hysterical."

Lady Longhurst? The name was enough to send
Marissa down the stairs in her bare feet, not caring
if it was proper or not. Since she'd come to Abbey
Thorne Manor she'd been kicking society's rules and
conventions out of her path like autumn leaves.

"What is happening?" she said, glancing from
one to the other.

Morris answered her, his voice stiff and his gaze
a little wild.

"It seems that Lady Longhurst has been assaulted,
Miss Rotherhild."

"Assaulted?" Marissa cried. "Is she injured?"

"Aye, me lady," the lad said, eyes wide, relishing
the dramatic situation he found himself in. "A for-
eigner came and she offered him her—her hospital-
ity and he betrayed it."

Marissa turned to Valentine, seeking illumina-
tion.

"It seems Von Hautt charmed his way into Lady
Longhurst's house," he said, troubled anger in his
eyes.

The lad interrupted. "She needs you to come at once, me lord. Will you come?"

Morris cleared his throat, his jowls wobbling. "My lord, I don't think it wise of you to go riding off into the night. You barely know this Lady Longhurst."

"I know she's a lady in need of my help, Morris," Valentine retorted.

"I thought you said you weren't Sir Lancelot?" Marissa murmured, with a questioning glance. "You are acting very like him."

"I am behaving like a gentleman," Valentine retorted, and turned back to Morris. "Get Bartholomew, Pinnock, Nesmith up out of their beds, with whoever else who wants to come, and tell them to ready the horses. I'll be there in a moment."

"Make sure there's a horse for me," Marissa said briskly. "Lady Longhurst will appreciate a woman's support in such a delicate situation."

Valentine opened his mouth to argue, then seemed to think better of it. "Very well," he said. "You are probably safer with me anyway. I don't like the thought of Von Hautt wandering around the countryside unrestrained."

"I am more than a match for the baron," Marissa assured him.

"Of course she is." It was George, standing on the stairs and yawning. He rubbed his eyes. "I'll come, too, just to be on the safe side."

Valentine gave him a narrowed look. "I thought you were ill in bed, George."

"I was. I'm better now."

Marissa left them to it. She wanted to tell Lady

Bethany what was happening before she left for Canthorpe, and after a soft knock on her door, opened it a crack and peered in. Her gasp sounded very loud in the silence.

The room was lit by the moonlight coming in the uncovered window so there was no mistaking what she saw. Two people, Lady Bethany and Jasper, lay curled in each other's arms, their mouths ajar in sleep, the covers tucked around them. They looked remarkably handsome together—which probably had a bit to do with the moonlight—and very peaceful.

Marissa couldn't decide whether she was outraged or horrified or any of the other things a respectable young lady should be. But the truth was she wasn't particularly upset; she wasn't even particularly shocked. She was well aware of her grandmother's attitude when it came to making the most of her life; she even shared some of her ideals. Marissa could only wish the lovers well.

Gently she closed the door and tiptoed away.

By the time she'd dressed and made her way out to the stable, the men were assembled.

"I don't want to be uncharitable," she said in a low voice to Valentine. "Perhaps the lady really is in dire need. But why has she sent for you and not one of her closer neighbors or relatives?"

Valentine gave her a grin. "You're jealous, minx."

"I'm suspicious," she corrected him. It had been obvious to her from the first that Lady Longhurst had set her sights on Valentine, and husband or no husband she was most unhappy when he slipped out of her grasp. Now she'd found a reason to draw him back into her web, and she must have known he would respond to her plea for help—how could Valentine the proper gentleman refuse?

But Marissa was adamant that Valentine was *her* gentleman and Lady Longhurst was not going to use his more heroic qualities to trap him. If anyone was going to hunt Valentine then it was Marissa.

I am hunting him, she thought in surprise. *Is he the one I want to marry and live with happily ever after? Was George simply a wrong turn in my journey? Whatever the answer, this husband hunting no longer feels like a game; it is deadly serious. A matter of life lived to the full with the man I love, or a lifetime of regrets.*

Love? Marissa was dizzy. Was it true, did she really love him? Her practical side cast doubt upon her emotional response, until she felt as if there was a battle going on inside her. But there was no time to sit down and properly consider her situation. A moment later they set off, galloping into the night, heading for Canthorpe, and she knew she must put her own feelings aside and concentrate on the here and now.

"Do you think Baron Von Hautt followed you?" George called out, as the horses spread out along the narrow road. "Or is his spy supplying him with our information?"

"I hope he's not following us," Marissa said, glancing behind her. She might boast she wasn't afraid of the baron but that didn't mean she was keen to come face-to-face with him in the dark.

For the first time she began to have an uncomfortable feeling about this whole business. She'd been dismissing Lady Longhurst as a manipulative creature, but what if she was being unfair? What if she was wrong? Von Hautt was a dangerous man who had shown himself capable of any mischief, and for some reason he had a grudge against Valentine.

"What I don't understand is, where could he be living? He must be nearby. Surely someone has seen him?" George had brought his horse up beside her, calling across her to his brother on her other side.

"I've made inquiries about the village." Valentine began to catalogue his efforts to find the baron in a grim voice. "I've sent men out to scour the woods and the countryside for miles. But I always get the same answer—no one has seen him. I'm starting to wonder if he's a ghost and can appear and disappear at will."

"Not a ghost," George said. "A magician, a trickster, that's what Von Hautt is."

A short time later they saw the village below them, and then shortly after that, Canthorpe, the entire house ablaze with light. Several servants could be seen in the formal garden, either guarding the house or searching the grounds, or both. Valentine's group was allowed past after one of the servants held a lantern up to his face.

"I'm sorry, m'lord," he apologized.

"Is Lady Longhurst inside?"

"Yes, she is."

"My men are here to help in any way they can."

"Thank you, m'lord. I'll set them to searching the wilderness."

Valentine sprang down from the saddle, followed by George and Marissa, and hurried inside.

The maid Marissa remembered from their visit yesterday came flying across the hall, her cap askew, spirals of hair tumbling from beneath it and into her eyes. When she saw who they were she seemed to fold in on herself with relief. "Oh, my lord," she cried, eyes big and frightened. "Thank heavens you've come. This way. My lady is in the small saloon."

She showed them the way, glancing behind her all the while, as if worried she might lose them even over such a short distance.

"Lady Longhurst is a great beauty, so I've heard," George murmured in Marissa's ear.

She flicked him a look and recognized the knowing expression on his face. "Is that why you're here?" she asked disapprovingly.

"I want to see Valentine play the hero."

A frown creased her brow. "He said you met up with Von Hautt in Magna Midcombe and that he threatened you."

"Yes," he said with a grimace. "Not one of my finer moments."

"Why do you think he's pursuing your family, George? What has he against you?"

George shrugged. "In my opinion he has bats in his belfry."

The maid had reached the closed door to the small saloon. "Lady Longhurst is in here," she said in a quiet voice. She hesitated, and then tapped lightly. When there was no answer she tapped again.

"Open it," Valentine ordered.

With a jerky nod, the maid tried to do so, but the door was locked.

"Lady Longhurst," he called out, knocking loudly. "It is Kent. You sent word for me to come and I am here. Please, unlock the door."

"My poor lady is beside herself," the maid whispered. The tears in the girl's eyes welled over her lashes and began to trickle down her cheeks.

"When did Baron Von Hautt leave?" Valentine said.

"Hours ago, my lord. At least, we think he left. But my lady doesn't believe it. She believes he's still hiding somewhere about the house."

"Lord Kent?" a husky, wavery voice came through the door from the other side. "Is that you?"

"Yes, it is me. Unlock the door, Lady Longhurst."

The scrape of the key in the lock, and the clunk of the bolt being released. Valentine twisted the handle and the door opened wide.

There were candles everywhere—a year's supply of wax gone up in one night—and the blaze of light was so bright it made Marissa blink. Lady Longhurst stood in the center of the room, a shawl wrapped around what appeared to be her chemise, in her stockinged feet. Her hair was tangled and falling down around her face. She was more like a tragic victim than the beautiful elegant lady Marissa remembered. Her lower lip was swollen and caked with dried blood, and there was evidence of tears streaking her cheeks. She clutched the door key in her hands, twisting it around and around, while her gaze was fixed on Valentine.

"Lady Longhurst?" Valentine was as startled as Marissa.

"He seemed such a gentleman," the lady said, her face pinched and white. "Such a—a gentleman."

The beauty Marissa remembered was still there, but now there was a ravaged quality to it. She felt a wave of pity.

"Lady Longhurst?" she said gently. "Are you able to tell us what happened?"

The woman shuddered. "What happened?" she cried in a rising, wavering voice. "I was assaulted, that was what happened." She lifted her tangled hair from one side of her face, and disclosed a livid mark high on her cheek. Then she tilted her head, showing another mark on the side of her neck. "There are others," she said, "but I will not show them to you." She closed her eyes for a moment, withdrawing into herself. "What will my husband say?" she whispered. "Dear Lord, what will he say?"

Valentine took her arm, his touch, his voice gentle. "I am so sorry you suffered at Baron Von Hautt's hands. Can you tell us what happened after we left? It may help us to find him."

She looked up at him and her face came to life. Tears streamed out of her eyes, dripping down onto her shawl, while her mouth shook and trembled. Her hands continued to twist the key, until Valentine placed his hands over them, and held them tightly within his own.

"H-he seemed so cultured," she sobbed. "So continental. I believed he was the sort of man I could confide in, whom I could trust to . . . to . . ."

She looked up wildly, and it was Marissa who answered.

"I understand. He betrayed your trust."

"Yes," she spat. "He was a filthy creature of no conscience and no soul."

It took time and patience, but gradually the truth came out one painful piece at a time. Lady Longhurst had indeed found Baron Von Hautt charming and pleasant company, and she'd chosen to invite him into her bedchamber for some mutual enjoyment. She was a lonely woman, and now she admitted that her husband had a young mistress in London, so she was also feeling neglected. The baron seemed like the sort of man who would understand her offer was for a casual afternoon of enjoyment and after they'd both taken their fill then he would leave.

However it didn't happen as Lady Longhurst had hoped, and before too long she began to realize that she had made a terrible mistake. All began as it should, with wine and conversation in her boudoir, but his kisses were rough and painful, and suddenly Lady Longhurst no longer trusted him. She ordered him to leave, but he refused, and a moment later his façade of charming gentleman peeled away to reveal the real creature beneath. Despite her struggles and protests he would not desist in his rough lovemaking.

"He told me that to be hurt was what a woman such as me deserved." By now Lady Longhurst was sobbing bitterly. "He told me that only a whore would offer herself to another when she was already married. He said—said he needed to teach me a lesson about f-fidelity that I would never f-forget."

Once the story was told, Lady Longhurst became incoherent for some time, and Valentine carried her to her bedchamber, where Marissa and the maid put her to bed with a sedative. Eventually she fell asleep.

Marissa stroked her hair, looking down at the bruised and ravaged face, now pale and peaceful. She knew Lady Longhurst had been foolish and perhaps arrogant in her belief that her position would keep her safe, but she didn't deserve what had happened to her. She was not part of the quest for the rose and yet Von Hautt had chosen to make her suffer.

Leaving the maid with her lady, Marissa went to seek out Valentine. She found him in deep discussion with the servants, but when he saw her, he broke off and led her into a room where they were able to be private.

"I understand why she didn't call anyone who lived nearby Canthorpe," Marissa said unhappily. "She's embarrassed, vulnerable, and she feels as if it was her fault for trusting him. Baron Von Hautt must know that. What sort of creature is he, Valentine, to prey upon a sad and lonely woman?"

He reached to take her hand in his, squeezing her fingers comfortingly. "You were right to come, Marissa. She did need a woman's support."

After a little while Marissa managed to shake off the image of Lady Longhurst's bruised and injured body. "What did the servants say?"

"They say they heard nothing at all until Lady Longhurst began screaming and when they came to her aid they found her door locked. By the time they'd broken it down, the baron was gone, escaping through a window and into the garden."

"So he *is* gone?"

"It appears so."

Marissa sighed. "I am sorry I thought badly of her," she said. "No one deserves to be treated like that. He must be a madman."

"If that happened to you . . ." Valentine began and then shook his head, not wishing to finish. "I'd kill him," he growled. His eyes were blazing, his cheeks were flushed, the tendons in his neck standing out.

Shocked at his show of raw violence, nevertheless Marissa felt a purely feminine thrill. "He won't do anything to me," she reassured him, leaning forward to kiss his lips. "I know what he is and I would never trust him."

"Hmm, I seem to have interrupted an interesting moment."

George was standing in the doorway with a questioning look on his face.

Marissa moved to draw back, tugging her fingers from Valentine's, but to her surprise he held on to them and kept her close. George's eyes narrowed.

"That's enough, George," Valentine warned, before he could speak. "Marissa is upset. This has been a most unpleasant experience."

"She could always come to me if she's upset," he muttered sulkily.

"George!" His brother gave him a quelling look and for once George took heed, although his sigh was heartfelt. "The servants also told me that Lady Longhurst has a younger sister she is very fond of, who lives about five miles away. The sister has a new baby and they think that is one of the reasons she didn't send to her for help."

"I think we should send word to the sister that Lady Longhurst requires her help. If they are as close as she says then she must be told." Marissa looked to Valentine for support.

He smiled into her eyes. "I knew you'd think so. Let's do it then, before we go home."

Arrangements were made for a servant to go to Lady Longhurst's sister, informing her of the situation, and asking her to come to Canthorpe as soon as possible. By the time Valentine and Marissa were ready to leave, all was in hand, but George had agreed to stay, just in case.

"I'm sure you won't miss me," he said mournfully.

"I've continued the guard on the house," Valentine ignored him. "Just in case Von Hautt is still about, although I doubt he is. He's too clever to linger after something as dastardly as this."

"We must find him before he attacks someone else," George said bleakly, looking out into darkness that was beginning to lighten with the dawn. "He's a very dangerous man."

His words returned to Marissa as they rode away, and she knew it was true, and she should be wary and a little bit afraid. But the sun had begun to rise and suddenly the world was beautiful again. If Valentine was the man for her, there was no need to search anymore. She thought she might love him, and she thought—she hoped—she could convince him to love her.

Her own budding happiness made her feel guilty,

remembering Lady Longhurst. As they paused before the old moated manor house that she was beginning to think of as home, the light of dawn turned the bricks and timber to pink, while the rising sun reflected in the moat. And everything felt so wonderful and right, she was suddenly afraid.

As if the Fates were laughing at her, and preparing for her fall.

Chapter 22

Their horses crossed the drawbridge, hooves striking the stone, and into the courtyard of the manor house. Valentine looked up at the oldest part of his home, with its overhanging upper story of medieval black and white timber, small-paned windows shining in the sun. The walled garden was just coming to life with insects and birds, and servants were hurrying about their tasks for the day ahead. It was as if he'd stepped back into another world, for it was doubtful much had changed at Abbey Thorne Manor for centuries.

Valentine looked to Marissa, who was dismounting with the assistant of a groom. Once on the ground she shook her skirts into shape and brushed down her sleeves, reaching up to tuck a strand of hair behind her ear. She looked tired but no less beautiful and he accepted the knowledge that he wanted to pick her up and carry her to his bedchamber.

But there were other matters to deal with, and from the look on Morris's face when he came out to meet them, there was something very serious at the front of the queue.

"I did not know, my lord," he began, hurrying

after Valentine as he entered the house. "I had no idea until it was too late. I would never have allowed such a thing to happen if I'd had the least idea."

"What on earth are you talking about, Morris?" Valentine was weary and irritable.

Morris's eyes grew startled and wide, and his jowls began to quiver. "But . . . didn't Wallace speak to you, my lord? I sent him after you as soon as I knew."

"I haven't seen Wallace."

If Morris had been a lesser man he would have stamped his feet. "The fool probably went the wrong way. And after I gave him explicit instructions—"

Valentine was at the end of his tether. "Tell me what you're talking about, Morris, and tell me now."

"My lord, I have bad news." Morris stood stiff and straight, like a soldier facing the firing squad. "Someone was in your rooms while you were away. I didn't know anything was wrong until I entered to place some mail on your desk, and I saw immediately that things were not at all as you'd left them. I cannot say if anything is taken, my lord, but—"

Valentine gave a roar of rage. He began to run toward the stairs, the sound of his boots on the marble floor echoing all around them.

"Lord Jasper is looking through your papers now," Morris said hurriedly, his voice rising as he pursued his master up the stairs. "He thought it best to know the worst at once."

"Of course, Morris. Thank you." Marissa managed a fraught smile as she followed in Valentine's wake.

Upstairs, she found Lord Jasper and Lady Bethany busy making repairs to the room, both of them appearing somber and concerned. Valentine stood in the doorway like a man in shock, glaring around him at the chaos of papers and books that covered the desk, chairs, and floor. Books had been pulled from the shelves and lay tumbled in piles, while dried rose specimens, broken and smashed, were scattered throughout the room.

Marissa was too horrified to speak.

"He's been in here," Valentine said, cold rage in each word. "In my rooms. Touching my things. Reading my papers."

No one asked who he meant.

"I think it looks worse than it is, old chap." Jasper's voice held a soothing note. "Nothing is missing as far as I can see. It may not even be Von Hautt who did this, you know."

But Valentine shook his head. "It was Von Hautt," he said through gritted teeth. "This was all planned. Attacking Lady Longhurst and then drawing me away to Canthorpe. I thought he was behaving like a madman, but he's a madman with a purpose. He planned it so that he could sneak into my rooms. Invade my personal belongings."

"But even if that's so, he hasn't gained anything by it, has he?" Jasper insisted. "He already has the list of names. What is there here that he hasn't already got?"

"Perhaps he wants Lord Kent to feel unsettled," Lady Bethany suggested. "Knowing that his home has been infiltrated by the enemy will cause him a deal of suffering, and Baron Von Hautt seems to want him to suffer."

Valentine ran his hands through his hair until it stood on end, making him look even more dangerous. "How can we guess the thoughts of a lunatic," he muttered. Then he stopped, eyes narrowing, and spun around toward his desk. "Wait a moment . . ." Wildly he began to search through the mess of papers, some of which had fallen to the floor, or were about to.

Marissa came and stood beside him. "What is it?"

"The letter!"

"What letter . . . ?"

"My friend in London. The letter that told me the geographical locations of the last families on the list. It was here and now it's gone." He looked up, eyes blazing into hers. "Von Hautt has it."

"Are you sure?" She began to search through the mess of papers, carefully sifting them from one pile to another.

But Valentine already knew it was gone. He was striding across the room and then back again, so distracted it was impossible for him to keep still. "Oh yes, he has it," he roared with bitter certainty. "Now he knows where the last two families lived and he'll be able to get there before us. That has been his plan all along. To beat me to the rose."

"We won't be far behind." Jasper was all quiet menace. "Don't worry, old chap, he can't hide from us. We'll find the rose and we'll find him, and then we'll make him pay."

"How the hell do you know he hasn't found it already?" Valentine was beyond being rational or calm. "He could have it in his hands now. He wants to hurt me and he knows that by taking the one thing

I've been searching for all these years . . . How can I complete my quest?" His gaze sought and found Marissa's, his eyes full of agonized emotion.

She knew exactly what he was thinking. If Von Hautt had the rose then he'd failed. All the years of searching in vain.

She slipped her hand into his, warm and comforting, and watched as he forced himself to climb out of the pit of darkness. Valentine was no weakling, and he must be strong or Baron Von Hautt really would trample on his hopes and dreams.

"I'm sorry," he said in a more natural voice. "It was seeing what he'd done. I am recovered now. Forgive me."

There were understanding nods all around.

"Surely Baron Von Hautt cannot expect to appear in London with the rose and everyone to pat him on the back and say well done?" Lady Bethany said thoughtfully. "The truth about his behavior will come out and he'll be shunned by the very people he wants to impress. Where's the glory in that?"

"You are wondering what is the point of him winning the rose by foul means?" Jasper said with a nod.

"All that seems to matter to him is that he's won," Marissa replied, "not how that win was achieved. Defeating Lord Kent is what is driving him, not fame and world renown."

"What have you done to him that he feels so bitter toward you?" Lady Bethany said. "There must be something, Kent. You must search your memories until you find it."

Valentine sat down and put his head in his hands,

his shoulders hunched. "I don't know," he groaned. "I honestly don't understand any of it."

"Very well then, let's just consider matters calmly for a moment," Jasper said. "Von Hautt lured you away from Abbey Thorne Manor, using Lady Long-hurst, and when you'd gone he came up to your rooms and stole the letter." He paused, looking about. "Didn't someone see him? He must have passed through the house and there would be ser-vants, Morris, and so on. Someone must have seen something."

"Morris says not," Marissa murmured.

"Then someone must have let him in and guided him to the letter. All this," Jasper waved his unin-jured arm at the mess, "is for effect. To hurt you. To show you he is capable of creeping into your most private sanctum. How can you feel safe knowing that?"

"All along I've believed an enemy resides within my household," Valentine said. "There are things Von Hautt knows about me, about us, that only an intimate of my family could possibly know."

"So not a kitchen maid or a boot polisher," Lady Bethany said in droll tones. "This enemy must be someone who spends time in your company and is well known and trusted by you."

"One of us." Marissa spoke what they were all thinking.

Valentine looked bleak. "That makes it worse. A betrayal. This person and Von Hautt are comrades, working against me, and there's nothing I can do to protect myself."

"You need some sleep, Kent," Jasper said gruffly.

"You've been up all night. Lady Bethany and I will deal with the next name on the list and if there's a chance the rose still exists then we'll send for you."

Valentine wavered, obviously torn, but he was exhausted and he knew he'd be no good to anyone unless he spent an hour or two in bed. Reluctantly he nodded, and Jasper and Lady Bethany began to make their plans.

"George is still at Lady Longhurst's," Marissa added. "Someone should send a message to him and let him know what's happening, so that he can be on his guard, too."

It was agreed. Jasper and Lady Bethany would set off after breakfast, and Valentine and Marissa would remain at Abbey Thorne Manor.

"And we will all take great care," Lady Bethany said with grim seriousness, looking at each of them in turn. "It seems our little botanical adventure has turned into a dangerous melodrama, and I would not like to see any more of us hurt."

"We must be united against our enemy," Jasper said.

"Enemies," Valentine corrected him.

And with that somber warning they went their separate ways.

Chapter 23

"What do you think of my granddaughter and your friend Kent?" Lady Bethany spoke into the long silence as the carriage bowled along a lane beneath a blue summer sky.

"Think of them?" Jasper appeared surprised.

"Haven't you noticed there is a certain frisson between them, whenever they are together? Really, Jasper, you can't be that unobservant."

"I suppose I have noticed a change in Kent since Miss Rotherhild arrived."

"That's better. A change in what way?"

"Well, he's far more jittery, as if he's living on his nerves." Jasper shifted uneasily on his seat. "Didn't you tell me your granddaughter came here with an eye for George, my dear? I'd hate Kent to have his heart broken by a fickle miss."

Lady Bethany bristled in defense of her granddaughter. "Marissa is not a fickle miss, Jasper, far from it. And as for George . . . if you knew how drab the poor girl's life has been you'd forgive her for setting her sights on the first man she met who was good-looking and the slightest bit interested in anything other than plants."

"I suppose so," he said uncertainly.

"I know so," she replied forthrightly. "But when we arrived at Abbey Thorne Manor and she came face-to-face with Kent—and he with her, I might add—she realized George wasn't the one. She has had stars in her eyes ever since."

Jasper smiled. "Do I have stars in my eyes, my dear?"

Lady Bethany pretended to peer closely into them, her face expressionless, but there was a flush on her cheeks that betrayed how she was really feeling. "There may be one or two," she admitted at last.

Jasper sighed contentedly. "Who would have thought that in the twilight of my years I would find the love of my life."

Lady Bethany slipped her hand into the crook of his arm. Falling in love was a wonderful thing, there was no doubt about it, but she'd lived long enough to accept it didn't always end happily or well. She had come to Abbey Thorne Manor for Marissa's sake, never expecting to meet a man with whom she could feel such an affinity.

The strange thing was that she'd recently given up on any more affairs of the heart. She was, she'd told herself, too old for the highs and lows of passionate love. These days a warm fire and comfortable slippers had become far more important than a man's companionship.

But even while she was preparing to make her bed and lie in it, she'd admitted that she missed the feel of strong arms about her, and the exquisite physicality of a masculine body pressed to hers. It wasn't even as if the act of connection mattered greatly to her anymore; it was the being close, being stroked and loved, and the feeling that she wasn't alone.

And then, quite unexpectedly, she met Jasper and found everything she'd decided to give up on.

He matched her intellectually as well as physically, and he made her smile. She looked forward to his company. She even felt the aches and pains of old age less since they'd become friends. Lady Bethany was feeling young again, like a girl in the throes of her first passion.

She closed her eyes in the shadow of her hat, enjoying the moment. Because for a woman of her years every positive moment was important and must be thoroughly enjoyed.

Valentine was asleep, or so he thought. In his dream he was resting in Marissa's arms and she was stroking strands of his hair back from his brow, her fingers gentle and soothing. She murmured his name and then kissed him lightly on his lips. It felt so perfect he told himself he didn't want to wake up, but it was already too late.

He opened his eyes.

She was looking down at him, her dark hair loose about her face, her dark eyes wide in her pale face. She smiled, but even so he sensed her tension.

"I missed you," she said. "I know we cannot be together in the way I want, not yet, but I thought it wouldn't matter if we slept in each other's arms."

Valentine knew what he should say.

Doubt took away her smile and her lashes drooped. "I'll go. I'm sorry."

In answer he pulled her down, tightening his hold on her, drawing her in close against his shoulder, feeling the soft relaxing of her body against his. She was, he couldn't help but notice, wearing a white nightgown with long sleeves. It was virginal and would act as a reminder to behave himself.

"I prefer you stay," he admitted, his breath warm in her hair.

"I prefer to stay, too," she whispered with a sigh.

"Von Hautt—"

She placed a finger across his lips and shook her head, her hair tumbling around them. "Don't let's talk about him." Her gaze was pleading. "Let's forget about him, just for now."

He kissed her fingers, and took them in his own. "Are Jasper and your grandmother back yet?"

"Not yet."

He lay back and closed his eyes, and she snuggled into his arms with obvious pleasure. He held her, forcing his mind away from carnal thoughts, enjoying the closeness. How long was it since he'd held a woman like this?

Too long.

He'd been alone for so many years he'd forgotten the joys of having someone to share his bed and his life with, remembering only the negatives.

She tugged the covers up over them, her limbs tangling with his, her cheek upon his pillow, and smiled sleepily. "What would Morris think if he saw us like this?"

Valentine gave a mock shudder. "Nothing, probably. His expression would be enough to send you screaming back to your room."

"Morris doesn't frighten me. He's very loyal, isn't he?"

"He's been with me for a long time. Since my father died. I don't know how I'd manage without him; he's like one of the family. There isn't much about us that Morris doesn't know."

"You don't think Morris could be your spy?"

The idea was shocking. Morris? In cahoots with Von Hautt? It was like suspecting George, and Valentine found he couldn't do it. He shook his head. "No, not Morris."

She murmured a reply but he could feel her growing limp as she drifted into sleep. Her breathing deepened. He watched her, sleepy himself, pretending just for a moment that he could have her beside him every night, that this was the beginning of a lifetime with her as his companion. The fantasy wasn't as difficult to visualize as he'd thought. He'd reached the point where his son was smiling up at him with Marissa's eyes and he was instructing him in some piece of botanical science, much to Marissa's disgust, when commonsense put a stop to it.

There was the rose to find and Von Hautt to defeat.

If Morris isn't the spy, then who?

Doubting his faithful retainers made him feel grubby and he closed his eyes and returned to Marissa instead.

Soon he had followed her into sleep.

As far as finding the rose went, the purpose of their journey had been a waste of time, although on a personal level Jasper and Lady Bethany had enjoyed themselves immensely. The manor of the de Turville family had been destroyed by fire many centuries ago and what remained was then taken by the local farmers to build their barns and byres and houses.

Jasper made a careful search across the overgrown patch of ground where the manor once stood. Lady Bethany refused to help him, saying she valued her skin too much, preferring to watch him from the safety of the carriage as he cursed and thrashed his stick through the weeds and brambles.

But it was all to no avail, and after Jasper declared that if the rose had ever existed here then it existed no longer, they turned for home.

"That leaves William Beauchamp," Lady Bethany said, after ticking the list of crusaders' names off on her fingers. "He is our last and final hope."

Jasper looked morose. "Poor Kent. He thought he had a real chance of finding the rose. I don't know what he'll do if this fails."

"He'll keep looking, surely?"

"Oh yes, he'll keep looking, my dear. But he knows, just as I know, that there is the distinct possibility it no longer exists. That no matter how hard and how long he searches for the wretched thing he's never going to find it."

"Is he the sort of man who'd become embittered?"

Jasper considered the question seriously. "I wouldn't have said so, although lately he seems to have become rather desperate about the whole thing."

Lady Bethany waved a lazy hand at an insect that

had decided her chip straw bonnet would make a nice home. "You do realize, Jasper, that my visit is coming to an end."

He turned to her with a startled look. "Good heavens! You're leaving, my dear?"

"You know Marissa and I must return to our home in London, Jasper. And who knows where we'll be this time next week! Probably in the wilds of Sutherland, hunting for mosses in knee-deep snow. My son-in-law is relentless when it comes to his chosen field."

"Good heavens," Jasper repeated, clearly shocked at the prospect. "We can't have that. I'll have to come and rescue you, my dear. Carry you off on some romantic tryst, eh?"

Lady Bethany smiled a little smile. "I would like that," she said. "It sounds very agreeable."

"Should I rescue your granddaughter, too? Or do you think she'll be all right?"

"Oh yes, I think so," she said. "If I am right, Jasper, then we'll have a wedding to attend before too long, and I will be able to boast to all my friends that I was instrumental in bringing it about."

"And were you, my dear?"

"I played my part, Jasper. I intend to claim the credit anyway."

He laughed, and she laughed with him.

After a moment he grew serious. "I'm an old bachelor, my dear. Set in my ways. I never thought I'd . . . well, I've no idea what I'd be like as a husband at my age."

Lady Bethany patted his hand, where he held

the reins. "I don't want another husband, Jasper. I'd much prefer a good friend."

"Would you?" He seemed struck by the thought. "I thought all women were keen on bagging a husband."

"Not all, I promise you."

"Friends then," Jasper said. "Very good friends."

They drove on in silence, both very content with the future they envisioned.

Chapter 24

The door opened a fraction and Augustus Von Hautt's heart began to speed up. Sometimes lately his heart beat so hard that it hurt his chest, and he had to put his hand over it, to hold it in. This was one of those moments.

"There you are," the familiar voice said, and the door closed again. "I was worried."

"You told me to come here when I needed to."

"Of course I did. Are you hurt?"

He shook his head, shivering a little. He'd lit the fire but the chimney was full of soot and wouldn't draw properly.

"Look. I have some food for you. Eat up and you'll feel better. You always feel better when you've eaten."

It was true, he did feel better on a full stomach.

"Why did you frighten Lady Longhurst?"

He met those familiar eyes and looked away. "She deserved it. My mother . . ."

"Augustus, you can't go about punishing people because they remind you of your mother. You loved your mother, you know you did."

"I hardly knew her."

"Well, *she* loved *you*."

He finished the food and pushed back his chair with a sigh. He did feel better now. But so weary; his eyelids were drooping.

"You're the only one who has ever loved me, Bobo," he murmured, using the old childhood name, the sound of it comforting him.

He could hear the fire being stoked, the warmth spreading through him as he dozed. He knew there were things to do, important things. He had to find the rose, but that could wait until tomorrow, when Valentine set off after the final name on his list.

Beauchamp.

Was it fate? Or just luck? Well, whatever it was, Augustus was pleased things had worked out this way. The end was coming.

Soon he would have completed his life's work and he would finally be able to rest.

Chapter 25

Valentine hadn't visited the town of Bentley Green before, and he found it an industrious little place. Bentley Green was a market town, and because it was market day there were numerous people about, competing with the noise made by the farm animals penned in the market square. Stalls had been set up, selling eggs and cheeses and other farm produce, while children played at tiggy around the barrows and carts. Marissa laughed at a farmer who stood with his booted feet apart, discussing the weather and shouting encouragement to his flustered wife, as she chased an escaped goose through the melee.

They left their horses and carriage at a stable and set off to find what information they could on the Beauchamps. Before too long George declared he was hungry.

"We should have bought another picnic basket," he added. "Why didn't you think to tell Mrs. Beamauris to pack it, Valentine?"

"I have more important things to think of than your stomach, George."

"Nothing is more important than my stomach," George declared.

Marissa giggled.

She seemed happy today and he played at being happy, too, although he was beginning to wonder if he'd ever find the Crusader's Rose. The rose had filled his life for so long that he didn't know what he'd do without it, and yet, strangely, the idea did not fill him with despair. Not when Marissa was by his side.

There were two taverns in Bentley Green: the Fox and Hounds, which had a private parlor, and The Crosskeys, which didn't. They chose the former.

At first the landlord of the Fox and Hounds was reluctant to hire the parlor out to them.

"We have plenty of so-called gentlemen willing to pay to seat themselves in here away from the common folk," he said suspiciously, looking Valentine up and down. "Why should I let you have the whole parlor for only three persons when I can fit a full dozen in there?"

"Because I am Lord Kent and I do not want to share," Valentine said in a cold and haughty voice.

The man returned his stare, and then gave a respectful nod. "Fair enough then, Your Lordship. This way."

Valentine caught George's grin at Marissa as they made their way down the narrow, musty passage. "Valentine is an approachable fellow most of the time, but don't ever forget he's a lord of the realm."

"Being a lord of the realm comes in handy," Valentine retorted, "as you may find out one day."

"Never," his brother said firmly. "I am not hanging out for your title, Valentine. That is yours to pass down to your son."

Caught by surprise, Valentine's gaze slid to Marissa and quickly away again. She was looking down, her face in shadow, but he was certain he saw the curve of her mouth, and her dimple, and wondered what she was thinking.

The parlor was shabby but at least they were able to eat their meal in peace, and the food was well-cooked and plentiful. The landlord followed the serving girl in and asked if all was to their liking. From his change in attitude it was obvious he'd made inquiries about Lord Kent and, liking what he'd heard, hoped to do further business with him.

Valentine took the opportunity to question him about the Beauchamp family.

"Beauchamp? Aye, I know them. What do you want with them, if I may be so bold, Your Lordship?"

"That's none of your business. Answer the question."

The landlord of the Fox and Hounds seemed to respond well to Valentine's autocratic manner. "They used to live in the great house about two miles south of Bentley Bottom, but one of the Beauchamps had a liking for London gambling tables and they went bust and lost it, oh, probably two generations ago. Now and then the place gets leased by visiting gentry, but it's been empty for a year or more. Too big, you see, and in need of too many repairs."

"And what happened to the family after they lost the house?" Marissa asked.

"Some of them still live in the village but now

they's as poor as church mice. The rest are scattered far and wide."

"And this house . . . it was definitely the only one owned by them?"

"Used to be owned by them. Aye. There was another house on the same land before that one, but it was pulled down to make way for this present one. At the time the Beauchamp lady wanted everything bigger and better—she even had the flower beds and the orchard dug up, so's she could plant a garden in the new fashion. Ten years later they lost everything."

Grimly Valentine nodded his dismissal.

"She had the flower beds dug up?" Marissa repeated, when they were alone again. She didn't need to say more; they were all thinking it.

Is there any point in looking for the Crusader's Rose?

"We have to make certain," Valentine said. "Even if it is not the original building the land has been in the family for centuries. The rose may have seeded into the new garden."

Once more he was clutching at straws and he knew it, but he couldn't afford not to be thorough in his search. If he missed something and then Von Hautt found it, he'd never be able to live with himself.

Back in the market place, the stallholders were beginning to pack away their wares and the farmers were loading up their carts and preparing for the journey home. The weather had been fine for days, but now the summer sun had disappeared beneath a bank of cloud, and there was a distinct smell of approaching rain in the air.

It didn't take them long to collect their equipage and horses and set off to the south. Bentley Bottom was a scatter of cottages, soon passed. None of them spoke as they headed along the road, fields on one side and a thick copse of trees on the other. As they left the shelter of the trees Marissa suddenly made a little sound in her throat, and Valentine turned to see what was wrong.

She was staring to her left. "How utterly horrible," she said with a shudder.

The house was like a great dark bird, glaring down at them, and even Valentine, who was usually not susceptible to atmosphere, felt a prickle of dread.

"Good God."

"Is that it, do you think? The Beauchamp house?"

She sounded as if she hoped not, but he pointed out the faded name attached to one of a pair of crumbling pillars flanking a narrow lane. Beauchamp Place. They turned up the lane and drew closer to the house. There was a depressing decrepitude about the brick façade, and several windows were boarded up.

"No wonder it is unoccupied," he said. "I can't imagine anyone choosing to live here."

"It's like something from a fairy tale," Marissa said, managing a lopsided smile. "One of the more unpleasant ones."

"The garden doesn't appear to have been touched for a hundred years."

Marissa followed his gaze and her face fell. "Oh dear."

A ramshackle wooden gate barred their way, and

beyond it brambles grew rampant across what were now only memories of pathways and borders and arbors that must once have been neatly trimmed.

George stared. "How are we going to search this place? We need a team of helpers with scythes and shovels and—and pickaxes."

Valentine waved a hand dismissively. "I know what I'm looking for," he said, with far more confidence than he was feeling. He glanced at Marissa again. She looked cold and downhearted and he wanted to put his arms about her and hold her until she was warm. Instead he said, with polite diffidence, "Do you want to wait in the carriage, Marissa?"

She seemed surprised, and then pulled a scornful face. "No, of course not," she declared. "What a poor creature I'd be if I did that. I've been to worse places than this, believe me."

"But not with me," he said, the words spilling out before he could stop them. "This isn't the sort of place I would ever willingly bring you to."

Thankfully George was busy trying to open the gate and hadn't overheard him. But Marissa was watching him, her dark eyes seemingly trying to see inside his head and discover what he was really saying.

"What sort of place would you prefer to take me to?" she said quietly. With a sideways glance at George, still busy with the gate, she lifted her hand, and he knew she wanted to trace the shape of his mouth, just as he knew he wanted to press his lips to hers.

"There is a garden in Italy, growing on the side of a hill." His voice sounded shaky, uncertain, far from the autocratic tone he'd used in Bentley Green. "There is an orchard and you can pick oranges from the trees and taste the sun in them. They crush their own grapes and make their own wine. I've dined in a courtyard full of flowers and music and laughter, with moths dancing around the candle flames. Perhaps, one day . . ."

She was gazing at him, her expression soft and dreamy, a little smile playing on her lips. "Valentine . . ."

But then George came up, interrupting. "That gate will fall down if I get it open. We'll have to climb over it." He held out his hand to help Marissa down to the ground. "Do you think you can manage?"

She nodded. "I—I think so."

George tested the strength of it, putting his boot on the first wooden bar, before swinging his leg over the top and dropping down to the other side. Impatiently, Marissa gathered her skirts out of the way with one hand, holding her bonnet with the other and prepared to follow.

"No."

Valentine was down from the carriage before he had a chance to reconsider. He swept her up in his arms and held her nice and securely against his chest. Startled, she clutched hold of her bonnet, and looked up at him with wide eyes.

"That's better," was all he said. "George?"

George chuckled as he held out his own arms to receive her. "Ready."

"There's—there's no need. Really," she said breathlessly.

"My brother being gallant," George teased, "that's

something I haven't seen for a long time. Make the most of it, Marissa."

Valentine ignored them both, swinging Marissa up and over the top of the gate, and depositing her gently within George's grasp. A moment later she was on her feet in the garden, and Valentine vaulted over behind her, landing with a thump and striding off into the wilderness.

"Follow me," he called, heading into the dank greenery.

"Follow me," Marissa muttered an hour later, wiping a gloved hand across her brow, and glaring down at the remains of a tangled patch of forget-me-nots, the sticky seeds clinging to her skirts.

Since Valentine had marched off into the garden like an explorer heading into darkest Africa, Marissa seemed to have gotten nowhere despite hours of hard work.

"Anything that looks like a rose, call me to take a look," he had instructed before he disappeared entirely. "Remember, the Crusader's Rose should be flowering at this time of year, but if it's struggling in this mess it may not have the necessary light and nourishment to flower. The leaves are a pale green and the thorns have a reddish tinge and are hooked over like a hawk's claws."

George had dredged up a sigh from the depths of his being. "I hope you know you will be reimbursing me for this. My tailor's bill needs paying and I am going to tell him to send it to you. I'll probably need a new set of clothes after I've fought my way through this jungle."

"Then you should not have worn your London best, George. This isn't a stroll along Bond Street, you know."

George swept his brother's ensemble a scornful look. "One of the Kents has to keep up appearances, Valentine."

The two of them headed into the garden, still arguing, until their voices faded completely.

At first Marissa remained close to the gate, exploring the edges of the garden, but eventually she was drawn further and further into it. Narrow paths were still evident, their bricks moss-covered and slippery, while dark and mysterious tunnels of undergrowth tempted her away from the light. Soon she was barely aware of the two men, apart from the occasional snapping of a twig or the rustling of leaves, and even that began to blend in with the natural sounds of the place.

She was completely immersed and it was only when a rumble of thunder sounded overhead that she realized how much time had flown by. Surprised, she looked around her. The light was fading, as the approaching rainstorm trailed its dark skirts over Beauchamp Place. If it had been creepy before it was more so now. Almost as if something was watching her, waiting to pounce.

And gobble her up.

"Valentine?" she called, her voice a squeak. "George?"

Neither of them answered. She forced back her panic, reminding herself that until a moment before she had been deaf and blind to anything but the search for the Crusader's Rose, and no doubt they still were.

Marissa stood up on her tiptoes, peering through perennials that were now as big as small trees, but it was impossible to see through the close-growing greenery from here. She needed to find a high point.

The sky lit with lightning, and a moment later there was another growl of thunder. Marissa knew she'd had enough. Pushing her way along one of the paths, she glanced up at the Beauchamp house looming above her, its dark windows like watching eyes. Lightning flashed again and just for a brief second she saw a figure, standing within the frame of the window, silhouetted against the room behind him.

He was watching her and she stared back. His hair was pale. Fair, like Valentine's or George's? Or was it gray, like Baron Von Hautt's? Then the figure stepped back into the room and was gone, merging into the shadows.

"Valentine!" This time her voice was surely loud enough, but still there was no answer.

The wind suddenly gusted up around her, tossing leaves and branches. Rain splattered down in big drops, just a few at first, and then more rapidly. Wet now as well as frightened, Marissa forced her way through a great mound of tangled vines. Ahead of her lay a relatively open space, set in the middle of the garden. Low brick walls delineated what appeared to be the remains of a pond but was now little more than a muddy ditch.

There was something lying down there at the

pond's edge. Clothing and a pair of boots . . . Her heart began to beat harder. She reached the wall and climbed over it—it was only waist-high, but broken in places. Sharp rushes caught at her skirts and crackled under her shoes, but she no longer noticed. Now she was closer she could see exactly what was lying in the pond.

His boots were in the mud, his legs spread-eagled, while an outflung arm cradled his fair head.

She began to run.

Valentine.

Chapter 26

Marissa didn't remember moving, but suddenly she was kneeling beside him, turning him over with hands that were surprisingly steady. His skin was pale, but not deathly so, and a trickle of blood ran down the side of his face from the lump on his brow, just below his hairline.

He must have fallen, knocked himself unconscious.

But Marissa knew that wasn't what happened. She'd seen Von Hautt upstairs in the house, she was sure of it, and wherever the baron was disaster followed. He had already attacked Jasper, why not Valentine? Why not Marissa . . . ?

A prickling sense of being watched brought her head around, eyes wide, searching the surrounding garden, but there was no one there. She was alone with an injured man.

What about George? Had he been attacked, too?

Marissa didn't have time to go looking for him, and she wasn't going to leave Valentine alone here, helpless and hurt. She began to tug at him, grasping the folds of his jacket and pulling him further from the remains of the pond. It occurred to her that if he'd fallen the other way, with his head in the muddy water, he might have drowned.

What would her world be like without Valentine Kent?

She felt dizzy at the thought. Was this the moment when a respectable young lady should faint? Marissa decided she couldn't be very respectable because she had no intention of fainting. Instead she was angry, and getting angrier. Baron Von Hautt had attacked Valentine, her Valentine, and she was going to see that he was punished for it.

Valentine made a noise, a groan, and Marissa stopped tugging at him. He opened his eyes, their color even more striking in the gathering gloom of the storm, and peered up at her as if he didn't know who she was.

She cupped his face with her hands, her voice trembling with emotion.

"Darling Valentine, what happened?"

He looked at her blankly a moment more, and then all of a sudden understanding flooded his face. He tried to sit up. The abrupt movement must have made him light-headed because he stopped, cursing, and raised a hand to his head, examining the bump.

"Here, let me . . ." She tried to support him, but he didn't want her help, and a moment later he had pushed himself to his feet and staggered over to the wall. He sat down on the crumbling bricks, still pale, but his voice was strong with resolve.

"I have to find Von Hautt."

She came and stood before him. The rain was steady, and the feather in her bonnet was sodden, dangling down over her eyes and tickling her chin. Valentine's hair was plastered to his skull, and the blood from his injury was mingling with the water and running down his cheek. She reached out and, with her sleeve, wiped it away.

"What happened to you?"

"I was searching for the rose. I don't know how long he was watching me, but suddenly he was just there." He rubbed a hand across his eyes, hard, as if he was trying to clear his head. "He said, 'Give up, Kent, the rose is mine.' I tried to grab hold of him, but my foot caught in some brambles, and he laughed while I tried to get free. Then George was shouting, coming along one of the paths."

"I've been calling for George but he won't answer. Valentine, tell me he isn't hurt, too?" She was shaking now, from cold and reaction—the anger seemed to have shrunk to a little hard knot inside her.

He shook his head. "Von Hautt kicked out at me." He put his hand to his ribs with a wince. "I fell. Hit my head on something on the ground. A stone or a brick, I think. He was looking down at me, grinning, and he said . . . he said . . ." He closed his eyes and stopped, grinding his teeth.

"What did he say?"

But Valentine either couldn't or wouldn't answer her. He took a deep breath, wincing again from his bruised ribs. "George arrived and I heard them arguing. Then running. I tried to get up, to follow them, but I was dizzy and I tumbled over the wall and down into the pond. I must have lost consciousness. The next thing I saw was you."

"So George is . . . ?"

Marissa looked around. The rain was still coming down and she was as soaked as she could possibly be. She felt Valentine's hand close on hers and he began to rub it between his, as if to warm it.

"You're all wet," he said mildly.

"Yes, Valentine, it's raining." Her smile was lop-sided, but she hoped he couldn't tell how miserable she felt.

He stood up, slipping his arm about her and pull-ing her to his side. "Come on, let's find some shel-ter," he said, and together they stumbled toward the house.

"I saw the baron upstairs at the window," she said, brushing the soggy feather out of her face. "He might still be here."

Valentine looked up, his eyes glittering. "Oh, I hope so."

They reached the portico over the front door. A furious gust of wind blew rain into their meager shelter. Valentine cursed, wiping the rain from his eyes, and shoved at the door. It swung open.

Inside it wasn't as dark as Marissa had expected, although the smell of damp and rotten wood told its own story. Looking up, she saw that what had once been a stained glass window far above had broken, and rain was dripping in. Cobwebs hung in curtains from the corners and the pieces of furni-ture stacked and abandoned around the walls were coated thickly with dust.

"Where did you see him?" Valentine asked. There was a staircase rising up to a gallery, part of which had begun to come away from the walls. The or-nately carved railing where once Beauchamps had stood to admire their home was now warped and broken.

She did her best to explain, ending with, "But he could be anywhere now and . . . Valentine!"

He ignored her, already heading up the stairs, moving swiftly for a man who had recently been lying unconscious. Marissa went to follow him but she'd only taken a couple of steps when he turned to face her.

"No!" he roared. "Stay there."

His autocratic attitude didn't surprise her, and Marissa was prepared to argue. "I want to come with you!"

He jabbed his finger at her, emphasizing each word. "Stay right there until I come back."

"What if the baron—"

He was grinding his teeth again. "He won't because he's upstairs. I'm going to teach him a lesson in manners."

Marissa wanted to protest but he was already on the move again, as if he expected her total obedience. He reached the first landing and a moment later he'd disappeared down one of the corridors.

Did he really expect her to stand and wait for him? Stand all alone while he went off after the baron? After what happened last time the two of them met? Marissa had no intention of obeying him—he wasn't her husband yet, and even if he was . . . well, Marissa had her own thoughts on the obedience to which a husband was entitled.

As she climbed the stairs they creaked alarmingly. She slowed, moving more cautiously, testing each tread before she rested her weight on it. That was when she noticed the heavy layer of dust on the bare wooden treads and the clear footprints. She could see where Valentine had just been, but there was another set of footprints, an earlier set, sometimes overlaid by Valentine's.

Von Hautt?

Who else could it be?

The fact that the footprints were only going upward seemed to imply the baron hadn't come back this way. Marissa wasn't sure whether that was a good thing or a bad thing. Valentine might be struggling with Von Hautt at this very moment . . . .

She couldn't lose him now that she'd found him.

A wave of despair washed over her. It wasn't just her current situation. She knew why she felt so low. It was her rain-soaked condition. Her sodden skirts were dripping, her hat was falling to pieces, and her skin was cold and clammy. When she'd been on botanical expeditions before she'd been exposed to the sun and the wind, even the snow, and maintained her equilibrium, but she never could abide being rained on. Lady Bethany used to laugh and say she must be half cat, the way she behaved when her feet got wet.

Marissa pushed the feather out of her eyes again, and made her way across the landing. Valentine must be following the footsteps, too, she decided, because they were both going in the same direction. Abruptly a door slammed overhead, making her jump. She looked up, listening hard, but there was nothing more. The wind, perhaps? It was certainly moaning around the house, gusts shaking loose boards and shutters, tearing at roof tiles.

There was an open door to her left and she peered in. The room was empty, with wallpaper peeling from walls where damp stains made strange shapes. Dried leaves rustled in the corners, where they'd blown in through the broken windows.

"Valentine where are you?" she whispered, looking ahead into the deeper shadows, trying not to imagine the baron waiting to pounce on her. Her skin was icy and she held her arms around herself, seeking a little warmth, her shivering almost constant.

"Valentine? Marissa?"

It was George! With a cry of relief she spun around and hurried back to the head of the stairs. Relief made her careless and she came to a halt against the banisters, using it as a brake. The old wood cracked loudly under hands and she felt it begin to give way. She scrambled backward, almost falling, landing against the wall with a thud.

"Marissa, be careful." George was striding toward her up the stairs. "The whole place is about to come down."

He was soaked, his trousers splashed with mud and his hair slicked to his skull.

"Valentine was knocked unconscious," she gabbled. "I saw Von Hautt at the window and he's gone to find him."

George frowned as he deciphered this. "Well, he won't find him," he reassured her. "I've just chased him across the fields until I lost him in the trees. Our friend the baron is gone . . . for now at least."

"And it really was Von Hautt?" Marissa said.

"Oh yes. And Valentine's not badly hurt?"

"He's walking and talking."

George grinned. "He's got a hard head. I had to leave him when I took off after the baron, but I could hear him cursing after he hit his head on the brick, so I didn't think it was too serious."

Marissa decided if she'd been in George's shoes she would never have left Valentine. She gave a shiver at the memory of seeing his body.

"We need to find somewhere warm," George said, giving his jacket a sorrowful look. "When we find Valentine I think we should go back to the Fox and Hounds and ask our friendly landlord for some rooms and some hot baths."

"Nonsense!"

They both looked up as Valentine came around the corner and onto the landing. "We're going home to Abbey Thorne Manor," he growled. "If Von Hautt is watching the house—and he must be if he followed us here—then I want him caught and locked up as soon as possible."

"Valentine—" George began to protest.

"This is more important than you warming your toes in front of a good fire, George."

Marissa noticed a new smear of dirt on his cheek but no new injuries, although the bump on his head was turning a colorful shade of purple.

"Not me," George retorted. "I'm thinking of Marissa. She's frozen through. Look at her."

He did. His gaze narrowed, sweeping over her from head to toe, and back again. "She's certainly soaked," he said, "but then we all are. I thought this was what you liked, Marissa. The adventure, the chase."

"I do, but—"

"Well then, you should be prepared for a little hardship."

Marissa gave a violent shiver. Her bonnet slipped forward and the feather drooped over one eye. It was the final straw.

"I hate being wet," she said, her teeth clenched to stop them from chattering. "I hate it above all things. I have stood in the rain from the Faro Isles to the Scilly Isles, and I've hated it every time. And you promised me I would not get wet on your expedition. You *promised* . . ." She dragged her bonnet from her head and flung it on the ground. It landed with a sodden squish. For a horrible moment she felt like she was going to burst into tears.

"I'm sorry," Valentine said, biting his lip.

"You'd better not be laughing . . ."

"No, I-I'm not. We'll go to the Fox and Hounds in Bentley Green."

Marissa shook her head, frightened to speak in case her voice came out all wobbly.

"You don't want to go to Bentley Green?" Valentine hazarded, coming closer.

"Yes," she managed, "I do. But you need to see a doctor. Your head."

"My head's hard as a rock."

"Well it's not, is it? It was a rock, at least a brick, that did this to you."

"My head is fine."

"Nevertheless," George interrupted, "you will see a quack, or whoever passes for one in Bentley Green. Do you think Von Hautt meant to hurt you?" he added, before his brother could protest.

Valentine pushed a lock of hair out of his eyes. "I think he hates me," he said in a voice devoid of feeling. "He wants to see me suffer."

"But why?" George seemed bewildered.

Valentine gave him a look, as if he had more to say but wasn't going to say it in front of Marissa. Cautiously she began to descend the creaky stairs. *I don't care*, she told herself. *Let them have their silly secrets.* She crossed to the front door, her shoes squelching with each step. *I want a warm bath and a warm fire and dry clothing and warm sheets with a hot water bottle.*

Outside, the rain had stopped. The afternoon was lighter, and the rain clouds were breaking up as the storm moved on. She might have thought it a big improvement, apart from the fact the wind was icy. It felt as if it was blowing right through her wet clothes to her bare, shivering skin.

Behind her Valentine and George came out of the house and stood under the portico. They both looked at her, then away again. George even flushed. Something had passed between them; something about her, Marissa decided, irritably. Well they could keep their secrets, see if she cared.

With as much dignity as she could muster, Marissa headed down the path through the garden, trying not to wince each time the rain-soaked foliage showered her with drops.

I wish I'd never come, she thought miserably. *I wish I'd stayed at home. Why do I want to marry a man who brings me to a monstrous tumbledown ruin with an overrun jungle for a garden and then makes me stand in the rain?*

A warm, strong hand closed on her arm, and a

large jacket was placed about her shoulders. It was far from dry but at least it was warm from his body, and just for a moment she allowed herself to breathe in his scent.

"Poor Marissa," he said, his voice deep and husky, with a smile in it.

"Not poor Marissa," she retorted. "Courageous Marissa. Marissa who saved you from drowning in the pond."

He was silent a moment, and then he bent closer, his breath in her ear, the warmth of it making her shiver despite herself. "Sweetest, dearest Marissa, thank you."

She hoped he meant it, but she wasn't sure. She glanced at him sideways and saw that he was watching her, a sparkle in his eyes. How could he be so . . . so *alive* after all that had happened?

"Does it rain on that hillside in Italy?" she asked blithely.

He grinned. "If it does there's always the villa to shelter in."

Marissa opened her mouth to ask if the villa had a bed, and then closed it again. Time for talk about beds later, when she was warm again, and when they were alone.

Chapter 27

Baron Augustus Von Hautt raised his telescope
to his eye and watched the passing of his
enemy. Lord Valentine Kent was on the road below,
ignorant of the fact that he was under observation.
The baron smiled. He'd returned to the house as
soon as Kent left it, creeping in unseen, settling himself by the window on the top story. He knew the
place well and today he'd used that knowledge to
make a fool of his enemy.

All his life he'd felt second best.

Well, soon that would change. He would be a
hero, someone others admired and listened to in
silent appreciation, the sort of man who was invited
everywhere. His life would become what it always
should have been, had fate been different. All he had
to do was find the Crusader's Rose and destroy Valentine Kent.

He used to think the two went together, that by
being the first to discover the rose after all these
years he would automatically blight Kent's future
happiness. But now he saw another possible avenue
for his revenge.

Marissa Rotherhild.

It had been clear to him from the first moment he saw her, as he stood looking into the candlelit rooms of Abbey Thorne Manor, that she was something out of the ordinary. A rare and precious treasure, like the Crusader's Rose itself. He'd seen her again at Montfitchet, and been even more struck by her.

That's when he'd decided to have her as well as the rose.

Well, why not? To be truly destroyed, Valentine Kent must lose everything he treasured—and Von Hautt believed Kent was enamored of Marissa Rotherhild. For years he'd watched him, secretly, and he'd never seen him like this, as if he was on the verge of an epiphany.

Augustus wanted nothing more than to ruin it. He hadn't meant to give away his plan, but while Kent lay on the ground in the garden, at Von Hautt's mercy, he hadn't been able to resist gloating a little. He'd leaned down and whispered, "The woman will be mine. Remember all you have lost while I am . . ." He'd used a filthy term, but one he knew Kent would understand. The coarseness of it added to the effect, despoiling what Kent believed was wholesome and pure.

Kent had promptly tried to throttle him but instead he'd fallen and struck his head. Not dead, though—Von Hautt had time to check before the brother came after him and he had to run.

Was Kent remembering his words now, as he hurried toward Bentley Green? Was he grinding his teeth in fury, imagining what would happen to his woman? Von Hautt smiled. He hoped so. He hoped Kent was sick with fear. Let him suffer.

Before the final confrontation.

Chapter 28

The landlord of the Fox and Hounds was obliging enough, especially when Valentine offered to pay extra for the carrying up of water for the hot baths. He made sure that Marissa was bustled upstairs first, a kindly maid fussing over her. Valentine and George settled down in the parlor with some brandy and a warm fire, awaiting the arrival of the local doctor.

"Well, he isn't really a doctor, but he makes do as one," the landlord said cryptically as he closed the door.

George grimaced at his brother. "I hope it's not some old warlock with a jar of leeches."

Valentine grunted, taking a gulp of his brandy, and watching his boots steam as he stretched them out before the fire. After a moment he said, "I'm going to get him, George."

George didn't ask who he meant. "Did he really say that?" he said quietly. "Perhaps you misheard."

"I didn't mishear," Valentine growled, glaring at him. "He said it deliberately, watching my reaction. It was me he wanted to hurt, not Marissa, but he's willing to use her."

"There's something deep here, Valentine. Who is Baron Von Hautt, really? What of his family, his past? We don't know much and I have a feeling we need to delve into who he is if we want to solve the mystery."

Valentine stared thoughtfully into the flames. "He's been around as long as me, he's about my age, and his family is Prussian. His father was a soldier, I think, but I can't swear to it. Someone told me once that his background was murky, and it doesn't surprise me. That's all I know for certain. I promise you I haven't done anything to make him swear revenge on me."

"So you haven't seduced his sister or stolen his family inheritance," George said thoughtfully. "It can't be anything obvious then, Valentine, but there is something. Perhaps it's time we found out just what his problem is." George looked up. "Oh by the way, was your rose in the garden at Beauchamp Place?"

Valentine shook his head. "Roses were few and far between."

"That's it then." George tried to sound cheerful but his sideways glance was wary.

Valentine said nothing. He didn't want to talk about his failure to find the rose. There were too many unknowns, too many decisions to be made, and he didn't want to face any of them just now. He'd deal with the problem of Von Hautt and then he'd decide what came next.

"I don't think Marissa should stay at Abbey Thorne," he said at last. "I want her to return to London with her grandmother, where she's safe."

George raised his eyebrows. "Good luck with that, brother."

Valentine gave him a baleful look. "You think she'll refuse?"

"I'd wager on it."

"Can't you persuade her?"

George looked pensive. "I'm beginning to realize I was mistaken in her character. She always seemed a fun sort of girl, undemanding, not complaining if a chap happened to be late or forgot to mention a boxing match he was going to. But now . . . I don't think we'd suit after all. I have a feeling the banns would hardly be called and she'd be nagging me to do something I didn't want to do."

Valentine was staring him. "Yes, you're probably right," he said at last, and turned back to the fire.

Typical of George to decide Marissa wasn't the woman he thought her, in the middle of a crisis. Still, it was one less worry for Valentine. Now he knew George wouldn't accuse him of stealing his ladylove; he might even be grateful to his brother for taking her off his hands.

Valentine tried to smile, but couldn't.

The memory of the baron's expression, the gleam in his eyes, was enough to set his anger bubbling and boiling all over again. Trying to steal the rose was one thing but threatening darling Marissa . . . well, that was quite another.

By the time Marissa had soaked in a hot bath and dried herself before a fire, her underclothing was also dry enough to be worn. Her outer gar-

ments were still too wet, so she had no choice but
to don a woolen dress that had once belonged to the
landlord's mother. It was a little big but not overly,
and the style was very old-fashioned, with the waist
several inches above Marissa's actual waistline, and
the skirt lacking the yards of cloth now so much
in vogue. Still, it was better than nothing, and she
felt able to enter the parlor feeling more like herself
rather than that tearful creature of the rainstorm at
Beauchamp Place.

The parlor was stuffy and warm, with a not unpleasant odor of drying cloth. George looked up at
her with a wry smile. He was standing by Valentine's
chair, while a stranger bent over him and examined
his head. If this was the doctor, Marissa thought, he
was old and grizzled and well into his retirement.

"Aye, you've had a nice bump on the head there,
m'lord," the fellow said, straightening up. He turned
his lined face toward Marissa, and smiled a kindly
smile, his eyes crinkling up.

"This is Miss Rotherhild," George introduced
them. "Marissa, this is Doctor Arnold." He widened
his eyes slightly.

"Doctor is a courtesy title," the man said, not
losing his good humor. "I am an animal doctor, Miss
Rotherhild, but the folk of Bentley Green call upon
me for most of their ills."

"Oh." Marissa didn't know whether she should
be appalled or grateful. "And how is Lord Kent,
Doctor?" she asked tentatively.

Valentine shuffled about at the sound of her voice.
"Perfectly well," he interrupted.

"He will soon recover, miss," Doctor Arnold assured her. "He is a strong and healthy young man, as fit as a horse."

George found that hilarious and doubled up with laughter. Doctor Arnold smiled at him with good humor, not at all insulted.

"Is it true it was Baron Von Hautt who struck you?" the doctor asked, and suddenly his smile was gone and the lines on his face deepened.

"Do you know him?" said Valentine.

He gave an unwilling nod. "Always a troubled soul, that one. But he had no one else and I was better than nothing, I suppose, after his grandmother passed on."

Marissa drew closer. "Is your name Beauchamp, sir?"

"Aye, it is. Arnold Beauchamp."

"Do you mean Von Hautt is a Beauchamp?" George cried.

"On his grandmother's side, aye. He used to visit her as a child and she'd tell him all about the family's past glories. Rubbish most of it, but he believed in it. I think it gave him something to hold on to after his father died at Waterloo."

Valentine stiffened. "My father died at Waterloo, too," he said.

"He still comes and stays in the house like it belongs to him. I've sat opposite him and listened to him planning to make the place as grand as before, with him king of his little kingdom."

"Perhaps he will," Marissa said.

But the old man shook his head. "He has no fortune, his title is a hollow one. After his father died the brother stepped in and took what was left, although he couldn't take the title. Augustus has nothing but dreams. As I said, he's a troubled soul."

More than a troubled soul, thought Marissa, remembering what he had done to Valentine. Whatever his problems Von Hautt could not be allowed to run amok any longer.

And from the expression on Valentine's face she knew he agreed.

When George went upstairs to take his bath, Marissa broached the subject.

"We must find him and stop him before he causes any more harm," she said, walking about restlessly in the stuffy parlor. "He's dangerous, Valentine."

Valentine was watching her pace back and forth, a frown between his brows, but when he spoke his words weren't what she expected. "What *are* you wearing, Marissa?"

She turned to stare at him. "My dress is wet, remember? I'm surprised you would bring that subject up after you broke your promise. The landlord found it for me. It belonged to his mother."

His mouth twitched but he smoothed it out when her eyes narrowed warningly. "It looks like something from a museum, but a very fetching something, I might add," he said hastily. "Perhaps they'll have something similarly museumlike for me."

"A doublet and stockings? I do hope so," she retorted. "And those shoes that curl at the toe."

"I think only jesters wore them," Valentine said. "A pity."

She sank down in the chair beside his and, kicking off the clogs her host had found for her while her shoes dried, lifted her stockinged feet to join Valentine's before the fire. They sat a moment in companionable silence as a clock ticked on the mantel.

"Do you think Baron Von Hautt will visit Doctor Arnold tonight?" she said at last, smothering a yawn. "He seems to be the only friend he has in Bentley Green."

"No. I think he will realize we mean to spring a trap on him and he'll stay away."

"Or he might think we'll think that and come anyway."

Valentine chuckled. "Your mind is torturous, minx, but nevertheless you may be right. I'll send George to stay with the old man just in case."

"George will love that," Marissa said, with a raised eyebrow.

"It's time he earned his place in the Kent family tree," Valentine replied unsympathetically.

"But you don't believe the Baron will go there?"

"No, I don't believe he will." He smiled at her and reaching out entwined her fingers with his.

Marissa turned to the window, where rain was still softly falling.

His fingers tightened gently on hers, bringing her attention back to him. "I'm sorry I broke my promise. I'll never do it again."

"I hope not," she said, but her heart had begun to beat a little erratically. Was he saying there would be more promises?

"The quest for the rose is over," he spoke quietly, without emotion.

Her gaze searched his. "And you haven't found it. I'm sorry, Valentine."

He bent his head to kiss the back of her hand, and smiled up at her. He looked weary, with shadows under his eyes, but there was also a gleam in his eyes that spoke of his refusal to let defeat bring him down.

"I haven't quite decided what it means to me," he admitted. "Disappointment, certainly. My quest has turned out to be a bit of a flop, I suppose. But I'm not as shattered as I might have expected to be. I did my utmost and if I failed then I did so honorably; if there is such a thing as an honorable failure."

"Valentine . . ."

There was a twist to his mouth that made him seem vulnerable and endearing. "Somehow after what we now know about Von Hautt the rose doesn't seem quite so important. More like a boyhood dream that I should have grown out of years ago."

"You're nothing like him, Valentine."

But she could see he didn't believe her, not entirely. There were so many parallels between the two men. She reached up to gently brush aside his hair, to better see the lump on his head.

"You'd never do this to anyone, Valentine, not even for the Crusader's Rose. I'm sorry that you didn't find it at Beauchamp Place."

He met her eyes, his own blazing.

"No, don't feel sorry for me. I'm far from needing any pity. I may not have found the rose, but I've found you. Actually, I should be celebrating. It took the ending of the quest, and Von Hautt, to make me realize how empty my life had become until you arrived at my door. I've been a coward, Marissa, hiding from life in case I get hurt again, but I'm not going to hide any longer. I'm going to face whatever comes my way."

Marissa felt her heart swell in her breast, full of emotion and passion for this man. Tears stung her eyes. "I'm glad," she said in a shaky voice.

There was a tap on the door and the call that supper had arrived. The meal was as good as before, and they ate heartily and then sat contentedly by the fire until it was time for bed. George went off, complaining, into the night, to spend his time keeping watch at Doctor Arnold's house.

"I shouldn't think he'll come," Valentine assured him.

"Oh, I wish he would!" George declared. "I'd like to show him what I think of him."

Valentine considered his brother and Marissa thought he might begin a homily on overly hasty behavior but instead all he said was, "Take care."

With George gone the room seemed very quiet, and when Valentine yawned, Marissa rose to her feet and wished him goodnight. He smiled at her sleepily. "See you in the morning, minx," he said.

Marissa hesitated, and then reached out to touch his cheek. "I don't know what I'd do if something happened to you, Valentine," she said, her dark eyes reflecting the firelight.

"Nothing will happen to me," he replied, but he reached up to take her hand in his. His fingers were warm, alive, comforting. Marissa trembled.

It was as if their passion, always so close to the surface, broke free. He pulled her down onto his lap, holding her close, his breath warm against her hair. "Marissa," he groaned.

Her mouth trembled as she lifted her face to his. "Earlier you spoke to me as if you had made a decision about our future," she said. "Tell me what you've decided, Valentine. I need to know."

The moment stretched out and then his arms tightened. "Let's go to bed, Marissa," he said in a deep, husky voice that took her breath away. "Let's go to bed right now."

Chapter 29

Her mouth was warm and passionate, and he kissed her as he lifted her in his arms, finding it difficult to stop long enough to open the door. The passageway was in darkness, only a dull murmur of sound coming from beyond another door that led out to the front of the building. He kissed her again, before starting up the narrow, creaking stairs to the landing, and then stopped to kiss her once more.

Marissa wrapped her arms about his neck, her fingers twining in his hair. "Mmm." She ran her tongue along his bottom lip, as if he were a delicious dessert. The soft warmth of her body shifted in his arms. He tightened his grip and moved toward his chamber, ducking his head under the lintel as he pushed open the door.

His bed was turned down, the pillows fluffed up, and a lamp burned low on a table. Valentine carried Marissa to the bed and kissed her again, before he lay her down on the mattress. She sank into it with a gasp, struggling to sit upright, but he didn't give her time to escape.

She gave a squeak as he landed beside her and then they both went still, staring into each other's eyes.

It struck him, as it had the first time he saw her, just how beautiful she was, with her flawless pale skin and dark hair. Her thick, dark lashes swept down over her velvet brown eyes, then lifted again, and he looked deep inside her. This was a woman who had felt alone and isolated, who'd sought to follow her own dreams, and make her own happiness, with a determination and passion and intelligence that he couldn't help but admire.

She would make him the perfect companion. They would never grow bored with each other, and although they may well argue they would always find a way to compromise. Despite the brevity of their acquaintance he knew now he couldn't live without her, and he wasn't going to fight with himself any longer.

"I love you," he said.

The corners of her full mouth lifted, and that irresistible dimple appeared. He bent and set his lips to it, and then kissed her mouth. She arched up against him, slipping her hands inside his jacket and then, as if that wasn't enough, tugged his shirt out from his breeches and touched his skin.

He shuddered, feeling the rush of blood to his head and his groin, taking all thought of caution with it. He reached for the fastenings of her prehistoric gown, fumbling at buttons and hooks and laces. Finally he tugged it over her head and flung it to the floor. They were both panting now.

"You may as well be wearing a medieval chastity belt," he groaned, flicking a finger over her underwear.

Marissa glanced down at herself and giggled. Then her face grew serious and she said, "I wonder if Richard de Fevre's wife was forced to wear a chastity belt before he left for the Crusades?"

"Taking the key with him, do you mean?" he mocked.

She looked appalled. "Would he have done that, Valentine? Left her like that for years? And what if he didn't return, what then?"

Valentine smiled. "I think the idea was to leave a spare key with a trusted friend or servant, so that his wife could be released if he was captured or killed."

"How unfair," Marissa retorted.

"Unfair in what way?" he asked, beginning to undo the buttons of her chemise, one by one, disclosing her pale skin and soft curves. A dark rose nipple butted his hand and his mouth watered.

"Unfair that de Fevre would force his wife to take a vow of chastity, whether she wanted to or not."

He'd opened her chemise fully now, and was working on her stays, fingers trembling slightly in his haste to have her naked.

"Perhaps she wore it willingly, Marissa."

Marissa looked uncertain, seeming not to notice he'd now divested her of her corset and was working on the ties of her bloomers. "I don't think so. Women are not great believers in being uncomfortable just to prove a point. They're practical creatures."

That made him stop and raise his eyebrows.

"Really? So you think I am a romantic dreamer with no notion of reality?"

"I think you are a little removed from the outside world, but that's to be expected of a man who is an expert in roses."

He sat back on his haunches and stared down at her, then he folded his arms for added effect. She blinked. He waited.

"Why have you stopped?" she said in a little voice.

"I thought you must want me to," he retorted.

She smiled. That dimple again. His heart began to beat quickly in his chest, echoing the beat of his blood as he looked down at her charming disarray.

"I'm a little nervous," she admitted. "I talk when I'm nervous."

"I've noticed."

Now she looked contrite, but there was a mischievous gleam in her eyes. "What can I do to make up to you, Valentine? There must be something you'd like me to do?"

"Well . . ." He pretended to consider the question. "You could take off your stockings for me. Slowly."

She bowed her head submissively. "Yes, Valentine."

He watched as she stretched out her leg, and reached down to untie the ribbons holding the stocking up over her knee. Slowly she rolled it down, taking her time, arching her foot. His gaze was fixed on the line of her leg but then he noticed her breasts were rocking gently with each movement she made, and it was too much for him. He reached for her, planting openmouthed kisses on her, finding a turgid nipple and drawing it in.

Marissa clasped his head and held him to her, her head thrown back and her eyes shut as she gave herself up to the wondrous sensation.

He found her other breast, giving it the same treatment, and then he was pushing down her bloomers, while she wriggled eagerly, trying to help. Her skin was feverish, and he could smell the musk of her arousal. It only added to his own need.

He nudged her thighs apart and began to stroke her slick flesh, playing with her, causing her to gasp and moan and press against him, seeking the release she knew he could give her. But this time Valentine knew it was going to be different. This time he was finally going to claim her.

He knelt above her, and began to remove his jacket. Now that he was no longer touching her, Marissa opened her eyes, pushing her hair back out of her face, where it had tumbled wildly. Her cheeks were flushed and her eyes gleamed softly. He drew his shirt over his head and tossed it after the jacket. Then his hands went to the buttons at his waist, while she watched with flattering attention.

His body was hard, straining toward her, and she reached out to grasp him in her hand, moving closer, focused on what she was doing. As he looked down at her, wary and yet excited almost beyond control, she began to lap at him with her tongue.

Valentine felt desire roar through him, drowning out everything, as her warm lips closed over the head of his cock. Bending over him as she was, he could see the smooth line of her back, the bones of her spine drawing his eye down to the rounded curves of her bottom.

He knew he could let her have her way, spill into her mouth, and she would not be shocked or outraged. But such pleasures were for later. Now he just wanted to take her as he'd dreamed of so often.

Gently he lifted her, hands spanning her waist, and as she gazed at him with passion blurred eyes, he began to kiss her mouth. She tasted of him, and there was something arousing about that, if he wasn't already aroused nearly beyond bearing. She fell backward into the soft mattress, taking him with her, and their bodies slid and pressed together, naturally shifting into the best fit.

Her nipples were hard little beads against his chest, and he bent to kiss her breasts, his hand reaching again for the heat between her thighs. She was ready and he put the head of his cock against her, easing himself the first inch. She didn't stop him or stiffen, rather she seemed to melt around him, urging him on to fulfillment.

"You must be patient," he said in a hoarse voice. "I don't want to hurt you."

He pushed further, feeling the resistance, and waited until any discomfort had passed. She groaned, hands sliding down to his buttocks and clasping him urgently. He was deeper now, and suddenly her maidenhead gave and he slid up to the hilt, nudging at her womb. She jolted and he felt her breasts rising and falling quickly, her hands still on him.

"Marissa," he said, hoping she was unharmed, hoping all was well.

She moved, just a little, experimentally, and when it didn't seem to hurt, she moved again. Her hot, tight body clenched around him and he groaned and thrust against her, his control slipping. Her breath was warm against his shoulder, and he felt her teeth nipping at him.

"Minx," he managed, as he began to move against her, with a mixture of urgency and tenderness.

Her breathing was quickening again, but this time it was passion, and he felt the telltale signs within her as her pleasure began to peak. He shifted slightly, nudging deep inside, his rhythm quickening, the muscles of his buttocks and thighs tightening with the effort. And then she began to cry out, arching her back and clutching at him frantically. With a groan of relief he let his own control slip, and felt himself spilling within her, the ecstasy shaking him and tumbling him, so that he clung to her.

"Valentine," Marissa whispered.

It was some time since either of them had spoken and she wouldn't have now except that she felt the need to say something.

He grunted, his hand resting on the curve of her hip, his face in her hair. He'd rolled over onto his side, his body still connected to hers, and held her in his arms while they caught their breath. Marissa could feel the tingles and tremors in her body still, the momentous pleasure they had experienced together. If she'd ever doubted they were meant for each other then she did no longer.

"You don't regret it?"

He lifted his head and opened one eye, peering blearily down at her. "Good Lord no! What a bloody silly question."

"Well, it was you who said only a cad would ruin me," she said mildly. "I thought I should ask."

He chuckled and hugged her closer. "I'd only be a cad if I didn't marry you after I'd ruined you."

"Is that a proposal?" she said quietly.

"Will you marry me, Marissa?" He was smiling but there was a seriousness in his expression that told her he was in earnest.

She could have accepted immediately; it was on the tip of her tongue to do so. But she wanted to wallow in the moment, enjoy the pure bliss of knowing her future happiness was certain. And, if she was really honest, there was still a tiny kernel of doubt. Her practical side was telling her, loudly, that she'd sworn never to marry a botanically inclined man, and here she was considering spending the rest of her life with one.

You'll be standing on rainy hillsides with freezing fingers while he ignores you and croons over his latest find . . .

No, he wouldn't do that!

Defiantly, Marissa nuzzled against his throat, enjoying his scent. Her leg was resting on his thigh, and now she felt his cock twitch against her. He moved as if to draw away, probably believing once was enough for a virgin, but she was not having that.

"First, can we do it again?" she asked innocently.

"Minx," he growled, clasping her in his arms.

"*Your* minx," she said, with the sense that she was burning her bridges, and then gasped as he began to show her all over again how wonderful they could be together.

Chapter 30

Valentine opened one eye. The room was still, apart from Marissa's gentle breathing as she slept. Any doubts he'd had were gone, laid to rest by the knowledge that he'd made the right choice. For a moment he allowed himself to enjoy the feel and sound of her, as she lay next to him, and to imagine what it would be like in the years ahead, going to bed with her and waking up to her every day and every night.

But there was something he must do first, a dark shadow that could not be allowed to intrude upon his happiness and Marissa's safety any longer.

He rose, stretching, and went to the window, lifting aside the blind to see outside. The yard was in shadow, moonlight barely penetrating beyond the crooked rooftops of neighboring buildings. As he'd expected, no one was about.

Making as little noise as possible he pulled on his clothing, and then sat down to put on his boots. Marissa didn't wake, for which he was grateful. She would argue with him and want to come with him, and he wasn't about to put her into any more danger. Which was why he hadn't told her what he intended.

She'd be angry about that, too, but he'd face her recriminations later. Running his hands through his hair, he went to the door. He glanced over his shoulder one last time, at the shape of Marissa in his bed, and smiled. Who would have thought his life would be transformed so swiftly and so completely by this woman?

Valentine wasn't a violent man, but if violence was necessary to stop Augustus from ruining their future then he would use it. He found his hands had folded into fists, and he opened them, forcing himself to be calm. Tonight he'd end this matter, one way or the other, he told himself, as he closed the door quietly behind him.

The landing was chill, and as he stood a moment getting his bearings, words echoed softly in his head.

"I will steal her, and when I do I will use her until every part of her smells of me. And even if she should live a hundred years and wash a hundred times every day she will never rid herself of my memory. And neither will you, every time you look at her and hold her and kiss her. You will think of me, Valentine."

Remembering made him icy with rage. Normally he thought of himself as a hot-blooded man with a fiery temper when it was roused, but not this time. The anger he felt toward Von Hautt was glacial, and he knew when he got hold of the other man he would find it difficult to control his fury.

The parlor was dimly lit, the fire had burned

down to mere coals. He warmed his hands as he waited for the innkeeper to bring him a tankard of ale while his horse was being saddled. They'd made the arrangement last night, out of Marissa and George's hearing, and now it was time.

"Your horse is ready," the man said, entering the parlor, his eyes reddened with lack of sleep and his hair on end.

"Good," Valentine said, taking the ale and gulping it down.

"How is your head, sir?"

He'd forgotten about his head, he'd had far more enjoyable things to think of. "Better, thank you."

"Are you sure you don't want me to send for your brother, so's he can go with you?" he said.

"Quite sure." Valentine noticed he didn't offer to come himself, but even if he had he would have refused the offer. This was something he wanted to do on his own.

The horse's breath was steamy in the damp air, and quickly he mounted and set the animal at a walk out of the stable and into the yard. Water dripped from the roof and ran down his back, and he grimaced, shrugging his shoulders. A light rain was still falling but it wasn't enough to worry him and he set off.

The road from the village to Beauchamp Place was empty and Valentine set his horse at a gallop beneath the night sky. The worst of the rain might be gone but the road gleamed wet and there were numerous puddles, reflecting the moon as it darted behind clouds and peered out at him through the cold mist. Swaths of white hung in the dips and hollows, and seemed to spin like webs about the horse's hooves. Valentine rode on.

Soon the dark shape of the manor house loomed to his right, and as he slowed to observe it more carefully he spotted a gleam of lamplight in one of the upstairs windows. Just a brief flicker before it was hidden again. He was there then, his arch enemy; Baron Von Hautt who hated Valentine with all his heart.

It was time to confront him and discover why.

Marissa opened her eyes and moved in the bed. At once she felt unfamiliar aches and twinges, as if her body belonged to someone else. And then she remembered. In a way she *was* someone else. She was Valentine's lover. She had given herself willingly to him and stepped into a new phase of her life.

As she thought of the pleasure they had taken with each other her smile grew. She could hear the deep rumble of his voice in her head: *Minx.* He'd asked her to marry him. She felt immensely privileged and lucky. Valentine had tried to convince her he was staid and tedious and she'd grow tired of him, but she knew that wasn't how she saw him at all. She had finally realized that it didn't even matter that he was involved in botanical pursuits—surely she could deal with that? She would even join him on his expeditions—she pictured sleeping under the stars in Valentine's arms.

But Marissa had been on too many expeditions with her parents to believe such things were necessarily romantic. Could she really endure journeys to uncomfortable and far-flung places for the sake of being the wife of this admirable man? Marriage would be a fine balance, between pleasing herself and pleasing her husband, but as long as she didn't begin to resent the latter it might work.

When Marissa began her husband hunting she'd imagined finding herself marrying George, but it had all turned out differently. Anyway, she would have been miserable with George. In nearly all ways, Valentine was her perfect mate, and if she refused him then she would be miserable for the rest of her life. She must take that leap . . . or regret it forever.

It was time to say a long and lingering yes.

Reaching out her hand, she expected to touch his warm flesh, and to draw herself closer to him.

He wasn't there.

Her first thought was he must have risen for some reason and would be back soon, but when the moments ticked by and nothing happened, she began to worry. She sat up, pushing her hair out of her eyes and looking about her. The room was empty. Dark and cold and empty. Even his side of the bed felt chilled, as if he'd been gone for a long time.

"Valentine?" she called softly, knowing even as she did so that he wouldn't answer. She would have felt his presence if he was close by, and she did not.

Tossing back the covers, she slid from the bed to the floor, shivering. The blind was slightly disarranged and she went to the window to look through the small, smeared panes.

The yard was empty.

Something was stirring in her, a whisper of fear, and she stilled to listen to it. Where could he be?

Had George sent for him? Or had he gone to George to check how he was doing? It seemed unlikely, and surely he would have said something to her if the explanation was that simple. Instead he'd crept out of the bedchamber, silent as a ghost, not wanting her to wake and . . .

She frowned. Not wanting her to ask questions and perhaps argue with his choices?

Of course!

He'd gone to find Augustus Von Hautt and he didn't want Marissa to come with him.

Feverishly she began to pull on her clothing, the hand-me-down dress over the top of her underwear and stockings. She would need her boots and a cloak or some thick outer garment to keep her warm. And a horse, too. She couldn't follow Valentine without a horse.

He'd gone back to Beauchamp Place, she knew it, the knowledge solid and sure within her. He believed the baron had returned there after they left and he was going to capture him and . . . But what else he meant to do Marissa wasn't sure. That was another reason she really needed to find him and make certain nothing desperate happened between the two of them, more especially to Valentine.

Very worried now, she went to find the chamber belonging to the innkeeper and tapped on the door. She had to knock louder and repeatedly before it was finally opened. The man looked grumpy and didn't try to hide it behind any false politeness.

"I need a horse and a cloak and my boots," she informed him in a firm voice, before he could begin to complain. "Lord Kent has set off alone into danger and he needs me."

He wanted to argue. She could see it in his eyes and his impatient shuffling, but he must have seen something in her face that persuaded him he would be wasting his time. Eventually he shrugged and sent her to the parlor while he dealt with her requests.

Marissa paced back and forth in front of the dying fire, the moments stretching out while she imagined all sorts of horrid things happening to Valentine, but it really wasn't very long before the innkeeper returned with her dried boots and an old musty cloak that swallowed her up, and told her he would be saddling a horse for her with his own hands.

After he'd gone his wife crept into the room, her plump face creased with worry.

"You'll take care now, miss?" she said, eyes anxious beneath the frill on her nightcap. "A young lady like yourself shouldn't be riding alone in the dark, you know."

"I will be careful," Marissa replied, lacing up her boots, "but I must go. I can't sit here and wait and wonder what is happening."

The woman nodded as if she understood. She glanced at the doorway, and then stepped closer and pressed something into Marissa's hands. Her voice was a whisper. "I've had this since we was robbed five year ago. It is clean and working, so don't fear it will explode in your face. If you need to use it, aim a little to the right of your target, as it don't fire exactly straight."

Marissa looked down. She was holding a silver pistol with a pearl handle, small enough to be concealed in her hand. When she looked up questioningly at the woman, she found her blushing.

"A gentleman give it to me," she said, eyes flickering sideways. "My husband don't know, so please don't tell him, miss."

Ah, a lover, perhaps? Someone who'd cared enough about her to ensure her safety? Marissa smiled and reached to touch her hand reassuringly. "Thank you," she said. "You are very kind. I will only use it if I must, and it will remain a secret between the two of us."

"Well," the woman blushed, "I'm glad. T'ain't every day we get to have a lord stay at the Fox and Hounds."

"Aye, just as well," her husband muttered behind her, making her jump guiltily. "Been run off our feet with all his orders we have."

Marissa slipped the pistol into her pocket, out of sight. The pair of them accompanied her to the stable and watched her ride out into the yard, the horse's hooves clattering loudly on the cobbles. She thanked them again and kicked the beast into a canter, and then a gallop, her borrowed cloak flapping about her.

She remembered the way but even so everything looked different at night. There were odd shadows and shapes, as if what was ordinary by day had suddenly become threatening and extraordinary.

"You're being silly," she told herself firmly, as the miles to her destination shortened. "Valentine needs you. Just keep remembering that. He needs you . . ."

* * *

Valentine had left his horse hidden at the edge of the garden and made his way through narrow paths and overgrown tunnels toward the front door. He planned to test it first and if it was locked then he would try the back door that led to the servants' stairs.

The light was still plainly visible, a soft glow through the broken shutters in one of the upper windows. Possibly Von Hautt didn't realize the lamp was showing or that the shutter was broken, but Valentine thought it more likely that the man was so arrogant he did not consider the necessity for circumspection.

He reached the front door and stood a moment, listening, but there was nothing more than the soft patter of rain and the creaking of the crickets from the garden. Resting his hand on the damp-warped paneling, he gave the door a push. It remained shut. Next he rested his shoulder against the paneling and pushed harder. This time the door moved, slightly, inward, but it was as if something was preventing it from opening fully.

Setting his boots at an angle against the surface of the porch, he gathered his strength and shoved the paneling, hard. This time it moved further but there was a tremendous groaning, grating sound that echoed through the entire house.

Valentine froze.

He knew, with a sense of grim acceptance, that the baron must have heard it. Even if he was sleeping such a hideous noise would wake him at once. His plan to catch his enemy unawares was now impossible. He could abandon it and return to the inn or carry on regardless.

Making up his mind swiftly, he peered through the gap in the door. There was a dresser that had been set against it and had now moved enough to allow him to squeeze in. Valentine paused a moment, holding his breath, but there was no sound or movement from the stairs, and he quickly crept across the entrance to one of the doors and slipped inside, pressing himself to the wall behind it.

Just in time.

The stair treads groaned as someone descended. Valentine set his eye against the crack in the half-open door. At first he could only see a shadow, but as the figure moved closer he was able to make out Augustus Von Hautt, his gray hair silver in the faint moonlight from the high windows, wearing the same long jacket over his riding clothes. It was only as he turned to look about him that Valentine saw the pistol in his hand.

For what seemed a long time the baron peered into the shadows, rather like a hunting animal seeking its prey, and then he moved toward the rooms on the other side of the hall and began, systematically, to search them.

It would only be a matter of time until he found Valentine.

There was a chance, however, he could get away while the baron was in one of the other rooms. Valentine waited until he was out of sight, and quickly came through the door, meaning to make his way into the shadows farther down the hall. He'd only taken a couple of strides when the worst happened.

"Halt!"

Slowly he turned to face his enemy.

Von Hautt was standing, booted legs apart, the pistol trained on him, a smile on his youthful face. "Ah, Valentine," he said, with deep satisfaction. "I hoped it might be you."

Valentine found himself rigid with tension and he forced his muscles to relax. He needed to get the baron off his guard.

"I saw your footprints in the dust," the baron went on, waving the barrel of his pistol in the direction of the floor. "But I thought it best to play a game with you, let you think you could escape. You are behaving a little like a rat in a trap, Valentine. I had thought better of you. Why did you not call out. Face me man-to-man."

Valentine gestured at the pistol. "For the very reason I see before me now. You are armed, Von Hautt, and I am not. I do not trust you."

Von Hautt looked insulted. "You do not trust me?" he said haughtily. "That is ironic, my friend, considering how your family has treated mine in the past."

Valentine tried to understand what he meant but could not. His bafflement must have been obvious, and it made Von Hautt angry.

"Do not pretend you do not understand!" he shouted. "I know you are well aware of what your father did, and the consequences for me. Do you think I would allow you to escape the punishment you deserve? Do you?"

And he raised the pistol until the barrel was aimed at Valentine's heart, his finger tightening on the trigger. Valentine felt light-headed, and yet he could not run. He could not move. Marissa, he thought, with an ache of longing. The life he'd dreamed of, the happy future he'd imagined with her, would never now come to pass.

Chapter 31

Marissa saw the house at last. It really did look like a dark bird of prey against the sky. The moon had slipped beneath the clouds and the rain had returned, just lightly, but enough to cause the cloak to become damp and her face damper as she struggled to see ahead. Now she turned the horse up the narrow lane to the gate where she had been earlier today, and saw that Valentine had left his own mount hidden by the overgrown garden.

Seeing it there was comforting. He was here after all. It was only as she glanced up at the manor house that she saw the wedge of light coming through the shutters in the upper window, and her heart sank again.

Augustus Von Hautt was here as well.

Quickly she climbed over the gate, jumping down onto the muddy ground, and began to make her way toward the house. As she drew closer to the portico she saw that the front door was ajar, leaving a black and sinister gap. She hesitated, uncertain whether to approach any closer in case someone was waiting for her on the other side, but then she heard the voices.

Two voices. Although she could not make out what they were saying she recognized one of them instantly as Valentine's, and the other she was almost certain was the baron's.

They were inside the house, beyond the narrow opening in the door. Marissa crept closer, onto the portico, and edged toward the voices.

"Why should I believe you?" the baron shouted suddenly, making her jump. Valentine replied, sounding calm and unflustered, and she knew he was trying to defuse the dangerous situation.

She peeped through the gap and into the house only to pull back almost immediately with shock. But she'd seen enough.

Valentine was seated on the stairs, hands clasped loosely between his knees, head tipped to the side as though considering what he'd been told. Von Hautt was standing before him, his back to Marissa, but she could see he was holding a pistol pointed in Valentine's direction.

Her own hand slid into her pocket and closed around the petite weapon the innkeeper's wife had given her. Peering at it in the faint moonlight, she managed to cock the firing mechanism. It was just possible that she may be able to slip through the gap in the door and creep in behind the baron, taking him by surprise, forcing him to surrender his pistol.

And if he refused to surrender? Or threatened her?

Marissa knew she would have to shoot him.

"Your father seduced my mother and abandoned her," the baron was saying bitterly. "When I was born she died, leaving me to the scorn of my relatives. My father hated me, too, because I was not his. But I am your brother, Valentine. You cannot deny me that, at least."

His words were wild, bizarre, and as far as Marissa knew completely untrue. Where could he have got such a story? From the expression on Valentine's face he was wondering the same thing.

"Did you know my father was also a seeker after the Crusader's Rose?" the baron went on. "He had heard the legend from my mother's family, that one of her distant ancestors helped to bring the rose back to England after the Crusades, and he wanted to find it. He was told of your father, Valentine, and that he, too, was on the quest."

"I didn't know," Valentine said with feeling. "Why didn't you tell me this before?"

"Because I hate you," Von Hautt spat. "You would take everything from me, if you could. It is I who should be Lord Kent. I am the eldest born son. But how to prove it? How to satisfy your English blue bloods that I am as good as them."

"I assure you, Von Hautt, my father is not yours. It simply cannot be. My father was never in Prussia in his life."

"Because he told you so?" Von Hautt mocked. "You are a fool. Of course it is true. My grandmother told me the truth when I was a boy. She said my father was a wealthy and aristocratic gentleman, a lord, and that he lived close by Bentley Green in an old manor house and that he also had an interest in roses. Who could it be but your father?"

Valentine looked away, as if considering the question, but he was clearly finding it difficult to answer without antagonizing the baron.

Marissa moved into the gap, careful not to let her cloak brush against the warped wood. At first she was half hidden by the dresser that seemed to have been used to bulwark the door, but she knew she couldn't stay there indefinitely.

"I wanted to find the rose before you, to prove to you I was the better of the two of us. I wanted to be like one of the knights of old, honorable and good. You believed that, too, didn't you?"

"When I was a boy, yes, I did feel like that," Valentine said, sounding as if his throat was dry. "But now I see there are other things more important."

"You are wrong. You don't deserve to find it."

"At least I didn't cheat and steal."

Von Hautt went white.

"You have a spy in my house! Tell me who it is?" Valentine roared, rising up from the stairs.

Von Hautt's grip on his pistol tightened and he took up a firing stance. "Sit down!" he shouted.

Marissa's heart was thudding. The two men were yelling at each other, their voices echoing up into the dusty heights of the old house. The tension grew unbearable. There was no time to wait; it must be now. She came around the dresser toward them, knowing they wouldn't hear her anyway with the noise, but she'd reckoned without the moonlight.

She hadn't realized the clouds had cleared away and the moon had come out, bright and beaming, and was shining through the gap in the door behind her. As she moved her shadow stretched across the floor and fell upon the men.

Von Hautt spun around, eyes wide, the pistol wavering as he saw her. There was a moment, just a moment, when she read the shock and fury in his gaze, and then Valentine called her name and was running toward her and she knew if she didn't fire now then one or other of them would die.

She pressed the trigger.

The retort wasn't very loud. Von Hautt had not fired and she saw that he was still upright, still standing facing her and Valentine, who by now had reached her.

Von Hautt looked down at his torso. "You shot me, Miss Rotherhild," he said in wonderment. There was a hole on the left side, but very small, and although blood was beginning to seep onto his clothes it was very little. He put his hand over the wound and actually laughed. "Next time you play the heroine, you must use a real gun and not a toy," he teased.

"Put your pistol down, Von Hautt," Valentine said firmly. "It is over."

The baron tipped his head to the side. "What is over, brother? The quest for the rose? Maybe. But I am determined your family will recognize me for who I am."

Marissa's hand had stolen into Valentine's and she felt his fingers squeeze hers. For comfort or for warning? She glanced up at him and couldn't decide.

"I wish I could recognize you, Von Hautt. I will need to investigate the matter further. But I swear to you I have never before heard of the things you are telling me."

The bitterness in Von Hautt's smile made him

almost ugly. His strange cold eyes slid to Marissa and narrowed. .

"But you see, brother, that isn't good enough. My mother should have had justice, but she died with the condemnations of her family and her husband ringing in her ears, the same sneers and jibes I have heard all my life. I do not forgive. I want justice. An eye for an eye."

Valentine seemed to know what was coming. Marissa felt his body stiffen, felt the surge of energy within him. His hand on hers tightened painfully. "No," he said.

"Don't move, Valentine," the baron said in an icy voice.

"What you're suggesting is monstrous," Valentine growled, and pushed Marissa behind him. "I warn you, I will not allow you to touch her."

Understanding came to her as she stood, frozen, at his back. Von Hautt meant to seduce her as he believed Valentine's father had seduced his mother, only in this case there would be no seduction. Von Hautt would take her as he'd taken Lady Long-hurst—brutally and without pity.

She pressed her face into Valentine's jacket, finding comfort in his solidarity. "I want to marry you, Valentine," she whispered. "I'm so sorry I made you wait for my answer."

He glanced back at her and their eyes met.

"And I want you to know how much I love you," she said, her voice breaking. "In case . . . in case . . ."

"I will never let him hurt you," he said gruffly.

"Monstrous?" the baron was too busy ranting to

notice their private conversation. "Shouldn't your father have thought of that before he destroyed my mother?"

"Von Hautt," Valentine said wearily, "how can I make you understand that I am completely ignorant of any wrongdoing by my family to yours?"

"You're my brother," he cried, and there was something dangerous and, at the same time wounded, in his tone.

Valentine fell silent.

Marissa dared to peer around her bulwark. Von Hautt appeared to be swaying from side to side. The pistol was still pointed at them, but he was having difficulty keeping it level. And his face was paler, with a shine of sweat on his skin. Her gaze dropped lower and, with a cry of horror, she saw that the hand he was holding over his wound was now red with blood.

"You need a doctor! Please, let us help you, Baron."

He turned to stare at her as if he'd forgotten she was there.

"Yes," Valentine added, in that same soft tone. "Let us get you help, Augustus. Look at yourself. You're losing a great deal of blood."

He looked down in surprise. "But it was such a little hole," he muttered. "How could such a little hole bleed so much?"

Valentine took a step forward and then another. "Come, brother," he said, "let me help you."

The baron stumbled, losing his footing, and then his legs gave way completely and Valentine caught him as he fell, the pistol clattering to the floor. Carefully Valentine eased him down on the floor, while Marissa knelt beside them.

The baron's eyes fluttered and then opened wide. He stared up at Valentine and then he smiled.

"Brother," he whispered.

Chapter 32

Old Doctor Arnold finished washing his hands in the bowl by his side and began to dry them carefully. His gaze rested on his patient lying still in the bed, the covers folded neatly over his chest, his face as unmoving as the effigy on a tomb.

"Will he recover?" Marissa said anxiously.

Valentine took her hand in his. "It isn't your fault," he assured her, but he could see by her expression that she felt differently. "You had no choice," he went on firmly. "He was beyond reasoning with. You saved our lives, Marissa."

"Perhaps he wouldn't have harmed me after all," she said, without much conviction.

"He would have tried, but I wouldn't have allowed it. He'd have had to shoot me first." His words sounded heroic, very different from the man he'd always thought himself, but Marissa made him feel like a hero—capable of anything.

She gave a woebegone smile, tears sparkling in her eyes, and wished everyone would just go away so that he could hold her as he longed to.

"I have hopes he'll recover," the doctor interrupted.

"I've done what I can but I'd be happier if he could be seen by someone more, hmm, specialized."

"Of course. We will see to it," Valentine spoke with authority. "Can he be moved?"

"Better not," the old man said. He reached out and placed his gnarled hand on the baron's brow, and it was like a caress. "Is what you've said really true? Did he say those things about his mother?"

Valentine nodded. "Yes."

Doctor Arnold shook his head. "I blame his grandmother for filling his head with such nonsense. I know there was talk of Augustus being a by-blow from his mother's affair with a fellow officer of his father's, but it had nothing to do with your father, my lord. That was his grandmother's doing, trying to make a silk purse from a sow's ear. I think Augustus must have imagined the rest. Poor troubled boy."

"What's important now is to help him recover physically," Valentine said.

"And then what? I have heard of the terrible thing he did to Lady Longhurst. Perhaps it would be better if he died."

Valentine felt Marissa's fingers tighten involuntarily in his, and knew the baron dying wouldn't be better for her. He'd cursed himself for going off to capture Augustus. He'd been furious, eager to come to blows with the man, hoping he would not meekly hand himself over until Valentine had got a few good blows in. What he hadn't expected to feel was pity. The baron might be a dangerous lunatic but he was also a lost soul.

His quest to find the Crusader's Rose would never

seem the same again. It was time to put it away and concentrate on the here and now, the people in his life who mattered, the woman he loved.

The crackle of the fire brought him back from his thoughts.

"We will see to his comfort, whatever happens," Valentine assured Doctor Arnold. "I will take responsibility for him, never fear."

"You are very good, my lord."

Comforted, the old man rose and after another glance at his young relation, left the room. Valentine followed him out, and when he returned he found Marissa seated by the bed. She looked up, and there were dark shadows under her eyes.

"George has gone to London to bring the best medical man he can find back to Bentley Green," Valentine said. "The innkeeper's wife is a good and reliable woman, and she will watch Von Hautt. Doctor Arnold is nearby as well. There is nothing more we can do, my love."

"I know. I know you have done everything in your power, and more, to save him. I know he is dangerous and disturbed and he has done terrible things, but there is something horribly sad about his story, Valentine."

"Yes."

They were silent for a moment, both lost in their own thoughts.

"Can we go home now?" Marissa said softly. "I would like to go home, Valentine."

He smiled. He did not ask her where she meant; he already knew it was Abbey Thorne Manor that was home for them both.

* * *

There was a great deal to tell Lady Bethany and Lord Jasper, and arrangements to be made for the care of Von Hautt. The doctor George brought with him to Bentley Green thought the baron would be better off in a private sanitarium where he would receive all the care and attention he required, as well as be watched around the clock, and he was moved there at once.

"I'm sorry, but I can't feel for him," Lady Bethany said, as they sat down to dinner a week later. "And what will your parents say, Marissa, when they hear? They will blame me, you'll see. It will be all my fault."

"Perhaps we can distract them with some good news," Valentine interrupted, looking a little self-conscious.

They all turned to him, a mixture of surprise and anticipation on their faces. George, with whom he'd already shared the news, chuckled.

"I expect to hear myself thanked in the wedding speeches," he said smugly, "because without me this would never have happened."

Valentine gave his brother a long-suffering look. They'd discussed the matter at length and he was still doubtful whether George had told him the truth—that he'd engineered the whole thing for Valentine's sake—or he was simply saving face. Whatever the case he was glad George bore him no ill-feelings; indeed quite the opposite.

Lady Bethany was beaming. "Wedding speeches? Oh, Marissa, does that mean . . . ?"

"Good heavens, Kent! Congratulations to you. To you both."

Smiling, Marissa and Valentine accepted their good wishes with obvious pleasure.

"Morris! Fetch the best champagne," George ordered. "Lord Kent is to be married!"

Morris looked properly astonished, but there was a satisfied gleam in his eye as he wished them well. When the champagne was brought and the toast made, George demanded to know what date the wedding would be set for. "As I may have to rearrange my social schedule," he explained thoughtfully.

His brother snorted, but before he could offer his own observations on George's schedule, Morris cleared his throat and intervened.

"I think, my lord, it depends on how soon and how large you wish the wedding to be."

Valentine glanced at Marissa.

"My answer to that is as soon as possible," he replied.

"Then, if you forgive me, m'lord, it would be difficult to arrange a large wedding in limited time."

"What about a small wedding?" he asked, beginning to look a little desperate.

"We could manage a date one month hence," the indefatigable Morris said evenly.

"A whole month!" Valentine cried.

"Any sooner and I fear the celebration might be lacking. I should dislike it very much if Abbey Thorne Manor was not at its best for the occasion. And if Your Lordship and miss require suitable clothing for the ceremony, there are seamstresses and tailors to be consulted," Morris went on firmly. "I presume you do want to look spick-and-span on the day, my lord? If you do not look like a proper bridegroom then I fear I will not be able to take charge of the arrangements."

It sounded like a warning and Valentine sighed. "Very well, if I must, Morris. I will leave it in your capable hands."

"Oh yes, Marissa, you must have a bride's dress!" her grandmother declared, looking twenty years younger. "How exciting! Your mother refused to allow me any part in her wedding. They were married in a forest and she held a bouquet of ferns, pouf! This time I insist upon being consulted before any decisions are made."

"Of course, Grandmamma," she said quietly. "I have no argument with that. Your taste is impeccable."

Lady Bethany barely had time to preen. "My dear, we must go up to London immediately and begin. Where will the ceremony be held?"

"In the village church," Valentine said quickly. Then, with a wry glance at Marissa, "If that is acceptable to you, Marissa?"

She wasn't meeting his eyes, which worried him, but her voice was adamant. "The village church would be perfect. I don't want it in London. Then Father and Mother would feel obliged to invite all of their botanical friends."

Lady Bethany shuddered. "Oh lord, yes, how revolting. Of course some of them will still turn up, you know that. They will probably set about collecting botanical specimens in the churchyard. No, we must keep it small, and hope for the best."

"I—I would like my friends from Miss Debenham's to come, but other than that . . ." Marissa said.

"It will be necessary to invite some of the local families," Valentine said. "And George and Jasper," he added with a grin. "Afterward we will take our honeymoon on the Island of Reunion, or Bourbon as the French are currently calling it."

Valentine was becoming rather worried about his wife-to-be's lack of joy in this talk of the wedding, and he was glad to see Marissa's face brighten at the mention of the honeymoon. "Why there?"

"Because it is a paradise, my love, and you deserve a paradise."

"And there are a great many roses growing there," George added mockingly.

"Well, yes, there *are* roses," Valentine admitted, with a frown at his brother. "We may need to travel overland through France and Spain, and perhaps even the deserts of Arabia. We may be gone for a very long time."

Suddenly he was no longer certain whether he was doing the right thing. Perhaps Marissa would prefer a honeymoon in Brighton or Cornwall. Doubts grew inside him and for a moment Vanessa's poison bubbled up, threatening to ruin all his happiness.

Marissa's hand rested on his, her smile warmer than the sunlight through the window, soothing his fears. "I shall love it, Valentine." Her smile faded slightly. "But are you sure you can spare the time away from your work? Your studies?"

"I believe my work can wait," he assured her.

"Then, yes, I would love to travel with you to Bourbon."

George shook his head in despair. "I had thought better of you, Marissa. Does this mean you have been infected with the disease of rose collecting?"

Marissa laughed but to Valentine it sounded slightly forced. "Not at all, although I do admit to a partiality to their scent."

"In some parts of the world, I believe, women bathe in rose petals steeped in water," Valentine said to no one in particular.

Marissa bowed her head but he saw by her wicked smile that she was not expecting to take such a bath alone.

Lady Bethany was still mulling over "the dress" and had taken a small notepad from her reticule and was writing upon it with a pencil. Jasper watched her, bemused, but with a fond glint in his eye. He was not such a selfish creature that he wanted his ladylove's complete attention, especially when he knew this wedding gave her such pleasure. Who would have thought both he and Kent would fall in love like this?

Abbey Thorne Manor was about to enter a new era and Jasper was glad to be a part of it.

But the question of the Crusader's Rose niggled at the back of his mind, reminding him of the unfulfilled quest. A pity it would never now be found, but at least they had done their utmost to discover the truth.

And besides, if it hadn't been for the rose then

Valentine would never have met Marissa, and he would never have met Lady Bethany.

"What did George mean? That this was all his doing?" Marissa demanded, curled beside Valentine as they sat in the candlelit darkness of the yellow salon.

He explained how George now insisted their meeting had been part of his plan to find the perfect wife for his brother. "I don't know whether to believe him or not, but he insists it is the truth."

Marissa was inclined to be annoyed at first, feeling herself used, but when she saw that actually Valentine was touched that his brother thought so much of him that he'd gone to such lengths, she couldn't stay cross.

"I will have something to say to him next time we meet," she said with a thin smile. "The perfect wife indeed!"

"But you are," Valentine murmured, bending to kiss her softly on the lips. "Perfection in all things."

"Now you know that isn't true," she retorted, flushing. "If you really believe that you will be sadly disappointed."

He tried to hush her with another kiss. "I will never be disappointed, minx."

"Valentine, please, I'm serious," she said with a searching look. "If you think I am perfect then I will become seriously worried."

He laughed as if she'd made a joke, and drew her closer.

Marissa gave up, resting her head on his chest.

She wished she could put into words the confusion and doubt. The truth was, this sense of panic had first assailed her when Valentine began to talk about the wedding. He'd said he wanted a small wedding, as soon as possible, as if he was afraid she might change her mind and bolt. She knew that wasn't really true—he just wanted to be with her, as she did him, and it seemed as if the formal arrangements were getting in his way. But there was a sense of being rushed, perhaps even forced into the marriage, before she was ready.

What if she was making a mistake?

Marissa was beginning to feel trapped, but when she thought of the alternative she knew she didn't want to escape. The trouble was, at the moment, she didn't know what she wanted. Except perhaps to let things be—to enjoy herself and forget about the future.

Everything was happening so fast.

"I will accompany you back to London." Valentine's voice interrupted her growing desperation, and she was glad.

"Yes."

"I have to speak to Von Hautt anyway."

She looked up at him anxiously. "I suppose you do."

"Not just because of what has happened, Marissa, but because of all the things he knew about me. About us. Someone in my house is a spy and I need to discover who it is. I want to know, when you come to live here with me as my wife, that you will be safe."

His words soothed her, reminding her of why she

loved him and wanted to marry him. "Do you still have no idea who it is, Valentine?"

He shook his head. "No idea. Most of my servants have been here for years, some of them decades. I can't imagine any one of them turning traitor."

"Perhaps they don't think of it like that. Perhaps their loyalty is to Baron Von Hautt for some reason or another."

"Well, I cannot tolerate anyone in my house whose loyalty is not primarily to me. To us."

"Do you think this person, whoever they are, would harm anyone, Valentine? Surely not."

Valentine thought it possible, but he didn't want to alarm Marissa anymore, so he shook his head and said he didn't think so. But as he held her soft, warm body to his, he knew that it was very important to persuade Von Hautt to tell him the truth before the wedding.

If anything were to happen to Marissa . . .

"What is it?" she asked, looking up at him with wide, dark eyes. "Valentine you're trembling!"

He caught her searching hands, holding them firmly in his. "Did I tell you how much I love you?" he said earnestly. "And how much I'm looking forward to you being my wife?"

"Have I told you how much I'm looking forward to *being* your wife? And how much, how very much, I love you?"

Their kiss was full of wild passion, almost as if they were afraid it might be their last, and a raging desire caught hold of them. There was no time to do more than lock the door, and then Valentine lowered her down onto the sofa and began to undress her, kissing every inch of flesh as if it was newly discovered.

Marissa, lost in the touch and feel and taste of him, felt the first dizzying tug of completion as he used his fingers and lips on her, before thrusting deep, not slow and gentle this time but urgently, roughly. They both groaned at the end, clutching each other, gasping for breath.

For the first time Marissa understood the fragility and pain of love, as well as the pleasure. What if she were to lose Valentine? Guilt over her doubts filled her. It would serve her right if she did lose him.

"Marissa, what is it?" he murmured, and she realized she was clinging to him far too tightly.

"Nothing," she said, with a smile that didn't quite remove the worry in his eyes. "Everything is perfect, Valentine. How could it be otherwise?"

But he knew her too well and he sensed the doubts that she did not dare to speak aloud. Marissa prayed she could find some peace within herself before her wedding day arrived.

Chapter 33

London was warm, and dusty with the rush of traffic through the busier parts of the city, while the quieter squares drowsed in the sunshine, their parks and gardens a place for sitting and strolling and enjoying the shade. Valentine had brought his own equipage and he and his brother went directly to their London house in Mayfair, while Marissa and Lady Bethany returned to the Rotherhild house in Chelsea.

"You are very quiet, my dear," said Marissa's grandmother. "Are you worried that your parents will not like your intended? I'm sure they will heartily approve of him."

"But it is their approval I'm afraid of, Grandmamma! He is exactly the sort of man they will love, and therefore the sort of man I always swore I would never, never marry."

Lady Bethany chuckled. "I see what you mean. Well, all is not lost yet. Perhaps we will discover some dreadful flaw in his character that will set them against him, and then you can elope with him."

The idea had its merits, and Marissa found herself

considering it seriously. But no, how could she? They were to be married in the village church near Abbey Thorne Manor before her close friends and family, it was all settled—in Valentine's mind, anyway, she thought disloyally.

"Marissa?" her grandmother repeated for the third time, beginning to look worried. But it was too late to tell her what was really going on in her mind. The door was opening to them and her father, Professor Rotherhild, was coming downstairs.

"Marissa, there you are," he said, a bundle of papers under his arm, looking as if he'd just stepped off a windswept moor. Tall and thin, he was the opposite of her mother, who was short and plump.

"Yes, Father, here I am."

"Mama-in-law," he added, with a brief nod to Lady Bethany, who nodded back.

"Father, I wonder if I might speak to you and Mama? I have something to tell you." Marissa decided there was no time like the present to share her news.

"Do you?" He looked down at his notes, then longingly toward the sanctuary of his study, before sighing. "Very well. Your mother is in the back sitting room. We will join her there."

Lady Bethany rolled her eyes, but Marissa refused to feel any upset at her father's obvious lack of interest. When they entered the small, cozy sitting room, her mother looked up with a warm smile, her graying dark hair tied back in an untidy knot, her clothing covered by an apron as she sorted some dried plant specimens.

"Marissa!" She held out her hand, and Marissa

hurried over to kiss her cheek and receive a hug. Lady Bethany followed, and when her daughter asked if Marissa had worn her out in Surrey, assured her that she was perfectly well, better than she'd felt for years in fact.

"Humph," the professor said, but everyone ignored him.

"I have something to tell you both," Marissa announced, hands tightly clasped. "I am to be married."

Their faces fell, just for a moment, as if they were not pleased. But the next moment they were smiling, putting on a good show for her sake, and her father came to clasp her in an awkward embrace, saying with false heartiness, "Well done, Marissa. I'm sure you and young George will be very happy together."

Marissa froze. Of course they would think she meant George. How could she not have remembered that?

"No, Father," she began, "it isn't—"

But he wasn't listening. "Eleanor," he was saying to his wife, "we must be sure to book the botanical society rooms at once! We will have the reception there after the wedding. And for her bouquet, what do you say to a selection of ferns among the roses?"

Lady Bethany looked from one to the other and shook her head in disgust. Marissa's voice rose in dismay, not sure whether to laugh or cry at the confusion.

"Please, Father, Mother, listen to me!"

The sudden silence was unnerving. Her parents were gazing at her in consternation, but in another moment they would be peppering her with questions, so she made the most of it.

"I am not marrying George. I am marrying his brother, Valentine."

Consternation turned to astonishment. "Who?" her father burst out, while her mother put her palms to her cheeks in shock.

"Valentine, Lord Kent. He has asked me to marry him and I've consented."

"But . . . what of George?" her mother cried. "I thought it was George you were fond of. I don't understand. Dear me, Marissa, this is all very disturbing."

"Marissa is engaged to marry Lord Kent," Lady Bethany said loudly and clearly. "It is not disturbing at all, Eleanor. It is a very good thing."

Her father was frowning and then suddenly his brow cleared. "Lord Kent?" he said. "Of course, Lord Kent! The rose authority. Well, this is a pleasant turn of affairs. Not that we didn't like George, Marissa," he added hastily, catching his wife's warning glance, "but Lord Kent is so much, eh, eh, more suitable."

"Oh yes, in every way," Lady Bethany agreed knowingly. "Wait until you meet him."

"I thought he was a recluse?" the professor said.

"Not at all," Marissa replied. "Although he does prefer the country to London, it is his work that keeps him from socializing as he might wish."

"Is he in London now?" her mother asked, eyes wide. She was beginning to remove her apron, as if she was afraid Valentine might be about to walk in on them.

"Yes, he is. I have taken the liberty of asking him to dine with us this evening, Mother."

Eleanor's expression showed sheer panic at the thought of impromptu entertaining, but Lady Bethany patted her arm reassuringly. "I will speak to cook, my dear, don't worry. All will be as it should be. Now," she looked about with a beaming smile, "I will take a short nap. You have no idea how exhausting it was in Surrey."

After her grandmother had wafted from the room, Marissa's parents moved closer, expressions uneasy. "What has she been up to?" Eleanor asked in a long-suffering voice. "I do hope she's behaved herself, Marissa. You know what she can be like."

Marissa smiled a wicked little smile. "She has made the acquaintance of Lord Jasper, Mother, who is a friend of Valentine."

"I knew it!" the professor declared. "She looked far too pleased with herself. Is he completely unsuitable? You'd better tell us at once."

"He's very nice, really. You will like him, I'm sure."

It took some persuasion for them to believe Lady Bethany was genuine in her affections, and that Jasper was a suitable companion, but eventually they seemed to accept Marissa's assurances.

"We are very happy for you, my dear," Eleanor assured Marissa, when she rose to go upstairs to unpack and wash off the dust from the journey. "Lady Kent," she added, trying it out. "I never expected you to marry a lord. Although my mother came from an aristocratic family it has never been something we thought it necessary to aspire to. It is so much more important to be happy, don't you think, dear?" she said, looking at her husband.

But Professor Rotherhild had his own ideas on that.

"A rose expert for a son-in-law," he murmured, rubbing his hands together. "How thoroughly satisfactory, Marissa. Yes, indeed, you have done us proud."

As Marissa went up to her room she wondered if her spirits could sink any lower.

That evening, when Valentine arrived, he was shown into the drawing room—reserved for important visitors only—and her parents greeted him like a long lost friend.

"Lord Kent," her father said, beaming as he stepped forward to take his hand. "How do you do? It is a very great pleasure to meet you, and in such happy circumstances."

"Thank you, Professor Rotherhild." Valentine smiled his charming smile. "I have heard a great many good things about you and your work."

"My wife, Eleanor," the professor said, as Marissa's mother came forward with a shy smile.

"Ah, Mrs. Rotherhild, I believe you have an interest in carnivorous plants? I've always found them fascinating but I admit to knowing very little about them."

Her eyes lit up. "Yes, indeed," she said breathlessly. "You must see my collection and judge for yourself."

"I look forward to it."

By the time dinner was announced, Valentine seemed to have won them over completely. Marissa didn't know whether to be relieved or horrified. Some rebellious part of her had always wanted to choose a husband her parents would dislike for one reason or another. In her youth she'd visualized tears and pleas for her to give him up, rather like the stuff she had read in the penny dreadfuls the maids smuggled into the house for her. Emotionally exhausting, now she thought about it properly. She had to admit it was much more comfortable having a future husband who was liked, and yet the idea of a replica of her parents continued to worry her.

As they walked into the dining room, her arm in his, Valentine looked down at her, a crease between his brows, and asked her if anything was the matter.

"No. That is . . ." She sighed and shook her head. "I am being unreasonable."

"About what, minx?"

"They think I have chosen them the perfect son-in-law," she admitted hurriedly, nodding at the professor and Eleanor.

He looked confused. "But isn't that a good thing, Marissa? Or would you prefer them to be disappointed?" His brow cleared and he laughed. "Oh, I see. They wanted you to marry someone like themselves and you think you have. What, after you'd sworn never to follow in their footsteps?"

"Valentine—" Hearing it spoken aloud made her feel as if she was being ridiculous making such a fuss.

"Don't worry," he said, his warm breath brushing

her ear. "I have no intention of spending my days crouching on hillsides while you stand in the rain. In fact, I want you to write me a list of all the things you find unacceptable in a botanically inclined husband and I will study it carefully."

Marissa laughed shakily. "I couldn't do that," she protested.

"Of course you could. I insist. You are my number one priority, Marissa. I want you to be happy."

Marissa wondered if it was possible for her to love him any more. She told herself she would not make a list, but the idea was tempting. Putting her fears down on paper might help to negate them.

Over their meal, the conversation turned to the proposed wedding arrangements.

"The village church?" her mother repeated uneasily, with a glance to the professor. "Are you sure, Marissa? I think your father has other plans."

"Nonsense, Marissa, we will arrange for the Royal Botanical Society rooms," he said loudly, rubbing his hands together at the thought of greeting his guests in such hallowed surroundings.

"I'm afraid we cannot manage that," Valentine said smoothly. "Marissa and I will be leaving almost immediately after the wedding. We are going to spend our honeymoon on an, eh, expedition."

He'd chosen the right word. Marissa watched as her parents' disappointed expressions turned to understanding. To sacrifice everything for the sake of an expedition was completely acceptable in their minds.

"And what are you hoping to find?" The professor listened politely as Valentine outlined some of his plans, but Marissa could tell he was really just waiting for the moment when he could launch into a monologue detailing his own many expeditions.

Poor Valentine, she thought. Although, she narrowed her eyes at him, he didn't appear to be suffering. Of course he wasn't; this was his life. And it would be hers, too, when she was his wife.

"He is a fine man." Her mother had come up to her while she was deep in thought. "Handsome and intelligent and charming—a gentleman. We like him very well already, Marissa." She paused. "That said, I want you to be sure this is the life you want. I know what it is to feel pressured into making choices you do not wish to make, and I have never wanted that for you."

Marissa could imagine Lady Bethany's disappointment when her only child took a path so different from her own and it gave her a little more understanding of her mother. She was also touched Eleanor was willing to forego an alliance with the wealthy and charming Lord Kent for the sake of her daughter's happiness, when she knew things must have been very different for her.

But despite all that, she wished her mother hadn't asked.

"Marissa?" Eleanor said anxiously, reading something of her doubt in her face.

"I love him, Mama." She spoke with absolute certainty on that point at least.

"But is that enough, my dear?"

Marissa almost groaned aloud as her mother spoke the very question that was tormenting her day and night.

"I would be very hard to please if it were not," she said ambiguously.

Her mother looked into her eyes and to Marissa's relief accepted her statement as a yes. "Then," she said a little tearfully, "there is nothing more to be said."

Chapter 34

The private sanitarium was tucked away in a quiet street in Kensington, a solid redbrick building with discreetly barred windows. Valentine was shown into the office by the superintendent himself, a competent-looking man of fifty or so years with a comfortable paunch, called Gouch.

"Sit down, Lord Kent."

Valentine sat down on the chair opposite, trying not to let his impatience show. "How is Baron Von Hautt?"

"He is well enough, I believe. The mania appears to have subsided, but we keep him very quiet here, no excitement. I don't know how he will react to seeing you, my lord. We must be very careful."

Valentine didn't want to be careful and he hoped Augustus would react by telling him everything he needed to know.

"Forgive me," Superintendent Gouch's eyes were watchful, "but are you and the baron related? It is just that he persists in calling you his brother. At first we thought it was just the term for his fellow man, brothers-in-arms and all that, but we've begun to believe he genuinely thinks you are his blood relative.

Is that a fact, or simply one of his many delusions?"

"Unfortunately it is a delusion," Valentine replied. "But it is one I encouraged when he first spoke of it to me, and I am not adverse to keeping up the pretense if you think it will make it easier for me to converse with him. It is very important that I do so."

Gouch hesitated. "May I ask why, Lord Kent?"

Valentine leaned forward. "I am about to marry."

"Well, I must offer you my congratulations!"

He smiled and yet he found a little niggle of doubt, as he remembered Marissa's recent introspection. But now was not the time to worry if she was having second thoughts.

"Thank you. When my wife comes to live at Abbey Thorne Manor I want her safe. The baron knows of someone in my household who is my enemy, and I cannot be happy until that person is found and removed."

"I see. Yes, I quite understand your concern. I'm sorry I had to ask, my lord, but you see we must protect our patients as best we can."

"I understand. Now, may I see the baron?"

The superintendent rose. "This way, Lord Kent. Follow me."

Lady Bethany seemed to know exactly what she was looking for, and directed Marissa into a number of exclusive little establishments where the service was discreet and the staff eager to please. By the time the morning was over, she had ordered a wedding dress of exquisite pink satin and lace, matching slippers, and several outfits for their extended honeymoon.

"But won't I need serge or something stronger for climbing and walking?" Marissa asked. "You know what father's expeditions are like." The thought depressed her but she knew from past experiences it was better to be prepared.

Surprisingly, Lady Bethany laughed. "I don't think Kent has much climbing or walking in mind, my dear. He's far more interested in discovering everything about you than delving into the local flora."

Marissa felt her cheeks flushing. "Do you believe that, Grandmamma? How can you know?"

Lady Bethany lifted her eyebrows. "Surely you can see how besotted he is with you, Marissa?"

"I worry—a little—about . . . things. What if in a year or two he locks himself away in his study and I never see him? What if he insists on traipsing all over the country on wild searches for new roses?"

"My dear child, if you are worrying about that then you should act now, while he is putty in your hands. Insist he give up his roses or you will not marry him."

"Oh no, I couldn't!" she cried. "That is who he is, and if I am not prepared to marry him, roses and all, then I should tell him no."

Lady Bethany shrugged. "As you will. Did you take my advice about the hat?" she added, with a sideways glance.

Marissa couldn't help but smile. "I did. Thank you."

"And if Kent was a hat . . . ?"

Marissa laughed. "If he was a hat then I would purchase him in a heartbeat and—and never let him go."

Her grandmother's face softened. "Good," she said, as if that was the end of that. She became preoccupied again, tapping her cheek with her fingertip. "Now, what else do we need? Nightdresses! And I believe I know exactly where to find them."

Augustus was seated by a window, gazing out into the garden at the back of the house. His gray hair was cut shorter than before and he looked thinner, tall and gangly, rather than the imposing figure Valentine remembered from their previous encounters.

The superintendent spoke his name, and introduced his visitor in a jovial tone that rang false, and then, with a nod at Valentine, left them alone. Valentine walked over to the window, seating himself in a chair nearby, but Augustus did not make any sign that he knew he was there.

"How are you, Augustus?" he ventured at last.

Slowly, as if the words barely registered, the baron turned and looked at him with his cold, pale eyes.

"It's Valentine," he said, leaning forward. "Your brother."

Augustus smiled, just a flicker of his lips, and then made a slight gesture toward the garden outside. "The rose isn't there," he said, his voice dry and husky. "I've checked."

"The rose is lost," Valentine replied, with a grimace. "We must both accept it."

But Augustus didn't seem willing to let it go. He

frowned and then shook his head. "I have seen it."

Valentine felt shock ripple through him. He waited
for the baron to go on, and when he didn't, urged
him with, "You've seen the Crusader's Rose?"

"Yes." The baron swallowed, as if his throat was
too dry, and looking around Valentine saw a jug of
water and a glass, and poured some out, handing it
to him. He drank thirstily. "A year ago. In a church.
There was a great bunch of roses and it was there,
right there. I could hardly believe my eyes. But when
I asked the vicar he did not know where it had come
from, and although I questioned his wife, too, she
could not say who had given it."

Valentine sat, trying to think, wondering if it was
true or simply one of Von Hautt's fantasies. "So you
never found the origin of the rose in the church?"

"No."

"Where was this church?"

A sly look came over his face and he tightened his
lips childishly, as though that way he could prevent
any words from escaping.

"Augustus," Valentine said with a sigh, "we are
brothers, remember? You can tell me."

But he shook his head.

Valentine let the silence continue a moment. He
told himself there was no point in continuing with
questions about the rose. What he really needed to
do was ask Augustus about his accomplice.

"I need your help in a very important matter,
Augustus."

The pale eyes turned to him, watchful, curious,
waiting.

"Who is it at Abbey Thorne Manor who helped

you? I know there was someone. Will you tell me their name?"

Augustus's face brightened and he smiled. "Bo-bo," he said promptly.

"Bo-bo? Who is Bo-bo?"

That secretive look again, and the overemphasized tightening of his lips.

"Don't you want Bo-bo to come and visit you here?"

He did; his eyes gave him away.

"If Bo-bo is to visit you, you must tell me who Bo-bo is."

The baron was torn. For a moment Valentine hoped he had won and that he would hear the name he desperately sought, but then the baron seemed to change his mind. Or lose interest. He shrugged and looked away, back to the window. His voice was so quiet Valentine had to strain to hear it.

"Bo-bo said never to tell."

"Augustus . . ."

"The rose isn't in the garden. I've checked. It isn't there."

Valentine tried again, and again, but it was no use. Augustus had moved on or forgotten or he simply wasn't interested in telling him. Eventually he had to give up and leave the baron to his solitude. At least he had a name, as bizarre as it sounded.

Bo-bo. He repeated it to himself and thought it sounded vaguely familiar. For a time he tried hard to remember why, but the fleeting memory would not come to him and he had to let it go. Perhaps it was just wishful thinking.

He glanced back at the redbrick house as he left.

He knew he would come again—he felt a responsibility. Augustus may not be his flesh and blood brother but they were joined together in other ways.

Valentine even felt a sort of pity for him, now that the danger he'd posed had passed. The baron would never know the happiness that Valentine knew, would never have a future to look forward to. His life was effectively ended.

Valentine hoped that the baron didn't understand that.

Chapter 35

That evening Marissa and her family dined at Valentine's house in Mayfair—a house that was to be hers, too, soon enough. It was set in a square behind leafy gardens and looked grand enough to intimidate people far more socially ambitious than the Rotherhild's. But Valentine soon put them all at ease.

"My family has lived here for a hundred years, as you can see by the rather drab portrait gallery upstairs. I'm afraid it has been a long time since the house entertained anyone other than relatives and the occasional friends."

"You must throw a ball as soon as possible," Lady Bethany declared, her sharp eyes darting about as she considered the possibilities.

"What a good idea," George said. "Invite as many beautiful women as you can and I will choose one for my wife. It's only fair after you stole mine, Valentine."

"George, what nonsense," Marissa retorted. "We would never have suited. We are much better as friends."

George appeared shamefaced but anyone could

see he didn't mean it, and he was soon smiling again.

Lord Jasper was also dining at the Mayfair house, and Marissa noticed her parents' exchanging puzzled looks at the obvious affection shown between him and Lady Bethany.

"Don't you think you're a little old for such nonsense?" Marissa overheard her mother saying after the meal, when the women withdrew to the formal drawing room. "I thought maturity brought a degree of wisdom, Mother."

"Good heavens, I am not dead yet!" Lady Bethany retorted.

Marissa was glad when the men joined them, and grateful when Valentine suggested she come with him for a stroll in the garden.

Alone with him, she took a deep breath, lifting her face to the evening sky. Valentine smiled, bending to kiss her. "Have you changed your mind about marrying me? I'm sorry about the size of the house. I know it must be daunting. We can sell it if you like, or give it to George."

"I don't mind about the house," she said, reassuring herself as well as him. "And of course I haven't changed my mind. I'm surprised *you* haven't, now you've seen my family in all their eccentric glory."

Valentine raised his eyebrows. "I find them rather intriguing. I have only ever had the elderly aunts who brought me and George up, so I'm enjoying expanding. George told you I have a tendency to imagine people I meet as roses."

Marissa smiled. "He did. How do you imagine my family?"

"Your grandmother I can imagine quite easily. She is one of those wild roses that tends to throw out uncontrollable canes in all directions, but in the summer she's covered with flowers of such a glorious perfume that everyone puts up with her bad manners."

Marissa giggled. "And my father?"

"Well, I think he may be a tall bush rose with strong healthy foliage and a tendency to overwhelm any less vigorous plants in his vicinity."

"Hmm, I quite agree. What about my mother?"

"Ah, she is a small climber, easily managed most of the time, but occasionally she will grow in a direction you do not wish her to and there is nothing you can do about it."

Marissa laughed out loud. He observed her, eyes sparkling, before he leaned forward to kiss her.

She sobered. "And what of me, Valentine? What sort of rose am I?" She'd wanted to ask him that question ever since she met him, but some inner anxiety had always prevented her. She felt even more anxious as he observed her, a smile in his eyes.

"Marissa, you are an exquisite climbing rose upon a sunny garden wall, filling the air with the most beautiful scent, and your flowers are even more beautiful—full and generous and silky soft. There is no dishonesty about you, no artifice, and everyone who sees you loves you."

Tears stung her eyes at his rose-colored vision of her. "Oh, Valentine, I wish I was like that."

"What *is* it, Marissa?" He appeared genuinely concerned. "You don't seem yourself. Please, tell me what is wrong?"

But she couldn't; she wouldn't.

"It is just that I'm longing to be with you and I hate this waiting."

He kissed her again, more deeply, and she felt the warm tingle of desire flush her skin. But satisfaction of that desire was impossible, and she stepped away and shook her head.

There was a wicked gleam in his eyes. "There is a small summer house behind the orchard."

She glanced in the direction he pointed, biting her lip.

"There is a rather uncomfortable daybed in there, but I took the precaution of asking the servants to see that everything was aired and clean."

"Valentine . . ."

"Of course, if you'd prefer to remain chaste until the wedding, I understand."

Marissa caught his hand in hers and began to run, hearing his soft laughter. The summer house was charming, a white timber froth set in a small wilderness section of the garden. Once inside, Valentine locked the door then drew the shutters over the windows before lighting a lamp. Soft light spilled over lush furnishings, and Marissa saw that the summer house was more like a sultan's hideaway than the starkly furnished garden houses she'd known.

"Oh," she whispered in delight.

He began to remove the combs and pins from her hair, running his fingers through the tumbled mass. "The first time I saw you," he said, "I thought you the most beautiful woman in the world."

"Did you?" She reached up to stroke his cheek, then stretched up to kiss him, using her tongue.

He groaned, drawing her closer. "I'm already missing you," he said. "I need you in my arms, in my bed."

She reached for his jacket, slipping it from his shoulders and over his arms. When he tried to reciprocate with her clothing, she caught his hands and shook her head. "No, it is my turn," she insisted. "I've been dreaming of doing this. Let me. Please."

He subsided, and she unbuttoned the top of his shirt, drawing it over his head, murmuring her admiration. She ran her hands over his chest, following with her lips and tongue, exploring the hard nubs of his nipples. She took her time, enjoying the texture and taste of his skin, breathing in his masculine scent.

"I am only mortal, minx," he groaned at last.

Marissa looked up into his tense, flushed face and realized she may not have much longer to enjoy her power over him. With a grin, she reached to the buttons of his trousers, popping them open as slowly as she dared, while he looked down at her fingers, grinding his teeth.

She wrapped her hand around him, feeling the width and length and iron hardness. Leaning down, her hair shielding her face, she gently ran her tongue along him.

He caught up the silky tendrils and held them behind her head, and she realized he wanted to see what she was doing; that watching her was as exciting for him as this sense of control was for her. She slipped her mouth around him, freeing herself to do as she wished. He tensed, the muscles of his thighs bunching, and she heard the hiss of his indrawn breath.

"Hmm." She reached beneath the thick rod, exploring the balls, making him arch toward her. Her mouth took more of him in and she felt him give an involuntary thrust of his hips, seeking her moist heat.

Marissa knew he was enjoying what she was doing, and she was certainly enjoying it herself. When suddenly she found herself picked up and placed facedown on the daybed, it was a surprise. She protested, but he was already lifting up her skirts, sliding one arm under her hips, his fingers searching inside the opening of her bloomers.

Any protest she might have uttered died as she groaned and wriggled against him.

"I don't want to ruin your clothing," he said breathlessly.

"How . . . how dreadful that would be," she panted.

She felt him kneel behind her, widening her thighs, and then the blunt head of his cock nudged against her entrance. Marissa held her breath, her whole body rigid with waiting . . . And then he entered her with one smooth motion, going deep inside her, filling her until she became a part of him.

His hands closed on her thighs, holding her firm while he withdrew, just as slowly, and thrust deep again. Marissa copied the rhythm, moving with him, quickening the pace when he threatened to slow it down again.

"Patience, minx," he growled.

"You know that is not one of my virtues," she gasped.

He chuckled and his hand slid between her thighs, rubbing at the slick folds, and then squeezing the swollen nub. She cried out with shocked ecstasy, almost collapsing completely, but he wasn't finished with her yet.

As the tingles raced through her body, he was moving again. His hands cupped her breasts through her evening dress, and he said, in a rough, husky voice, "I wish you were naked, Marissa. I wish we were both naked. There are so many things I want to show you."

Why couldn't it always be like this? Marissa asked herself. When they were together, their bodies so in tune, she had no doubts.

Pleasure spiraled through her as he reached down to caress between her legs, and this time he joined her at the precipice, and they leaped together.

Valentine was sorry to have to hurry her, but he knew there would be questions asked as it was at the length of time they'd been gone. Quickly he straightened her clothes, casting a careful eye over her and nodding his approval. Then it was time for him to dress himself, buttoning his trousers over his still swollen cock, shrugging on his shirt and jacket and running a hand through his hair.

"How do I look?" he asked her.

She tipped her head to one side and that wonderful dimple appeared. "Perfect," she said.

"Ah, but will your father think so," he retorted, as he turned out the lamp and opened the shutters.

"You know he is ecstatic," she teased. "He is planning to show you his collection, so beware."

"Oh?" There was an interested gleam in his eyes.

"You *want* to see his collection," Marissa groaned. "I should have known."

"Marissa, you do know you are marrying a man whose life has been spent studying roses? I can't change what I am." He searched her face but this time she didn't look away or try to hide her feelings from him.

"Of course I know. And I love you with all my heart. Haven't I made that clear?" she said with a wicked glance. "Or should I show you again?"

He caught her hands before she could touch him. "As much as I'd love you to show me again," he said huskily, "we have to go back. Stop tempting me, minx."

Marissa watched him unlock the door, and followed him into the garden. The earthy smell and the sound of crickets greeted them.

"I spoke to Baron Von Hautt." Valentine's serious tone interrupted her pleasant thoughts. "He was lucid enough, but not particularly cooperative."

"Did he tell you who the spy at the manor is?" she said, straight to the point as they strolled arm in arm back toward the house.

"Yes. Not that it made finding him, or her, any easier."

"What do you mean?"

"The name he gave me was Bo-bo," he said, with a lift of his eyebrows.

Marissa repeated it softly. "How strange. It sounds like a—a pet name."

"That was what I thought."

"Someone must know what it means, Valentine."

"Let's hope so," he agreed.

They'd reached the house and their conversation had to be halted. As they made their way back to the drawing room, they came upon Morris, who had come up from Abbey Thorne Manor to take charge of the town house and run it in his inimitable style. He responded to Marissa's greeting with a bow, while his gaze slid briefly over Valentine's evening wear and his expression became pained.

"My lord, a note has come for you. I was told it was urgent."

"Thank you, Morris." Valentine took the folded piece of paper off the salver and opened it.

"How is everyone at Abbey Thorne Manor, Morris?" Marissa said, with a trace of longing she couldn't hide.

"Very well, Miss Rotherhild. They are all, if I may be so bold, looking forward to the wedding."

Valentine muttered a curse, causing Morris and Marissa to turn to him in surprise. He crumpled the sheet of paper in his fist. "Von Hautt has escaped. I don't know how or why," he went on, before Marissa could ask. "I need to go to the sanatorium and see the superintendent."

"I will come with you," Marissa said.

He opened his mouth to protest but she was determined and he must have seen it because he changed his mind, turning to Morris instead.

"Fetch the coach around, Morris, and make our apologies to our guests. Explain there's been an urgent matter concerning a—a relative."

"Very good, my lord," Morris said, seemingly unperturbed.

Marissa reached for Valentine's hand as Morris hurried away. He squeezed her fingers. "We must find him," he said quietly. "We must."

Chapter 36

By the time they arrived at the redbrick building in Kensington, all the lights were blazing and there were men moving about the grounds, some of them police constables called in to help. No one had seen Von Hautt since seven o'clock, when he ate a small supper and said he was weary and would retire to bed. It was two hours later that it was discovered he wasn't in his bed and, indeed, was nowhere to be found inside the building.

"One of the attendants discovered his clothing in a storage room on the ground floor," Superintendent Gouch admitted, when he had them seated in his office. He looked tired and worried, clearly shocked by the escape. "He'd changed into clothing belonging to the cleaners and walked out. I don't know how he did it. You saw him yourself, Lord Kent. He was barely able to speak."

"We must assume that was pretense," Valentine said grimly.

The man rubbed his hands over his face. "No one has ever escaped from this house before. Our record is impeccable. I don't know what will happen now. I suppose we will see a withdrawal of our more important patients. And I can't blame them. Who wants their lunatic relative turning up on their doorstep without warning?"

"You will continue the search?"

"Yes, of course, but I doubt we'll find him. If he has the wit to change his clothes then he must be capable of planning a route away from here. Indeed, he could be anywhere." He cast Valentine a shame-faced look. "He took some money, too."

Valentine stood up. "Thank you. We'll take up no more of your time. You will let me know if you find him?"

"Of course, my lord."

As they climbed back into the coach, Marissa was startled to hear Valentine say to the driver, "We are going home to Abbey Thorne Manor. We'll stop at the house in Mayfair first, but we need to set off from there as quickly as possible."

The coachman cracked his whip over the horses's heads and the vehicle lurched forward.

"Valentine—" Marissa gasped, falling back against the seat.

He turned to her urgently. "Where else would he go, Marissa? He's gone to find Bo-bo. And we must find them both as soon as possible."

He was right. This was their chance to discover the truth about the spy and to capture Augustus before he was able to vanish into the wider world.

Her parents were at first amazed and then ir-ritated by Marissa's determination to go rushing off with her intended for reasons she would not disclose.

"We were looking forward to seeing more of Lord Kent," the professor said. "This is very aggravating, Marissa."

Marissa could not help but remember her tenth birthday party, when her parents' plans took precedence, but she bit her lip and said nothing. Such ancient hurts no longer mattered to her.

"Is it proper for you to be entirely in Lord Kent's company?" her mother asked. "Perhaps you should remain in London until he returns."

Marissa had no intention of remaining in London. For the first time she admitted to herself that where Valentine went she would follow, no matter where that might be. Did that mean she was prepared to stand on rainswept hillsides with him? Or up to her knees in snow? The answer came loud and strong: Better that than waiting safe at home, frittering away her days with domestic duties.

At least they would be together.

"Marissa will be perfectly safe," Lady Bethany had come to her rescue, "because I am going, too."

"As am I," Jasper announced.

Professor Rotherhild threw up his hands.

George decided to remain in London and make certain Augustus didn't turn up on their doorstep. "I hate to mention it, brother, but you've been wrong before," he told Valentine.

In no time at all, the four of them were back in the coach and setting off on their impromptu journey.

As they traveled through London gradually the houses grew less and the fields and trees took over from the city, until they were in the countryside again.

Marissa closed her eyes, and let her thoughts drift. She remembered the list Valentine had asked her to make and spent some time thinking up dos and don'ts, but after a while it seemed silly to concern herself with what may never happen. Valentine wasn't the professor and she wasn't Eleanor. Just because she feared her life repeating itself did not mean it would happen.

Valentine might become distracted by his work, in fact she'd seen him just like that, but he would never neglect her. She was more precious to him than anything—he'd told her so. And she believed him. Marissa knew she must not confuse her future with memories of her childhood. Surely any doubts she had could be easily resolved? Valentine would listen to her; he'd already asked her numerous times what was wrong. It was her own fault she had refused to tell him.

Soon, feeling soothed by her own reasoning, she drifted into sleep. When she woke she was lying clasped in Valentine's arms, her head resting upon his chest, her face buried in his coat.

She lifted her head, wincing at the stiffness of her neck, and saw that his eyes were closed, his mouth slack. A glance at the other occupants of the coach showed that they were also asleep, Lady Bethany snoring faintly from within the hood of her cloak, while Jasper twitched in the throes of a dream.

Sitting up, Marissa peered out of the dusty window. The world was beginning to lighten with dawn and she knew they must be close to home.

Home.

She smiled. The word had never meant much to

her until now; the home of her childhood was not a warm and welcoming place. But Abbey Thorne Manor was different. Valentine had given her a wonderful gift when he made her a part of his family and his past, and she knew that awful sense of isolation, of not belonging anywhere, had finally gone.

She did not expect everything to be perfect and wonderful from this day forward—Marissa was too sensible to believe that. They would argue and they would find things to dislike about each other, they might even hate each other . . . briefly. But they would make it up, they would compromise, and in the end it would all go to making their relationship stronger.

That was love, the sort of love Marissa had been searching for all her life. And Valentine was her love.

At Abbey Thorne Manor the servants were only just waking up and beginning their daily household tasks. The coach had barely come to a stop when Valentine jumped out and ran across the inner courtyard into the manor through the back door. One of the housemaids stepped out of a side room, then shrieked when she saw him and leaped out of his way.

"M-my lord . . ." she wailed.

But Valentine didn't have time to apologize or explain himself.

Something had come to him during his fitful sleep in the coach. He'd remembered a long forgotten moment from his childhood, when his mother was still alive. He'd gone running up to her room to tell her about the caterpillar he'd found in the marigolds, only to be scolded for waking her and "frightening me half to death with that disgusting grub." Eyes filled with tears, biting his lip to prevent the unmanly moisture from falling, he dragged his feet back down the stairs to the kitchen.

"Poor little chap," a kindly voice had said, handing him a biscuit still warm from the oven. "Never mind. Your caterpillar will be happier outside anyway. In a moment we will go and put him back in the marigolds, so he can find his way home."

Valentine remembered the hurt dealt him by his mother fading, as they went off hand in hand to return his treasure to its home.

"I have a little boy just like you," the kindly voice said. "He isn't really mine. I am his nanny whenever he visits England. He is always finding creatures in the garden—he has quite a collection. He calls me Bo-bo, because he can't say my name properly. What do you think of that, Master Valentine?"

Valentine pushed open the kitchen door.

Mrs. Beaumaris looked up from the oven, her face flushed from the heat. She was startled by his sudden entrance, but there was something else there, some expression in her eyes that told him that he was right.

"Master Valentine, you did give me a fright," she declared, wiping her hands on her apron.

She came to stand before her scrubbed pine table. There were various ingredients laid out on its surface, ready to be put together and served for breakfast. Valentine could smell the mouthwatering aroma of bacon and sausage already sizzling. There was no doubt Mrs. Beaumaris was queen of her domain.

"We thought you'd be in London for a week or more. Is there something amiss?"

Her eyes held his, searching, making up her mind how she could throw him off the scent.

"It's too late for that," he said, and strode toward her. The table was between them and he rested his hands on it and leaned across eggs and cheese and milk, his gaze never leaving hers. "Where is he, Mrs. Beaumaris? I know he's here. He's a danger to himself and others. You know that. Tell me where he is so that he can be returned to the safety of the sanatorium."

"I don't know what you're—" she began automatically.

"Oh please, don't play games with me," he cut her short. "Give me some credit, Mrs. Beaumaris. I know the truth and I won't be fobbed off with fairy stories."

She wavered. He saw the indecision in her plump, good-natured face. And then she crumpled, dropping back into a chair as her legs seemed to give way, covering her face with her hands. "Oh, my poor boy," she sobbed. "My poor lad. What will become of him, Master Valentine, without his Bo-bo?"

Marissa was slower to climb out of the coach. She was stiff and sore from the long journey and the uncomfortable position she'd been in. Lady Bethany was moaning as she tottered about the yard, and Jasper was declaring he was ready for a roaring fire and a nice hot breakfast.

"Mrs. Beaumaris will accommodate us, I am

sure," he said, with a greedy gleam in his eyes. "I wonder if she has some of that delicious bacon I had last time?"

"Jasper, really, is your stomach all you think about?" Lady Bethany declared wearily. "Here I am, almost crippled, and you're worrying about your bacon."

"Now, my dear, that's not true."

Marissa was only half listening to their gentle bickering, her thoughts otherwise occupied with the baron and Valentine. It was chance that made her glance up at the gatehouse. It stood silhouetted against the dawn sky, a dark mass of stone with narrow windows like eyes. There was a figure standing on the square tower at the very top. Surprised, she raised a hand to shade her eyes against the glare of the rising sun, and realized that whoever it was had pale hair.

"Augustus," she breathed.

Lady Bethany jumped. "Where?"

"Up there!" Marissa cried, and ran toward the steps that led up into the gatehouse tower.

She didn't stop to think that what she was doing might be dangerous. The baron was here and she would face him and demand to know what he thought he was doing at Abbey Thorne Manor. She had bested him once and she would do so again. How dare he come and try to ruin her wedding and all her happiness? How dare he threaten Valentine?

Her shoes tapped on the stone steps, echoing the quickening beat of her heart, while her skirt and cloak brushed against the sides of the narrow stairwell. It was gloomy and dank, smelling of age, but she kept climbing toward the square of light at the top. When she finally reached it, stepping out onto the narrow stone balcony, she was out of breath. She clung to the stone balustrade with one hand, a brisk breeze tugging at her clothing and hair, as she gazed around for Augustus.

"Miss Rotherhild."

He was behind her, and she spun around, nearly falling backward down the stairs in her haste to confront him. Augustus was not a man she wanted to have at her back. She was remembering Lady Longhurst and the look on her face when she told them what Augustus had done to her. Shivering, she drew her cloak closer around her, as if it might protect her. Perhaps it was not such a good idea to come rushing up here alone.

As if he was perfectly aware of her state of mind, the baron smiled.

"I knew you'd come," he said, his pale gaze fastened unnervingly on her face. "As soon as I saw you I knew it was meant to be."

Meant to be? Before she could ask what he meant, he went on, his face blazing with purpose in a way that was beginning to terrify her.

"This is all mine, you know. I am the eldest son. I will marry you and we will live at Abbey Thorne Manor. There will be children, of course. I will need an heir."

Marissa tried to make her voice sound calm and reasonable, when all she wanted to do was scream. "I think Valentine might have something to say about that. I am engaged to him, not you."

He smiled at her as if she was flirting with him.

"Valentine understands. He owes me so much. He can never repay all his father's debts but he will try. I know he will. We are brothers, after all."

Marissa knew then it was useless to argue with him. The fantasy in his mind had grown to even more bizarre proportions and whatever she said he wouldn't be capable of believing her.

"Will you come down and talk to Valentine? You can discuss the—the running of the estate. You will have a great deal to learn."

He frowned. Practical matters had no place in his dreams of the future. "He has a manager, does he not? There will be no need for me to rub shoulders with the workers."

"You will need to give instructions. I think you'd better speak to Valentine." She was edging toward the stairs, drawing him with her. If she could get him down to the ground then there was a chance he could be recaptured, or at least Marissa would be able to escape.

Augustus shook his head. "Stay where you are, Miss Rotherhild. There is no need to talk to Valentine. He understands everything. He told me himself that he was giving you to me."

Goose bumps rose on her skin, and suddenly she felt icy cold. Augustus was so convincing she almost believed him, but in her heart she knew Valentine would never do such a thing.

"I am not about to be given to anyone," she said firmly. "I make up my own mind who I want to marry, not Valentine, and not you."

The baron looked amused, as if a piece of furniture had suddenly begun to air its opinions.

Marissa turned and took a step downward.

The next moment he had hold of her by the shoulders, pulling her backward, his fingers bruising her flesh. She struggled, kicking back at his shins, although her skirts impeded her efforts to escape.

"Let me go!" She struck back with her elbow, catching him in the stomach and he howled in pain. Marissa had forgotten his wound, but now it had the required effect, and he let her go.

Panting, her hair tangled about her face and shoulders, she stumbled away from him. Although bent over, his hand to his aching stomach, Augustus was watching her. His face was white, his mouth a rictus smile. He was standing between Marissa and the stairs. There was no other way off the tower, unless it was to jump.

She looked down and saw Lady Bethany's face turned up to her, her voice a thin sound, her words inaudible. There were others there, too, watching, horrified, as the drama was played out. She couldn't see Valentine and wondered in despair where he was.

"Let her go."

She thought she was imagining his voice, but when she turned Valentine's fair head appeared over the baron's shoulder as he climbed the last few steps to the top of the tower.

"Valentine," she whispered, too frightened to move. What if the baron attacked him and threw him over the edge?

But Augustus was beaming. "Brother. I'm so glad you've come. She is like a savage. I am going to have to teach her obedience. Tell her she is mine now. Tell her what we decided."

Marissa met Valentine's eyes and gave a little shake of her head, trying to make him understand that Augustus was not to be reasoned with. But Valentine must have seen that for himself.

"Refresh my memory, brother. What *did* we decide?" he asked in a calm voice.

"That I would marry Miss Rotherhild and live at Abbey Thorne Manor, because I am the eldest son. I am the heir."

Valentine paused and then shook his head, slowly, regretfully. "No, Augustus, I didn't decide that. I am marrying Marissa, not you. You need to go back to the hospital. You're not well."

"Please, Augustus," Marissa added, now that Valentine had chosen to be honest and no longer play along with the baron's fantasies. "They can help you there. Let us take you back to London."

He stared back and forth between them. To Marissa's relief he didn't try to argue or insist his own version of matters was the true one. Instead he went still, his expression solemn, as if he'd known all along.

"No, I am not going back," he said matter-of-factly. "I can't go back. Bo-bo understands. She says she'll look after me, just as she used to. She was my nanny, you know, when I stayed at Beauchamp Place. She's the only one who ever loved me."

I should hate him, thought Marissa. *He was going to hurt me. He's hurt others.*

But something in his voice, in his face, inspired

pity, too. Augustus had been hurt, he had suffered, and perhaps the madness had more to do with that than anything else.

"Bo-bo can come to see you, when you're settled," Valentine said. "I can arrange that. Come down with me now and we'll talk to her."

"Augustus!" The voice was a cry from the heart, and when they looked down they could see Mrs. Beaumaris below, hands clasped to her bosom, gazing up.

The sight of her seemed to stir something in him. Perhaps he saw how much he'd lost and would never have again. And perhaps he realized he didn't want to be locked up in London and it was better to be free.

Before either Valentine or Marissa could move, he took two strides to the stone balustrade and swung his leg over the edge. A moment when everything was still, even the breeze seemed to have stopped, and then he stepped into nothingness.

His coat floated outward, like dark wings against the soft pink of the sky, and Marissa remembered the first time she'd seen him on the hillside above Montfitchet. She turned away before he struck the ground, not wanting to see. There was a scream from Mrs. Beaumaris, shouts from the others, and then Valentine's arms came around her, pressing her close, and she wept.

Chapter 37

The little church was resplendent. Sunlight was shining in the stained glass windows onto the polished benches and pews, groaning with well-wishers. Aristocrats rubbed shoulders with plant enthusiasts who were squeezed next to the villagers. Enormous bunches of roses were everywhere, filling the air with their lush scent. Valentine stood before the altar, spick-and-span in his groom's clothes, while George and Jasper waited beside him. As the organist began to play the bridal march, everyone turned, craning their necks for a first glimpse of the bride.

Marissa started up the aisle on her father's arm. Her pink bridal gown seemed to glow like mother of pearl, her dark hair loose about her shoulders beneath a simple lace veil. Her face shone with happiness, her dark eyes finding Valentine, as he stood in the light that poured through the arched windows.

She felt strangely calm.

The emotion had threatened to overwhelm her while she was preparing and then driving to the church, but now she was here, a feeling of tranquility came over her. This was the moment she would pledge herself to Valentine; nothing could go wrong now. They were about to embark on the greatest adventure of all.

When she reached him, he was smiling, his blue eyes brighter than she'd ever seen them. "Minx, you take my breath away," he whispered, the words for her alone.

The vicar cleared his throat, beaming upon them, and began the service.

After a moment she felt Valentine stiffen. She glanced sideways at him, wondering what was wrong, and found his gaze fixed on something to the side, beyond where the professor stood with her dearest friends from Miss Debenham's Finishing School.

"Valentine?"

His eyes widened. "It can't be," he breathed.

People had noticed now. There was a murmur behind them, and the vicar was stumbling a little over the familiar words.

He stepped past her, ignoring the shocked expression of the vicar and the exclamations of their guests. "Valentine?" she hissed, and followed. He reached a large vase of flowers on a plinth and leaned forward, his face almost hidden in the flowers. With a trembling hand he lifted one of the roses free, causing several others to be disarranged and tumble about his feet.

"I say, Kent, old chap," Jasper said nervously, glancing around. "You are about to get married."

"Valentine, don't you think you should—" George began.

"Valentine?" Marissa put her hand on his arm.

But Valentine had turned to her and his face was ablaze. He took her hand and placed something in it. She looked down, confused, and saw that it was a rose. A rose the color of a Jerusalem sunrise, pink and gold and orange.

It took only a heartbeat for her to realize what this must be, what this must mean. Her eyes lifted in wonder to his.

"The Crusader's Rose," he said triumphantly. "I have found the Crusader's Rose."

The church erupted. Jasper was there, his hands shaking as he took the rose reverentially in his own hands, and then Lady Bethany was peering over their shoulders. It took some time for everyone to settle down. Eventually, Marissa was able to ask a question.

"But where has it come from?"

The vicar thought all the roses had come from gardens in the village and nearby area. Through a process of elimination they discovered this particular rose had come from Mrs. Horton's garden, at the edge of the village.

As soon as he heard that, Valentine took Marissa's hand in his, and they set off out of the church and along the village street, the congregation trailing after them. Marissa picked up her skirts, petals falling from her bouquet, while Valentine hurried along at her side. She didn't consider refusing to go or asking him to postpone his search. The Crusader's Rose had become as important to her as him, and it seemed right and proper that it should be found on this day.

Their day.

Mrs. Horton hadn't come to watch the wedding. She was old and unable to walk very far, and—the vicar said—it was decided by her relatives to let her rest at home. But she was in her garden when they reached her cottage, using a cane to stay upright, as she busied herself tying back an unruly clematis.

She looked up, mouth ajar, as Lord Kent and his bride arrived at her gate and proceeded into her garden, followed by a crowd of guests.

"Mrs. Horton," Valentine said, taking her hand. "Forgive our intrusion."

"It isn't an intrusion, my lord," she replied. "I wasn't expecting you, is all."

Her sangfroid elicited a ripple of laughter.

"This rose," he said, and he held up the Crusader's Rose. "Is it yours, Mrs. Horton?"

She nodded. "Aye, it is. Over here, my lord. You can see it's a fine strong bush. Likes a warm place, though. But if it's happy it flowers on and on."

Valentine stood staring at the rose bush, every inch of it covered in bright blooms. Marissa blinked back tears, knowing what he must be feeling, and managed a smile for the puzzled Mrs. Horton.

"Was this rose always in your garden?" she said.

"Goodness me, no, Your Ladyship! I was walking out by the manor one day—I was younger then, of course—and I spied it growing in a hedgerow. It was struggling there, but I liked the flowers, so I took a cutting and grew it myself. I hope you don't mind. It didn't belong to no one; it was just growing wild in the hedgerow."

"Mind?" Valentine said. "Mrs. Horton, you are a wonderful, wonderful woman!"

She blushed bright red.

Unable to contain himself, Valentine grabbed hold of Marissa and swung her around, her wedding dress belling out.

It was decided to continue the wedding ceremony in Mrs. Horton's garden, and it was there before the Crusader's Rose that Valentine and Marissa made their vows and were declared husband and wife, while everyone watched on.

"So romantic," murmured Marissa's friends from Miss Debenham's, as they wished her well. "You have found the perfect husband, even if he isn't the one you began with . . ."

"As long as he's the one I end with," Marissa said.

She looked up and caught Valentine's gaze, and knew that as nice as it was to have her friends here with her, she was looking forward to being alone with her new husband. Tomorrow they would set off on their honeymoon, just the two of them, and she couldn't wait.

Epilogue

Bourbon

It was warm, far warmer than an English evening. The insects hummed in the trees, as Valentine and Marissa walked down the narrow path toward the sandy beach. This was their last evening. Tomorrow they would be setting off on the journey home to England and Abbey Thorne Manor, to take up their lives as a married couple.

Marissa had enjoyed their honeymoon but it was time to go home, and she was looking forward to it.

She found herself missing the old manor house and the people she'd come to know and love, as well as her own family. Lady Bethany had sent a letter to say she and Jasper were well and Jasper was pestering her to marry him.

But there was a reason that made her a little nervous about returning, a reason she hadn't told Valentine yet. It was silly to doubt him, she knew that—she'd believed all her doubts were laid to rest. Perhaps it was because everything had been so perfect; she just didn't want to spoil it.

Valentine was growing restless, too. He was talking about the Crusader's Rose and how he meant to ensure that this time it remained in his family for many generations to come. Morris had written to say the cutting Mrs. Horton provided was growing strongly and would be ready for planting by the time he returned.

They slipped off their shoes and walked barefoot down to the edge of the sea. The water sparkled silver and gold, catching the setting sun and reflecting it back like thousands of precious stones.

"You're very quiet, minx," Valentine said quietly, his fingers entwining with hers.

She smiled at him, her dimple showing. "I was thinking how much I will miss our island."

"We could always stay longer."

She tried to read his face—did he mean it or was he trying to please her? She'd found that with Valentine it was always best to tell the truth. "Thank you, Valentine, but actually I am a little homesick."

His shoulders relaxed in relief and he leaned forward to kiss her. "Me, too."

They walked again, as the light faded. Lamps on fishermen's boats winked out in the dark ocean and the breeze tasted salty against her lips. A wave came in, washing over their feet, and they stopped to enjoy the sensation.

"Will it seem strange to you," she began tentatively, "sharing your home with me? After so long doing very much as you wished, day after day?"

"My dearest girl, how can you ask such a thing? You were right when you said I was hiding from life before you came along. I was too cowardly to take a chance, in case I was hurt again. I'd lost all confidence. But you've healed me. I will always be grateful to you for taking me in hand."

"Valentine, it is you who healed me," she cried, reaching up to fling her arms about his neck.

He held her against him.

Her voice was a warm mumble against his neck. "I'm asking you such a thing because I am concerned you will not be pleased with my news, Valentine."

He stilled, aware of all the things that could go wrong and how terrified he was of losing her. "What do you mean?"

She told him.

His heart was pounding in his chest. Slowly he let her slide back to the sand and, with a shaking hand, tilted back her face, brushing aside the wayward strands of dark hair. Her eyes were shining up at him, her mouth on the verge of a smile, but there was doubt, too, and the hint of fear.

"Thank you," he said, his voice deep and husky. "For making me the most fortunate of men."

"Babies cry, Valentine, and children can be noisy. And naughty—"

He laughed. "I know; I was both."

Valentine knew with a fierce certainty that when his son, or daughter, brought a treasure for him to see, he would not send them away. He would never make his child feel unwanted as he had, long ago.

He took a deep breath and told her so.

His wife listened, and then she looked at him as if he was the most wonderful man in the world. Valentine gave her another hug, enjoying her love for him, before they set off along the beach again.

There were plans to be made, dreams to be dreamed, a baby to prepare for, but for now they said nothing, simply enjoying being together.

Next month, don't miss these exciting new love stories only from Avon Books

In Pursuit of a Scandalous Lady by Gayle Callen
Entranced by a portrait and haunted by scandal, Julian Delane, the Earl of Parkhurst, will stop at nothing to learn the truth about the woman he believes to be the mysterious model... even if his quest leads to their utter ruin.

Touching Darkness by Jaime Rush
Nicholas Braden uses his psychic talent to hunt terrorists for a covert government program. Just as he realizes there's something off about the operation, he finds himself under the tempting spell of Olivia, a "good girl" with a wild side and secrets of her own.

The Rogue Prince by Margo Maguire
To the *ton*, the Prince of Sabedoria is a wealthy and powerful royal, but in truth he is a wronged man, hell-bent on revenge. Lady Margaret is chaste, an innocent, but a most tempting seduction ignites a passion she never knew she possessed.

The Notorious Scoundrel by Alexandra Benedict
Like an irresistible siren, orphan Amy Peel lures dukes and earls to London's underworld to see her dance—some say she is a princess, but only one man knows her darkest secret. Edmund Hawkins, pirate turned reluctant gentleman, will not let her out of his sight, especially when a growing threat mounts against the little dancer.

Unforgettable, enthralling love stories,
sparkling with passion and adventure
from Romance's bestselling authors

At Avon Books, we know your passion for romance—once you finish one of our novels, you find yourself wanting more.

May we tempt you with . . .

- **Excerpts** from our upcoming releases.

- Entertaining **extras**, including authors' personal photo albums and book lists.

- Behind-the-scenes **scoop** on your favorite characters and series.

- **Sweepstakes** for the chance to win free books, romantic getaways, and other fun prizes.

- Writing **tips** from our authors and editors.

- **Blog** with our authors and find out why they love to write romance.

- **Exclusive content** that's not contained within the pages of our novels.

Join us at
www.avonbooks.com

An Imprint of HarperCollins*Publishers*
www.avonromance.com